ESCAPE

L. A. DAVENPORT

P-Wave Press

PART ONE

CHAPTER ONE

DR HUNTER STOOD AWKWARDLY IN THE MIDDLE OF THE room, unsure what to do.

Maybe I could go for a swim. He stared at his suitcase, hoping he'd remembered to pack his trunks. Maybe a shower would be better, to freshen up. A wave of tiredness swept over him. Or I could just go straight to bed.

He glanced around the room again, taking in the heavy, ornate mirror, the richly upholstered furniture, the hand-painted French doors. All was in soft gold and ivory, with decadent hints of old colonialism. And none of it was 'him'.

He frowned and thought back to the intense heat that met him when he stepped out the plane, the boy trying to catch his eye at the luggage carousel, the bored taxi driver waiting outside Arrivals. That and the perfect blue of the sky as they followed the coast road to the town. But it had all seemed so remote, as if in a dream.

Snapping out of his reverie, he attached the Do Not Disturb sign and firmly shut the door. He hung his jacket on the back of a chair and put his mobile phone, wallet and pass-port in a neat row on the mantelpiece. He picked up his suitcase and lay it carefully on the bed. He took out several shirts and pairs of trousers, putting them in a neat pile. He picked up a neatly folded t-shirt, but froze when he saw the photo frame beneath. He dropped the t-shirt on the bed and stared. A torrent of emotions crashed through him and he was nearly sick.

How long did I manage, not thinking about her? He started counting up the minutes and hours, but realised there was no time, not one single second when she wasn't there with him in his mind.

He picked up the frame and stared at the smiling, happy woman. He could almost taste her in the air, almost hear her laugh, almost sense her skin. He placed the photograph carefully on the mantelpiece and positioned it so she gazed at the bed.

He clenched and unclenched his jaw, unable to tear himself away. Eventually, he turned back to the bed and, spotting his wash bag, grabbed it and marched to the bathroom.

CHAPTER TWO

HE GLANCED AT THE MARBLE SINK, THE PLUSH BATHTUB and the vintage shower, but he was confused, unable to process them. After staring blankly at the shower for several seconds, he decided he wanted to be clean. He pulled himself out of his clothes while the water warmed up. He knew he should have a cold shower but he wanted to burn away the sticky remnants of airports, taxis, trains and air-conditioned rooms. To burn away the last few weeks and every well-intentioned smile, every kind word, every moment of patient understanding. They meant well, of course, but all the same he wanted to shout into every one of their faces to, please, just leave him alone.

He stared into the mirror. His eyes were bloodshot and his mouth drawn. A desperation rose up and he wanted to scream, to punch, to kick, to throw something, to break something, anything, everything. But he just stood there and stared at himself, not recognising his own face.

I could smash the mirror.

He stared back at the face he didn't recognise, then

turned away. He watched the water crashing, bursting against the glass wall of the shower.

I could smash that too.

He imagined the water pouring onto the floor, mixing with the shattered glass. He imagined stepping on the broken shards, watching his blood mix with the water and flowing across the floor, then down into the sewers and out to sea.

Why am I alive? Why me?

He watched his hands open the glass shower door. He saw his feet, thinner than he remembered, step inside, and he gazed curiously as the steam from the hot water billowed up around him. The water seared his skin and he welcomed the pain. He stepped fully into the shower and winced as he forced himself beneath the burning cascade. He placed his palms on the wall and bowed his head, the heat scorching his neck and back. He shook as his tears fell into the water, lost forever in the churning torrent.

CHAPTER THREE

He let his towel fall as he reached the bed. He pulled back the duvet and slid into the soft, cool space between. Before he could pull the duvet over himself, he fell into a deep, deep sleep.

The room was calm and silent. Outside, the cicadas droned in the hotel gardens. The air lay still and he breathed deeply and regularly, the occasional twitch flashing across his face.

The heat left the day as the afternoon slowed into evening.

A small finch landed on the edge of the balcony and hopped along, looking for anything of interest. Unsatisfied, it flew off and swept over the gardens, darting back and forth, then wheeling over the swimming pool and the tennis courts. As it reached the bay, it turned and was lost in the falling light.

The cicadas droned on.

Abruptly, they stopped, leaving only silence.

The tinkle of laughter and a shrieked response. In the

distance, the slow crash of the waves against the cliffs below the hotel.

HOURS LATER, the room was long with shadows and the sun close to setting. All was cool and quiet, only the sound of his steady breathing breaking the silence.

From nowhere, banging and rattling started outside the room, as if someone was struggling to open a set of doors. His eyes opened instantly. The bedroom, now shrouded in semi-darkness, was strange and unfamiliar. Slowly, his eyes adjusted to the light and he recalled the flight, the hotel, the room.

Two men urgently and furtively whispered as they continued to struggle with a door. They seemed to be in the room with him, and he looked around in panic, realising after a few seconds that they must be just outside.

As abruptly as it had started, the banging and whispering stopped, and the room slipped back into silence. He fell instantly asleep. Just as his breathing became deep and regular once more, the banging and whispering started again, this time more urgently.

He placed his hand on the duvet ready to spring out of bed but, again, the noise stopped just as soon as it had started. After a pause, there was more whispering, and then footsteps down the corridor. He checked the bedside clock and, without registering the time, fell asleep again.

The cicadas struck up, their low drone filling the shaded room.

Indistinct voices drifted up from the gardens below.

The room became still once more, his steady breathing mixing with the call of the cicadas.

CHAPTER FOUR

SOMETIME LATER, HE LAY IN THE NEAR-DARK ROOM, WITH only the moonlight reflecting on the marble floor. He stared at the ceiling, tracing patterns in the ancient plaster, and listened to the start-stop of the cicadas. He tried to catch an animated conversation drifting up from an unknown bar.

He was disorientated, and lonely. Inexplicably, intense vertigo welled up and he became dizzy and nauseous. Now completely awake, it seemed more like early morning and time to go to work than late in the evening.

What was that banging and whispering ? What were they doing?

Hungry, he pulled himself out of bed and walked unsteadily into the bathroom. He splashed his face with cold water and stared at his reflection as he dried himself. He thought back to how he desperate he had been earlier and, revulsed, tried to push the memory away.

Back in the bedroom, he dressed slowly and deliberately in an open-necked shirt and fine-spun trousers, smoothing down the material and picking off loose threads as he went along. He carefully folded back his shirt cuffs to just below the elbow. He checked himself in the large mirror over the mantelpiece but he caught the eye of the woman in the photograph and turned away.

CHAPTER FIVE

THE HOTEL LOBBY WAS QUIET. EARLIER, IT HAD GLOWED IN gold and bronze in the afternoon light. Well-heeled guests had milled contentedly amid the clack-clack of expensive shoes and the soft ding of the elevators. Now, in the electric light of evening, the shiny decorations and highly polished marble seemed gaudy and overdone.

I wonder what all those people I saw earlier are doing now. He remembered a couple – him late middle-aged, overweight and tanned, her young, shiny and brittle – and wondered if they were, at that moment, having sex, or taking drugs, or both. He shook his head, surprised at his own assumptions. That stuff only happens in films.

He walked over to reception, and the concierge straightened up and smoothed his jacket as he approached.

"I realise it's a little late, but is there anywhere in the hotel I can get something to eat at this hour," he asked.

Before the concierge could respond, a tall, alert, overweight man in his early sixties appeared as if from nowhere. "Good evening, Dr Hunter," he said. The doctor turned, surprised to hear his own name. "I'm Charles, the hotel manager, and I'd like to welcome you to our little establishment."

"Thank you," Dr Hunter replied noncommittally.

"I do like to welcome each of our guests individually," Charles continued. "Are you suitably rested after your flight?"

Dr Hunter regarded Charles's cheery face. "Not as much as I'd like," he replied eventually.

"I'm sorry to hear that." He glanced at the concierge and nodded. The concierge went back to his computer screen. Charles continued: "I couldn't help overhearing you ask about the dinner options that we have available at his time of night." Dr Hunter nodded. "We have three restaurants at the hotel, all of which," Charles said, checking his watch, "are still serving."

"Okay."

"If I may, I'd like to recommend that you try the restaurant at the far end of the garden." Charles pointed towards a set of French doors and the darkness beyond. "It's a little way from here by foot, but it's by the sea cliffs and, on a beautiful night like this, nothing compares."

Dr Hunter gazed at Charles, unsure how to end the conversation, then looked down at his shoes.

"I am walking over that way," Charles said, undeterred. "If you would like to accompany me..."

"Sure," Dr Hunter said resignedly.

"Excellent." Charles turned to the concierge. "Could you call Stefano and tell him that number 22 is ready?"

The concierge looked up. "Right away."

Charles walked briskly towards the French windows and beckoned Dr Hunter. "If you'd like to come with me." Dr Hunter duly followed, although a few paces behind and giving the impression that he might wander off at any moment.

In the garden, the two men walked along beautifully laid-out paths lined with explosions of flowers, decorative plants and fragrant trees, with the occasional bench or fountain tucked discreetly away in recesses ripe for intimate conversation. All the while, Charles chatted happily about the history of the hotel, to which Dr Hunter paid hardly any attention.

"This wonderful old place has been many things over the centuries, you know," Charles said as they rounded a large rose bush, heavy with succulent flowers.

"Oh, really," Dr Hunter replied half-heartedly.

"Yes, indeed," Charles continued. "It started as a monastery in the late Middle Ages, and then became an institute of art and learning, famous throughout the Eastern Mediterranean."

"I see," said Dr Hunter, running his fingers through the leaves of a rhododendron in full bloom.

Charles turned and stared straight at Dr Hunter, who pulled up in surprise. "Then, I'm afraid to say, all that respectable scholarly learning went out the window."

"Oh yes?" Dr Hunter said, awkward at Charles standing so close.

Charles turned and continued walking down the flower-lined path, talking over his shoulder. "Yes, the place fell into, one could say, less reputable hands and became a brothel, among other things."

Charles turned briefly and smiled. "I think it's safe to say that the only lessons being learned here at that time were from the School of Life."

"Indeed," said Dr Hunter, his attention drawn by the heady waft of perfume from a nearby magnolia.

The two men rounded a corner, and a bar and tennis court appeared, brightly lit in the falling gloom. A few hotel guests were seated on high stools by the bar and at tables scattered under nearby trees. Charles smiled at a family seated at one of the tables as they passed and the father waved weakly back.

Charles continued: "After that particularly salubrious period in our history, the property was taken over by the family that currently owns the hotel."

"When was that?"

"Almost two hundred and fifty years ago. They initially used it as a home for themselves and their assorted relatives, but they soon started opening it up to travellers of the better sort, one might say. It was even a rather far-flung staging post on the Grand Tour, when that sort of thing was in vogue, although the constant meddling of outside powers stopped it really taking off as a destination."

The two men passed a large, azure swimming pool, glittering under hidden floodlights, then followed a path towards the clifftops that ended at an open-air restaurant.

"This place seems to have gone through a lot of changes over the centuries," Dr Hunter observed, examining the low stone balustrade that surrounded the gardens.

"Yes, but each one has never entirely erased the traces of the past," Charles replied. He stopped and turned to face Dr Hunter, looking him in the eye. "Everywhere, you will find clues to what has gone on before. Everywhere. Nothing that happens here is ever entirely forgotten or cannot be retraced." Charles paused. "One simply has to look hard enough."

Dr Hunter frowned as he regarded Charles properly for the first time, noticing the delicate green of his eyes, and the tired, watery bags beneath. "It sounds like a fascinating place to be," Dr Hunter said.

"That," Charles said, breaking into an enigmatic smile, "depends entirely on why you are here." He turned away and continued walking busily along the path towards the restaurant. Dr Hunter watched him walk away for a moment, and then followed.

As they reached the restaurant, Charles announced: "And

'here' we are, Dr Hunter. One of the finest sushi restaurants outside of Japan." He paused to let the words sink in. "And it's a pretty good Italian restaurant too."

Charles weaved between the tables and headed towards a bar at the far end, with Dr Hunter following. As they were approaching the bar, Charles pointed to an empty table. "If you would like to take a seat, Dr Hunter, I'll fetch you a menu."

He sat down at the tastefully and expensively set table and glanced around. There was a smattering of well-heeled diners dotted around the chic and understated restaurant, and he became aware of the low hum of indecipherable conversations mixing with generic European chill-out music emanating from unseen speakers.

To one side of the bar was a lounge area with low, soft sofas and even lower coffee tables. Two women, tanned, well-preserved, always noticing if they were being watched, sat chatting on a sofa. They didn't seem particularly interested in each other, although they laughed loudly and exaggeratedly every time the other said something intended to be funny. At the next table, a thick-set man in an expensive polo shirt was talking animatedly in Russian to another, less notable man. His companion listened carefully and nodded from time to time, but said nothing. They were finishing off plates of finely made sushi and throwing back glasses of sake like shots of vodka.

Charles reappeared and handed Dr Hunter a menu. "Thank you," Dr Hunter said without looking up.

"The specials are on a piece of paper tucked into the menu, should you be interested in trying them," Charles said. After a brief pause, he added: "Would you mind if I joined you for a drink?"

Dr Hunter was already studying the menu. "Fine," he said noncommittally.

Charles sat down opposite Dr Hunter and laced his fingers, smiling at his companion even though he was still fixed on reading the menu. "Thank you, Dr Hunter. I have to say, it's always a pleasure to have the opportunity of talking to someone like me."

Dr Hunter looked up, surprised.

"What I mean is that we don't get too many English guests here, and I'm one of the only non-locals on the staff."

Charles paused and looked around the restaurant. Dr Hunter went back to reading the menu. "You know," Charles resumed, "it's not so much England itself that I miss—my family send me mustard and tea, of course, and the occasional jar of Branston Pickle when I get desperate—but it's the conversation."

Without looking up, Dr Hunter replied: "Really? I haven't had the opportunity to experience a lack of it so far."

"No, of course." Charles turned to a passing waiter. "Two glasses of champagne, please." The waiter nodded and noted the table number as he walked on. Dr Hunter looked up from his menu again and frowned. Charles smiled apologetically. "A small celebration. Will you join me? It's on the house."

Dr Hunter down put his menu and folded his arms. "Okay. But what are we celebrating?"

"Life, Dr Hunter," Charles said, looking him straight in the eye. "It's all we have."

"Please, call me John."

"Thank you, John. I appreciate that." Charles smiled. "I realise, of course, that we should be drinking Prosecco, seeing as it's technically a little more local to the region than champagne, and some Proseccos are really rather excellent nowadays, but there are times when only champagne will do, don't you find?"

"Hmm, I suppose so," John said, unfolding his arms and placing his hands on the table. He looked around.

"Have you decided yet what you would like to eat?"

"No, not really."

"Then allow me. I'll have a word with the chef. He will make all of his most famous dishes for you," Charles enthused.

"Well..."

"My treat. The chef loves a chance to show off, and I love an opportunity to talk."

"Okay," John replied slowly.

"If you'll excuse me," Charles said, clearly delighted. He got up from behind the table and walked quickly away.

John picked up the menu, then put it down again without reading it and went back to looking around the restaurant. The Russian at the next table glanced at John from the corner of his eye.

After a couple of minutes, Charles resumed his seat, lacing his fingers once more. "That's all arranged then. I must say that you are in for a treat," Charles said, looking pleased with himself.

"Um, thanks, I don't think..."

"Not at all, it's always a pleasure to meet someone, let's say, cut from the same cloth."

John raised his eyebrows. "How so?"

Charles gave a mischievous smile. "Cambridge, I take it?"

"Yes. How did you know?"

Charles sat back in satisfaction. "Let's just say it takes one to know one."

He looked down at the table. "Still no drinks?" Charles caught the eye of a passing waiter. "Could you look into those two glasses of champagne we ordered?"

The waiter bowed his head slightly. "Yes, of course. At once." The waiter glanced at John and then scurried away.

John straightened his menu, then straightened his knife

and fork and refolded his napkin. "How long have you been working here," he asked.

Charles looked up at the sky. "Only for a short while, as it happens. I was in Germany for many years, and then Austria. Near the Italian border, in fact. While I was there, I picked up enough Italian to work in Venice for a while. And then, after various other stops along the way, I ended up here."

"Have you always worked in hotels?"

"In one form or another, yes. I had retired, but I was tempted back into the business."

John looked up, interested. "Oh yes? By what?"

Charles stared hard at John. "A death in the family."

John looked away. The two women who had been drinking on the sofa had left, leaving only their impression in the soft cushions. "I'm...sorry to hear that. Was it someone close?"

Charles laced and unlaced his fingers. "Yes, I'm afraid so. After that, I simply couldn't face being at home any longer."

"Yes, I can understand that," John murmured.

They fell silent, and John became aware once more of the low hum of chatter and the clinking of glasses at the bar. After a few moments, the waiter reappeared with two glasses of champagne and placed them carefully in front of the two men. The waiter looked at them, still lost in thought, and cleared his throat. "I am so sorry for the delay, Mr Charles," he said, "The barman was distracted by a large order for cocktails."

Charles glanced up at the waiter and smiled warmly. "Thank you." The waiter inclined his head fractionally and disappeared. Charles picked up his glass, inspected the bubbles and then raised it towards John. "To your very good health," he said.

Retreating from his thoughts, John picked up his glass and repeated: "To your very good health." The two men took a sip of the cool champagne. John luxuriated in rolling the golden liquid around his mouth, the bubbles bursting and the taste growing on his tongue.

Charles raised his glass again. "And may you find all that fate has in store for you."

John shot a glance at Charles and frowned. He swallowed the remnants of champagne and raised his glass again.

Charles looked briefly down at his hands and then around the restaurant. "You know, I tell a lie about not having spoken English in a while."

John put his glass down deliberately and looked straight at Charles. "Oh yes?"

"My goddaughter, who, I may say..." Charles learned in with a glint in his eye and lowered his voice, "is a very famous and extremely beautiful actress, stayed here recently." Charles leaned back again, examining John's face for a reaction.

"Uh-huh," he said, trying to sound uninterested.

"She tried to tempt me to go home and give all this up," Charles continued, gesturing around the restaurant. "She wanted me to enjoy a life of retirement and repose. But," Charles continued, "there are some things that are hard to let go of, once you have started them."

John looked around the restaurant and gardens admiringly. "Well, it certainly is beautiful here. I can see why you'd want to stay."

"But looks can be deceiving, don't you find, Dr Hunter?"

Before John could reply, a waiter appeared with a plate of beautifully prepared fresh sushi. He stared at the dish, unsure as to whether he really wanted to eat it.

"I promise you," Charles said, proud of the chef's creation, "that you will not be disappointed."

HALF AN HOUR LATER, John sat back and regarded the collection of small empty plates in front of him. He was satisfied and it had been delicious, but a wave of post-prandial exhaustion swept over him and his eyes became heavy.

Charles hadn't stopped talking for the entire time that John had eaten and, even now, he was explaining something in great detail. However, he was no longer fully aware of where the conversation was going or at what stage in the history of Charles's life they had reached.

He tried to concentrate. What was he saying? Ah, that was it. They had moved from Charles's life onto politics. He remembered Charles asking him his thoughts on the current crop of politicians running the country, a question that he had attempted to bat away but Charles had pursued regardless, launching into his assessment of each and every major public figure, once he saw that no opinions would be forthcoming from John.

He looked around the restaurant. There were fewer diners now, but the Russian at the next table continued talking animatedly to his near-silent dinner companion. John turned his attention back to Charles and tried to focus on what he was saying.

"...and that, of course, is one of the difficulties in trying to create a unified Europe," Charles said, leaning back with satisfaction at his argument.

"Uh-huh," John replied wearily, trying to stifle a yawn.

"Take Eastern Europe, for example. One of the biggest problems is the gravitational pull of Russia. It causes a destabilising influence, not only because it is a competing centre of power but also because it has, let's say, a complicated relationship with its neighbours."

"Yes," said John, half-listening. Charles leaned forwards. "And I think it's important not to forget how many millions of Eastern Europeans, and Russians themselves, were murdered by Stalin."

Before Charles could continue, the Russian sitting at the

next table made a loud shushing sound. John and Charles turned instantly towards him, Charles shocked as the Russian, with a sardonic grin on his face, slowly wagged his finger at him in admonishment. Charles turned back to John with an embarrassed smile. "Perhaps not all things are best aired in public," he said quietly.

John raised his eyebrows and ran a finger up the stem of his wineglass, and the two men fell silent. After a moment, John sighed and pushed back his chair. "If you don't mind," he said, "I think I'd like to go to bed. It's been a very long day, and I'm exhausted."

"Of course," Charles said hurriedly. "And here I am boring you senseless all night." Charles stood up and smiled at John. "Thank you so very much for your time, Dr Hunter. it was greatly appreciated. And I do hope that you enjoyed your meal."

"Please call me John. Yes, it was delicious, thank you. Are you sure...?"

"Not at all, it was a pleasure to host you."

John stood up and inspected Charles's face. "Well, thank you again. And good night."

Charles held out his hand. "Good night."

The two men shook hands and John walked back towards the hotel. As John reached the flower garden, he glanced back. Charles was still standing where he had left him, watching. John frowned, then turned and walked along the tree-lined path back to the hotel.

BACK IN HIS MOONLIT BEDROOM, he gently pushed the door shut and awkwardly pulled off his jacket, tossing it onto the bed. He then picked it up again, shook it out and placed carefully it on a hangar in the wardrobe. He sighed and glanced around the room, initially unsure what to do, then went to the bathroom.

He inspected his face in the mirror, pulling his skin and examining the whites of his eyes, now raw with tiredness. He washed his face slowly and deliberately, all the while staring at himself in the mirror. When he was done, he patted his face dry and carefully folded the towel onto the rail below the sink.

He pulled off his clothes on his way to the bed. He thought about folding them, but a wave of exhaustion swept over him and he let them drop to the floor. He clambered into bed and, as soon as his head hit the pillow, fell into a deep sleep.

Outside, the cicadas droned on in an endless roll, then stopped.

The room fell quiet, with only John's steady breathing breaking the silence.

CHAPTER SIX

THE BANGING AND TENSE, ANGRY WHISPERING RETURNED in an instant, slicing through the still calm of the night. John woke up, sharp and clear. He frowned and waited before springing out of bed, pulling on his shirt and trousers and rushing to the door.

He burst into the corridor, only to find it silent and empty. Puzzled, he looked down the corridor and saw the Russian entering his room. He stopped and stared at John and then glanced down at his bare feet. Embarrassed, John looked down too. By the time he looked up again, the Russian was disappearing into his room, the door closing behind him with a soft click.

John sighed. He turned to go back into his room, but something caught his eye. There, across the corridor, was a small gap in the wall. A gap that, he realised on closer inspection, was the outline of a concealed door. More than that, it was ajar.

John walked cautiously over and pushed the door open. Beyond lay a dark stone passageway that resembled something from a mediaeval prison. By the feeble light cast from the corridor, it was impossible to see where it led.

Checking to see if there was anyone around, he stepped tentatively into the passageway. He smarted at the rough, cold floor on his bare feet. Keeping one hand on the wall, he inched his way along, testing the ground before stepping forwards. Eventually, he reached what seemed like a corner but was in reality a dead end. John pushed gently at the wall to see if it would give, but soon gave up and made his way back towards the hotel corridor.

Back in the light, John padded down to the Russian's room and listened at the door but heard nothing. As he stepped back, he heard voices from the stone passageway. He rushed back to the concealed door but by the time he got there it had clicked shut. The door was now barely visible against the rest of the corridor. John ran a finger along the narrow gap that remained, through which issued a slight breeze. He glanced around and noticed a CCTV camera pointing straight at him. Realising his antics had been caught on camera, John cursed himself under his breath and went back to his room.

CHAPTER SEVEN

You walk along a busy London street, hand in hand with a beautiful, dark-haired woman. You talk animatedly, but your voices are distant, incomprehensible. The world is shining, luminescent even, though the sky is stained dark metal. You gaze at the woman. She smiles and talks, but seems far away. Her voice is increasingly indistinct and distorted and her expressions merge into one.

You walk on but she falls behind. She fades, and her hand slips from yours. You turn in panic and her twisted face melts into a silent scream. Her eyes rotate backwards, pulling her out of shape.

You follow her gaze and a police car skids across the road in slow motion, its siren slow and atonal. The car hits the pavement, flips and rolls towards the beautiful woman. It shatters into a crystalline tsunami of glass and refracted light that sweeps slowly towards her. You try to shout, to reach her, but you make no sound and cannot move. Your face tears in pain as the wave of glass and light envelopes her.

She is in a hospital bed, tangled, broken, covered in blood. Tubes pour from her nose, her mouth, her throat, her arms, her chest, all leaking blood. Her eyes leak blood, the bed leaks blood, and blood pours from the walls. She chokes on it as it spills from her mouth, her nose, her eyes.

You are trapped outside the room. You shout, bang on the glass, you try to reach her. You scream for help, but there is no one. There is only silence.

The walls of the hospital room drift away, the machines and tubes fade, and the bed melts into the endless darkness. The woman floats away and disappears.

IN THE DARK calm of his room, John's eyes were shut tight, twitching, lost in fitful sleep.

The cicadas were silent now. Somewhere, a woman laughed.

A tear rolled down his cheek.

PART TWO

CHAPTER ONE

EARLY NEXT MORNING, JOHN WALKED PURPOSEFULLY through the hotel gardens, dressed in swimming trunks and flip-flops. The pool was still and empty, only a couple of dry leaves floating on its unbroken surface. He stepped out of his flip-flops and dived straight into the azure water.

There was nothing and no one to accompany the sound of his slow, rhythmical swimming, save for the birds singing in the trees and the soft crashing of the waves below the cliffs.

HALF AN HOUR LATER, he walked around his bed in semicircles while he fiddled with his cufflinks. His mobile phone rang and he checked the screen before abandoning them and taking the call.

"Michael, hi. How are you?" He turned and looked out of the balcony doors and towards the sea. "No, it's lovely. The weather is amazing. It's a real paradise here."

He cradled the phone in his shoulder while he returned to the cufflinks.

"No, all fine, thanks. The hotel manager is a bit funny. He spent the whole of last night bending my ear."

He smiled at the response as he checked himself in the mirror. "I know. Isn't it just. But he means well I suppose, although he seems to talk in riddles half the time. He told me he hasn't had a proper conversation in English in ages."

He frowned as he looked around the room. "No, he is English, went to Cambridge, apparently. How he ended up working here is anyone's guess. Talking of work, are you handling the rota okay without me? Not too many tricky emergencies?"

He paced around the room, finally attaching the second cufflink. "I wish I could forget about work, Mike. Actually, I don't wish that at all. I wish I was back in theatre, scrubbed up and ready to go. Out here, I'm useless and lost."

He checked himself in the mirror and ran a hand over his still-wet hair. "No, of course. You're right. It's good to get away. I do realise that."

He stared at the photo of the beautiful dark-haired woman on the mantelpiece. "Maybe you're right," he said quietly. "I probably do need the rest. The one who needs it the most is always the last to know, right?"

He turned away and stared at the unmade bed. "No, thank you," he said, his voice thick with emotion. "I appreciated it. We all did."

He looked out at the balcony again. "Thank you...Okay, yes, sure. Speak soon. Take care, and say hello to everyone for me."

The call ended and, lost in thought, he let his hand drop down to his side. The phone slipped onto the bed as he stared into nothing.

CHAPTER TWO

THE BREAKFAST TERRACE WAS OVERHUNG WITH BUSHES AND trees and surrounded by a stone wall. With the canopies fully extended, as they were on this warm and sunny morning, it gave the impression of being a salon or small theatre. Adding to the effect, the space was crammed with tables and chairs, and, by the time John came down for breakfast, seemingly all occupied.

Unsure what to do, he hovered while the guests talked quietly among themselves and the waiters flitted between the tables. Eventually, a waiter appeared at John's elbow and took him over to a table in the far corner by the wall. He positioned himself so he had a view of the terrace and surreptitiously examined the other guests. Most were in their mid-thirties to late fifties. Everyone was tanned and healthy-looking and reeked of money and easy comfort.

He became aware of a conversation between two couples sitting at adjoining tables, both speaking in American accents.

"So, where have you guys just flown in from," one man asked.

The woman on the other table smiled and fluffed up her shoulders. "Paris. We were there for our honeymoon; a week in the George Cinq."

"Oh, how lovely," the woman on the first table chipped in. "So this is the second leg of your trip?"

The second man interjected: "Yes, we're doing a month-long tour of the Med. A few days here, and then we pick up a yacht and head over to Greece. How about you guys?"

"We're on our honeymoon too," the woman on the first table exclaimed. She gazed lovingly at her husband and placed her hand over his. John smiled to himself and fiddled with his napkin ring.

"What a coincidence," the other woman said, laughing inauthentically. "Where did you guys get married?"

"Florence."

"Sweet."

"Well, we're both on our second marriages, so we thought we'd go the extra mile, so to speak." The two women laughed.

"Right," the other woman said. "Same for us. We got married on a beach in the Caribbean."

"We hired a palazzo overlooking the Arno," the first woman shot back.

"Wow," one husband said, turning to the other. He smiled conspiratorially: "That must have cost you a packet."

The two couples laughed. John turned away to look at the other tables. Charles walked out of the hotel and checked each table before approaching John's and standing in front of him. John regarded the older man, squinting into the sunlight and cursing himself for having left his sunglasses in his room.

"Good morning, Dr Hunter. Did you enjoy your morning swim? I find it such an invigorating way to start the day, don't you?"

John frowned. "How did you know I went swimming? The hotel was dead. I didn't see anyone."

Charles smiled impishly. "I make it my business to know how each of my guests is getting on." John raised his eyebrows and then looked around the terrace, aware that the acoustics meant everyone could listen in on their conversation. Charles cleared his throat. "Would you like to try the special taster breakfast?" John looked unsure. He continued: "It's a little of everything that our head chef prepares each morning to awaken our guests' palates. As an introduction to his work, and as a start to the day, I can think of nothing better."

"Well..."

Charles smiled. "That's settled, then." He turned to a passing waiter. "The taster breakfast for Dr Hunter, here." The waiter made a mental note of the table before bowing his head and disappearing inside the building.

"That's Enrico, one of our finest waiters," Charles said proudly. "He has worked with me in three hotels across Europe now. We know each other, as the French say, like the inside of our pockets."

"It must be nice to have a relationship like that with a colleague," John observed.

Charles looked up to the sky and watched the birds turning on the currents. "In a place like this, Dr Hunter, to have someone you can trust is...essential."

John peered up, trying to glean some additional meaning from his statement, but he couldn't see beyond his business-like sheen, and did not wish to enquire any further without at least having had his first coffee of the morning. The two men fell silent and John returned to looking at the other guests.

"Do you have any plans for your first full day in our wonderful resort, Dr Hunter," Charles asked loudly.

John cleared his throat and shifted in his chair. "No, no, not really."

"There is so much to see here. The markets, the old

harbour, the beautiful hidden beaches, the rocky headlands and there are, of course, day trips to hidden grottos that shine like jewels. There is plenty, in short, to occupy and divert the curious traveller seeking rest and stimulation in equal measure."

John glanced around and caught the eye of one of the newly-wed couples.

"Okay, thanks," John said brusquely, "We'll see what happens."

Charles smiled and inclined his head. "Quite so. I should leave you to your breakfast, Dr Hunter. But should you require any advice or tips, or you would like to discuss any aspect of your stay further, please don't hesitate to ask for me. I am at your disposal."

John smiled awkwardly. "Thank you."

Charles walked briskly back into the hotel. Enrico appeared with a small plate of pastries, which he placed carefully on one corner of John's table.

"A little something while the chef prepares your hot dishes," the waiter said. "How would you like your eggs?"

John reflected for a moment. "Poached, please, with a runny yolk."

"And for your bread, sir? We have white, multigrain, rye... anything you want."

"Rye bread, please, toasted, and lots of slightly salted butter."

"Of course, sir. And what jams and confections could I get for you?"

"Actually, I don't like sweet foods. Could I have mushrooms or something like that with my eggs?"

"Yes, of course, sir. I shall tell the chef. He prepares a dish with two types of wild mushrooms, local herbs and a dash of sherry. It's not on the breakfast menu but I could ask him to prepare that for you, if that would be of interest?"

"That would be perfect, thank you. Also, I'm in the mood for a little spice this morning. Could you please bring me some cayenne pepper on the side?"

"With pleasure, sir. What can I get you to drink? We have the full range of hot and cold soft beverages, and the bar is available, should you wish to start the day with, say, something sparkling."

John smiled. "That won't be necessary, thank you. Just a strong black coffee. Not an espresso but stronger than an Americano, to be followed by a pot of Earl Grey tea and two slices of lemon on the side."

"Right away, sir. If you would like anything else, do not hesitate to ask." Enrico inclined his head in the same way as Charles, then disappeared back into the hotel.

John looked around the terrace and caught the eye of an elderly couple at a nearby table. "You certainly know what you want, don't you," said the woman in an American accent.

Before John could reply there was a scream from the other side of the terrace. A huge seagull had landed on one of the canopies and was flapping its wings and clumsily trying to find its feet on the slippery material. The woman who screamed looked aghast. "Oh my god," she exclaimed, and clasped her hand over her mouth.

The bird eventually found its footing and settled down on the canopy, carefully and deliberately folding its wings. The seagull stared straight at John, fixing his gaze and looking deep into his eyes as it tilted its head. John was transfixed and his stomach churned. The bird flicked its head down. John followed its gaze and saw the Russian man from the previous evening. The man glanced up at the bird and then at John, smiling quizzically at what John realised must have been his own confused expression. The seagull then turned its head slowly and stared back at John. Once it had trapped John's gaze once more, it looked straight back down at the Russian man. John's heart pounded in his chest and a hundred thoughts flooded his mind.

A waiter appeared from the hotel and shooed the bird away. It regarded the man with disdain and then slowly unfolded its wings and leapt into the air, flapping powerfully and lifting itself over the treetops.

John watched the seagull until it disappeared. The rest of the diners slowly returned to their breakfasts, and the hum of morning chatter resumed.

CHAPTER THREE

LATER THAT MORNING, JOHN WANDERED THROUGH THE busy, narrow streets of the old town, which were festooned with garlands and decorations from a recent local festival. Every available inch of space was filled with stalls laden with cheap gifts and trinkets, lava jewellery, tourist t-shirts, glistening cakes, shiny sweets, smoked meats, fruits in alcohol, plastic toys, leather gloves, silk scarves, disposable umbrellas and sports shoes, alongside pile after pile after pile of succulent fruits from across the Mediterranean.

There were sacks of grain, mounds of dates and figs, piles of local nuts, and iridescent bottles of gaudy local spirits, sparkling in the patches of sunlight that reached down between the buildings. Between it all, nestled cafés and tiny bars crowded with retired locals playing dominoes or chess, arguing casually or simply watching the world go by. Dogs who knew the street by nose threaded their way between the tourists, searching for someone to beg from, while cats sat on high balconies and watched the coming and goings with a disinterested air as they sunbathed in the hot sun.

John took his time to push through the crowds. He told

himself to slow down and turn off his ingrained city need to get from A to B in the shortest possible time. There is no A, and there is certainly no B.

He smiled as he passed a pile of particularly juicy and inviting dates, wondering why people in films are able to get away with stealing fruit from local markets while he would surely be caught. He watched an old woman talking to a young market-stall owner. They discussed their lives while she expertly chose fruit and vegetables and dropped bulging paper bags into a shopping trolley by her feet. The young man's attention was caught by a passing beauty in a tight dress, but the older woman soon recaptured his gaze.

John followed a middle-aged man on a scooter, with no helmet and a cigarette dangling from his mouth, as he slowly pushed through the crowd. The engine belched out clouds of thick, dirty smoke, and John wondered why he didn't simply drive down the main road rather than inching his way down this tightly packed lane. The crowds parted with some reluctance, and John used the opportunity to carve his own way through the melée, until he became fed up with the fumes.

EVENTUALLY, he reached a small square full of clothes stalls and cafes, and dominated by a large, old church that appeared to have been converted into a combination of working men's club and retirement home. He stopped and watched groups of old and middle-aged gents, and longed to join them. But he reminded himself that he hadn't learned a single word of the local language. In any case, wasn't in the mood to risk humiliating himself and be told he wasn't welcome.

After an old woman ran over his foot with her shopping trolley and made it clear that he had been in the way, John found a small corner café with a view of the square. He ordered a coffee, not knowing the word for anything else to drink, and chose a seat by the window so he could watch the world go by. After a few minutes, the smiling café owner brought him a tray with a metal cup of thick coffee and a piece of Turkish delight. John thanked him and resumed staring out of the window. The endless flow of people continued unabated and John revelled in the characters and mini dramas, the kaleidoscope of ever-changing colours and the richness of faces.

The coffee was strong, and John was glad to finish it when the thick granules at the bottom reached his lips. He watched a set of shutters open at the top of a building. A woman shook out a towel, her face tight with concentration and effort.

A seagull landed on a lamppost adjacent to the window, and stared straight at him. His mind flashed back to break-fast, then the photograph in his room and his stomach dropped. He looked down at his coffee cup and his heart pounded. When he looked up again, the seagull was gone. John tried to return to watching the passing crowd and follow its unfolding stories but he was disconnected now. Everyone in the square was on the other side of a screen and he was alone, trapped behind the glass. A swell of dark emotions overwhelmed him. A headache started behind his left ear and the blood coursed through his skull. He thought he might burst, as if he was trying to break out of his body.

His scalp crawled and he had pins and needles in his fingers. He wanted to get up, fling open the door of the café and run away. But there was nowhere to go. He was already somewhere else. Maybe I can take out as much cash as possible, get the first plane or train out of there and disappear?

But he knew that wherever he went he would be there, and it was to escape himself that he really wanted. To get away from the heavy weight of being inside his body, his mind. He looked at his hands. If only he could be atomised right there and then and flow into the sewer. To be thrust out into the sea, where he could mingle with the infinite water and never be seen again.

But it was no use. And what would it achieve? It would have no real impact, no real meaning. It was too late for all that. He had already been ripped apart. What would it mean to all those people in the square if he was to disappear? They knew nothing of him, nothing of his existence. To them, whether he was there or not was irrelevant.

What about at the hotel? He existed there, for the staff. How long would it take for them to notice he was missing? Until the end of his stay, when they expected him to check out? Presumably they would go to the police, once they realised he had not gone back to his room. They would make some basic enquiries and, once it had all blown over, they would declare the case closed and move on. And what would they do with his things? Doubtless they would dispose of everything. All those things he had deliberated and fretted over when he was packing, all those things he was so sure he couldn't travel without. They meant nothing to anyone else. Once a person disappears, the things that marked their trace have no significance anymore. They go back to being objects. All those proofs of another mind, another life, another set of connections and memories, made empty.

But what, exactly, would they do with his things? Send them back home? To his mother? Who else? She was his next of kin now. And what about the photograph on the mantel-piece? What would they do with that?

He made himself look at the world beyond the window. He tried to watch two female tourists deciding whether to try on some clothes in a flimsy curtain changing room behind a stall. He tried to focus on two policemen standing in the corner of the square, casually inspecting an abandoned scooter, but he couldn't concentrate. The same questions came flooding back, one after another. What would the police say if he disappeared? What would they say had happened to him? Death by misadventure, with the faint whiff of something untoward? And what would they think back at the hospital? His colleagues? His friends? God knows, but he was sure he would quickly be forgotten.

John inspected the granules at the bottom of his coffee cup and decided he wanted to leave. He pulled himself off the stool and paid the barman, tipping him generously. The man thanked John profusely, but John turned and walked out without acknowledging him.

CHAPTER FOUR

BACK IN THE SQUARE, JOHN SAW A SIGN POINTING TO THE harbour. It led him down a quiet side street dotted with restaurants and ice-cream parlours. Here, there were no locals getting on with their day, only throngs of holidaymakers ambling to or from the harbour and its tiny beach. Even at this hour there were lobster-red patches of skin crying out from under cheap holiday clothes. Everyone seemed tired and unhappy, as if they had endured an ordeal, yet about which they did not want to warn others.

He wandered on, weaving his way between the slow-moving crowds and large panels displaying photographs of identical-looking local meals. He thought about having a dip in the sea once he got to the beach, but remembered he had left his trunks drying on the balcony outside his room. He idly pondered buying new ones and using those, especially as he had brought only one pair with him, but it seemed a little wasteful given how often he went swimming during the rest of the year. A young family walked past and John stared at a blond-haired boy, wondering if it was the same one who had stood next to him at the baggage carousel in the airport.

Further on, the path turned and opened out onto a large square overlooking the old harbour and its small beach. John sat on a low wall that ran along the edge and gazed down at the sand, every square inch of which was covered with striped, lurid sun loungers in tightly packed rows, interspersed with umbrellas. John watched enterprising locals wending their way between the loungers, selling cold drinks and taking orders for lunch from nearby restaurants. The sea was full of holidaymakers shouting, jumping, swimming, laughing, playing, all hemmed in by buoys and ropes from the fleet of old fishing boats that came and went from the harbour. *Maybe it's a good job I didn't buy another swimming costume.*

DOWN IN THE OLD HARBOUR, John gazed at the cafés and small shops but didn't want to go in any of them. Waiters beckoned him in to their near-identical restaurants, trying two or three languages to see if he would respond, but he merely smiled weakly and walked on. He passed an old and dilapidated church and a dirty-looking English pub. Outside, an overweight couple sat drinking pints with an air of determined concentration.

At the end of the harbour, steps led up the opposite side of the bay and he followed them, hoping he wouldn't be too sweaty by the time he reached the top. Halfway up, he passed an old French couple, who expressed surprise and admiration at his efforts. He decided to test himself and adopted a steady, brisk rhythm, not pausing or slowing as the pain flared in his thighs and the strain became almost unbearable. He looked only at his feet and carried on and on, switching to two steps at a time, and panting and grimacing at each one.

He turned a corner and burst out onto a small turning point on the busy coast road, wondering why he had pushed himself that hard. He stood with his hands on his knees, gasping for breath, the blood pounding in his ears. The sweat poured out of him and he was glad of the gentle breeze across the top of the cliffs to cool him down. While he regained his strength, he gazed out over the twinkling azure sea and watched a seagull drifting across the air currents.

Finally catching his breath, John took in his surroundings and spotted a small shop. Stalls laden with fresh fruit and vegetables lined the entrance, over which hung a sign that English was spoken. Inside was a treasure trove. Initially wanting only a bottle of water, he soon changed his mind when he saw the counters full of cheeses and fresh cured meats and the racks of freshly baked bread.

He asked the owner, who spoke much less English than the sign suggested, for a cheese, tomato and roquette sandwich. He picked out some small, sweet grapes, plump Saturn peaches and olives from a huge vat behind the counter. Adding an apricot juice and the coldest bottle of spring water he could find, John asked the owner via sign language if there was anywhere nearby he could have a picnic. If he followed the coast road, the man said, he would reach a path signposted for, as far as John could make out, a palace.

Not particularly confident he would spot it, John picked his way along the main road, trying not to think about the rush of trucks, taxis, buses and mopeds that flashed by inches from his legs, each one spraying a fine mist of gravel and dust onto his bare skin. Eventually, he came across a sign to a Roman villa that pointed down between small holdings and ancient olive groves.

At the end, a small, crescent-shaped bay, hidden on all sides, opened out like a flower. He stood and took in the idyllic scene, grateful to have left behind the tourists and the traffic. He found a shaded spot looking over the bay and spread out his lunch. He watched a group of local teenagers cavort and frolic in a large rock-pool that seemed to have been carved out by ancient hands. He unwrapped his sandwich and relished the thick bursts of intense flavours and the coarse handmade bread. A tourist walked past and nodded at John, admiring his feast. He smiled and wrenched another mouthful from his sandwich, chewing it slowly.

He put the sandwich down and ran his fingers through some leaves. Sharp hairs bristled against his skin. He breathed deep the clean air of the sea, and listened to the laughing, teasing, unselfconscious teenagers, understanding nothing but sensing every contortion of emotion as they dived through the water and each other.

This is paradise.

He flicked a large ant from his sandwich and watched the animal turn itself in the dust and walk away. He took another bite and looked out to sea, watching the birds turned slowly on the air currents.

A cloud drifted by.

A tourist boat rounded the headland and made slowly for the bay. It stopped just in front of the entrance and several passengers dived off the side and swam ashore. They pulled themselves out onto the rocks and stood regarding the scene, first watching the group of teenagers, then spotting John on the path above before taking in the shape of the land and the rich vegetation.

Some stayed on the beach, looking out to sea, while others followed the numerous paths and threaded their way up the hillside. John watched a woman, perhaps in her late forties, as she climbed up the opposite side of the bay. Her dark hair flowed in waves and she walked with poise and grace. John watched her curves flex and adjust to her movements. At the top of the hill, she glanced in his direction and then out to sea. She adjusted the material on her swimsuit and breathed in deeply. John breathed with her.

After a moment, she dived off the cliff and disappeared from view. John started and got up to see what had happened to her. Seconds later, she reappeared, swimming slowly towards the boat. John imagined himself standing on the cliff, wondering whether he would dive in after her. He realised he would not. He could not. Not anymore.

He sighed and looked down at his legs, pale in the bright sunlight. When was the last time I sat in the sun? When was the last time we did? Pushing the thought away, he returned to his lunch, finishing the last of his sandwich and the fruit.

He watched an ant clambered over the hairs on his legs. Initially, he regarded it with curiosity. Then he wanted to kill it. Then to flick it away. Instead, he encouraged it run onto his hand, wanting to lift it carefully to freedom. But the ant didn't want to, despite several attempts, and persisted in clambering over him. A rage fired up inside him and he killed it, crushing it against his skin. The rage died down and, tinged with guilt, he examined the smear of red-black against his skin.

His minded drifted, alighting on the banging and whispering outside his door from the night before. What on earth where they doing? And what about the stone passageway? It didn't lead anywhere. What were they so desperate about?

Unsure what to make of it all, he looked up to find that the boat was gone, the teenagers were getting dressed and the bay was in shade. A breeze was getting up and he could see a storm cloud appearing over the horizon.

Paradise is over.

He packed away the remnants of his lunch and pushed his feet back into his flip-flops, the grains of sand and dirt rubbing against his skin. He sighed at the thought of having to walk back to town, and wondered if he could simply follow the road all the way back, rather than going via the harbour. Perhaps he could ask the teenagers for directions? No, he didn't want to talk to anyone. The thoughts in his head were too loud for him to speak. Anyway, the only way to get to know a place is first to get lost.

CHAPTER FIVE

THE STREETLIGHTS WERE SLOWLY FLICKERING INTO LIFE BY
the time John reached the town. The storm cloud had passed
without shedding a drop and the evening was turning balmy.
As John trudged along the road next to the narrow, winding
streets of the old town, he wondered whether he should get
changed before going out for the evening. He inspected his
shorts and loose, open shirt, both slightly the worse for wear
after a day's walking and sweating in the summer sun, and
pondered his visibly dusty feet.

Still making his mind up, John walked past a loud Irish
bar. Dozens of tables were strung along the side of the road
and each one was taken by couples, groups and lonely
drinkers from across the world, glumly sipping on pints of
Guinness in bored silence. John inspected their attire and
decided that there was no need to go back to the hotel and
change. He did, however, wash his feet at a water pump and
took a long, long drink from the splashing torrent, the cool
water unleashing a rush of freshness and energy within him.

After a few steps, his wet flip-flops were uncomfortable.
He stopped at a small bar by the edge of the old town and

drank a beer while he dried out. When he had finished, John asked the barman for a restaurant recommendation, fully aware that, in any case, he would recommend his cousin's place.

Pleasingly, it turned out to be a tiny trattoria lost in the backstreets, with a few tables ranged along a cobbled street. John drank a bottle of strong local white wine and took an octopus salad dressed in a delicately flavoured olive oil, followed by a green bean stew and tomato salad.

The street was quiet and most of the passers-by were townsfolk on their way home. At the next table, a young, sunburned couple from Germany seemed to be in the early stages of their relationship, still finding something funny in everything that was different, underlining their togetherness and connection. Maybe they're on their first holiday together. Maybe they're finding out if they actually like each other, away from the tedious distractions of daily life. The memory of earlier holidays and the sparkling brightness of a moment shared rose up within him, but he pushed it down as far as it would go.

The waiter asked if he would like a dessert. He deliberated the possibility of eating more, then taking a coffee and perhaps a small digestif, before strolling through the old town back to his hotel. It was the sensible thing to do, perhaps even the right thing to do and, given his situation, certainly what anyone would expect him to do. If he was with someone, it is what he would most likely have suggested.

But he was alone. He'd had a bottle of wine, and he didn't want to lose the comfortable warmth it had given him. If he went back to the hotel, he'd have to face the emptiness of the room, all that darkness and silence, the maddening calm and the mirrors staring back at him. He thought of her picture on the mantelpiece, and his own face reflected in the glass. All those memories would be waiting for him if he went back. He didn't want that. Not now.

When the waiter returned, he asked for a recommendation for a local bar. Something not too touristy but welcoming to strangers. The man described how to get to a place owned by his cousin, who had apparently lived in London for two years. While John half-listened to the directions, the German couple left and walked past. For the first time, John could see their faces, red from the unfamiliar Mediterranean sun. The woman, who was laughing, noticed John and instinctively became serious and glanced at the floor. John was puzzled and a little saddened. What did she see in me? What did I do?

As JOHN WALKED the narrow streets, a demon rose up inside him that he had not submitted to in a long, long while. He had sensed its approach several times of late but had known that to give in to it at this stage, in his current state of mind, would have been wrong or even potentially disastrous for him and those around him. But now, walking along a quiet street over a thousand miles and an entire universe from home, he wondered if, perhaps, he could at last let the demon in. Just this once. Maybe he could allow it to envelop him, to take charge of his senses, his hands, his mouth, his tongue, his eyes, and he follow it whatever it led.

The demon promised freedom from the weight that pressed down on him; from the dark, from the fearful shadows that awaited him whenever his guard fell; from the infinite exhaustion that clung to him and was there in the flickering of his eyelids; from the dense, thick fog that filled up his lungs, and the paleness that drained the life from his skin; from the dry distance between him and life; from being simply an automaton going through the motions of existence.

The demon told him he could escape all that, that he could be light and free, smile again, make jokes, connect with himself and other people.

Guilt at the idea of taking pleasure rose up too, but he pushed that back down. He knew he should go back to the hotel. He knew he should not have 'just one more drink'. He knew he should go to bed. He knew all this. And he knew what it would look like if it was known by people back home that he was having fun. But maybe they would say he needed to let his hair down and free himself, even if for a few hours. Perhaps some would even say that it was essential, after all he had been through in the past few weeks.

What is the point of being on holiday if you aren't there to get away, to slough off the skin of life and be fresh and new? Otherwise you may as well have stayed at home. Mind you, some might say he should never have gone on holiday in the first place. He reflected, however, that if one of his friends had asked him, he would have told them to go on holiday and make the most of it, to get out there, enjoy themselves, have a few drinks, get drunk even, and see what happens. To just...go with the flow. All the rest will still be waiting for you when you get back home. But, for now, you should forget all that and live a little. For now, you should drink.

BY THE TIME John had thought everything through, he had reached the door of the bar. He pushed it open with something almost approaching joy and quickly surveyed the room. The space was richly decorated from floor to ceiling with a thousand knick-knacks, old adverts on metal plates, banknotes, photos, drawings, traffic notices and musical instruments from all over the world. There were several tables scattered across the room and along the curved bar, which covered the entire length of one wall. Almost every table was taken by couples or groups of friends animatedly in discussion, and the ambience was infectious. No one looked up when John entered, although the barman, who was cleaning a glass while talking to a regular, saw him and motioned him to a free stool at the bar. John threaded his way between the tables and pulled himself onto the stool. He examined the impressive array of spirits above the bar and the fridges full of local and foreign beers.

While the barman finished his conversation, John took a proper look at the customers. All ages and types were there, although he was interested in a group of women sitting at one table. They were in their mid-thirties at least, and in full flow, heatedly discussing something that roused their passions. Each was dressed stylishly and in a manner that told the outside world that they were intellectuals. John wondered at their backgrounds, what they were discussing and what they all did for a living. One seemed to be a journalist and another an academic, although he realised that he was trying to read them using signs from his own cultural context. In any case, he'd be hard pressed to say why he'd come to those conclusions.

At another table, John saw a father and son having a drink together, both with the same face but at different ages, both holding their glasses on the table in cupped hands, as if drinking a hot chocolate and wanting to make sure they got the benefit of every ounce of warmth.

Before he could make any further presumptions the barman arrived and asked, in English, what he would like to drink. "How did you know I was English," John asked, curious at being so easily identified.

"I lived there for two years," he replied, smiling. "I know what an English face looks like." John frowned. "Yes, you have an English face," he said laughing. "What can I get you?"

John scanned the fridges, puzzling at the unfamiliar names and labels. "I don't know really. I'd like to try a local beer, something cold. What do you recommend?"

The barman casually pulled open the nearest fridge and tipped out a bottle with his finger, catching it as it fell. "This one is made near here. It's fresh and not too strong. They use the same mountain spring as the bottle water in the shops."

"Okay. Sounds good. I'll try that."

John watched the barman expertly flick off the metal top. "Do you want a glass?"

John shook his head and took a swig while the barman wiped down the bar. "That's really nice," John said, putting the bottle down with satisfaction. The barman smiled proudly. "What did you do when you were in England," John asked. "Your English is really good."

The barman looked out over the tables. "I worked in a pub in London, and then in a nightclub. So many drunk people! So many drunk girls! They used to laugh at my accent and teach me dirty words to say. I learned very quickly!" The barman frowned. "Excuse me."

He attended to another drinker and John swivelled on his stool to people-watch. He took another deep, long swig and revelled in the bubbles attacking his throat. The demon called out for more, more, more, so John finished the bottle quickly, asking for another as the barman passed.

Halfway through his second beer, the light, bubbly liquid mixed with his meal and he realised just how long it had been since he had eaten well and had some drinks inside him. The second soon turned into a third, and a light, cloudlessness lifted John and the corners of his mouth. He picked at the label on the beer bottle with his fingernail and watched out for more clues as to the identities of his fellow drinkers. Some had left and been replaced, while others, including the group of women, stayed on, still drinking and now talking more loudly and more animatedly than ever. John wished he could speak the local language and dive into the place like he would at home, with the potential of talking to anyone there. Who are they? What do they think about? What do they believe?

He ordered a fourth beer and the barman announced last orders. John checked his watch. Eleven-thirty already? "Is there anywhere I can go on to after here," John heard the demon ask.

The barman shifted on his feet and rubbed his chin. "Well, there aren't too many places like this open at this time. If you're looking for a nice place to drink with a nice ambience, there are a couple of hotels with bars."

"What about places that are a bit more interesting," the demon asked, with a sparkle in its eyes.

The barman smiled knowingly. "There's a small bar and nightclub at the other end of this street, but it's not very busy at this time of the week. There is one other...," the barman said a little reluctantly.

"Oh yes," the demon demanded.

"There's a more exclusive club on the road back towards the coast. I'm not sure they'll let you in with what you're wearing but, if you tell them Marco sent you, you should be okay."

John looked down at his shorts and flip-flops. "Thanks, Marco. I'll give it a try."

The barman leaned forwards and said quietly: "The cocktails are good and the staff are friendly, but you might pay a bit more than you would somewhere else, okay? And don't let them sell you anything you don't want."

John nodded and swivelled off the stool. He smiled at the barman as he closed the door behind him.

Outside, the temperature had dropped a few degrees, and John wondered whether he was doing the right thing. Maybe he should just go back to his room and go to sleep? The beers had taken care of his fear of being alone, and he knew that the memories, even if they did appear, would not now bring their full horror and pain.

Go back to the hotel. That would be the sensible thing to do.

As he crossed the road and followed the directions given to him by the barman, John listened to his flip-flops slapping against his heels and the distant revving of a scooter. I could turn back and go to the hotel. There is no need to go to this bar. After all, he clearly recommended it against his better judgement.

John stopped at a street corner and looked around. There was no one. In one direction lay the hotel, his room, sleep, the chance to be fresh and clear-headed the next morning, and the knowledge he had chosen the sensible option. In the other direction lay the bar, with its possibility for drunkenness, danger and, at the very least, spending too much money on average-quality drinks.

John stood and waited for something to tell him what to do. The demon was partially spent, its thirst somewhat slaked on the local beer, and his other self reminded him of just how tired he was. Unused to walking such distances in flip-flops, his feet were protesting and blisters were welling up.

In the distance, he heard a tipsy woman laugh loudly and then give a shriek of delight. He thought of the German couple and what they would be doing now. Would they would be having a drink, or already in bed, exploring each other's sensuality. Or asleep, too raw from their sunburn.

John smiled and raised his eyebrows. I don't know why I'm even debating what to do. He turned towards the bar, having known all along that the demon would win.

PART THREE

CHAPTER ONE

JOHN WAS LET INTO THE CLUB WITHOUT MENTIONING Marco's name. Once inside, he realised why—there were very few guests and the management were clearly in no mood to turn anyone away, no matter how badly dressed.

He stood awkwardly in the middle of the room, unsure what to do. One side was taken up with a shiny, American-style bar lined with stools and a small dance floor. The rest was filled with booths, most of which were empty. He was wondering what kind of place it was when a waitress came up to him in an outfit more suited to a prostitute and asked if he would like a private dance. He almost laughed at his own naivety. The demon may have brought him here, but not even that devious, craven, lying creature could have known he was being directed to a strip joint.

He refused politely, saying he wanted only a drink. And not 'a drink' in general, sonny, but just one and then you'll be on your way.

The hostess led him to a booth and he placed himself facing the door. He smiled at himself. If it ever got out that he had been to a strip joint, having his back to the performers would qualify merely as a technicality.

He played with a beer mat and tried not to look at the other customers, and didn't notice when another hostess came up to him and stood waiting for him to look up.

"What can I get you," she said eventually.

Startled, John stared at her, amazed by her beauty.

"What can I get you," she repeated.

"I'm sorry," he said, shaking his head. "I was in my own world."

Raising an eyebrow, she continued: "So, what will it be? Beer? Cocktail? Spirit? I would say wine but I don't think I can recommend what we have here." She spoke in a soft Eastern European accent, with tinges of East London.

"I'd like a...beer," he said. "I was drinking something in a bar just now. It's local, made from the spring water, or so the barman told me."

"We don't have that, but is sixteen sixty-four okay?"

"Yes, that's fine," he said, disappointed. "Thank you."

"Fifty centilitres, or a bottle?"

John inspected the shiny taps lining the bar, which seemed barely used. "A bottle."

"Okay, I'll be right back." She turned on her heel and walked away. Much as he didn't want to, John couldn't stop himself staring at her. She was so different from everyone else working there. What is it about her? She's so...what? Magnetic? No, that's not it. It's much more than that.

He longed for her to come back, his stomach turning with anxiety and excitement. Christ, pull yourself together, man. Just forget the beer and go straight back to the hotel.

But he wasn't ready to leave. The demon was curious and wanted to stay. At home, he wouldn't allow himself to go to a place like this, but here, away from everyone...

He tried to convince himself he was studying humanity;

that no human experience is invalid; that one cannot know oneself, or indeed anyone else, if one does not understand what drives people to do what they do, no matter how we judge them. He paused for a moment, then laughed. Who are you trying to kid? You just want to be here because it's better than being back there. Besides, he wanted to know more about her. No, he wanted to know everything.

He glanced around the bar again. He looked down at the table and laced and unlaced his fingers. He inspected his hands, then looked up at the ceiling, noting the ventilation ducts and the wires criss-crossing between them. He glanced over as someone came through the door. He didn't recognise him, and then wondered why he would. No one here who knows you. You are alone. There is no one to judge you, and no one to criticise. You came here because you need some time out from the weight of it all. Enjoy it. After all, isn't that what we're supposed to do? To live in the moment and take things for what they are?

The waitress placed the bottle of beer beside his hands. He looked up and smiled. "Can I ask you a question? Where are you from? I've being trying to place your accent ever since you came over."

She tried not to look as if she had been asked that question by every man she had ever served, but couldn't stop herself from flashing a sarcastic smile. "Where do you think my accent comes from?"

He realised it was a stupid question, and that he'd only asked it because he didn't want her to leave. But aren't all opening questions stupid?

"Oh, I don't know. I'm rubbish at this sort of thing." He smiled and she waited patiently. The silence become awkward. "Maybe Eastern Europe," he suggested.

She laughed and he realised it was blindingly obvious she was from Eastern Europe. "Poland," he ventured.

She stared straight into his eyes. "Maybe." She turned to leave.

"Am I close?"

She stopped and half-turned back. "That depends," she said.

"On what?" He took a swig of beer, grateful for something to do with his hands.

"On how many drinks you buy." She started to leave again.

"You're a hard woman," he called after her.

She spun around on her heels. "I have to be with you men. You're all the same."

"What? No we're not," he said defiantly.

"Oh yes?" She stepped back towards him. "What makes you so sure? All you men on holiday, saying you want a little conversation and a drink, but it always turns into more, if you can afford it."

He sat back and took another swig. "But that's where you're mistaken. I didn't know what this place was before I came here. I thought it was just a bar. The barman in the last place sent me here."

She laughed patronisingly. "That's what they all say."

He smiled. "Maybe, but maybe it's true sometimes."

"What difference does it make? You're all the same in the end."

He laughed. "I don't think we are 'all the same'. Yes, I'm lonely and would like to talk to someone, but I'm here by accident. I could have gone straight back to my hotel, and I nearly did, but I was curious."

The young woman thought for a moment and then stepped in closer. "Are you still curious," she asked. He smiled nervously, unsure what to say. She saw his expression and winked. "It's okay, Mr Accident. I'm only teasing you. I won't make you do anything you don't want to do."

She stepped back and he took another swig of beer. "So, where are you from," he asked. "Really."

She looked at him seriously. "Who cares? Really. I mean, we're all from somewhere, right? And we all ended up here tonight, and that's all there is to it."

He wanted to say something smart but couldn't think of anything.

"Why don't you ask me my name," she said.

"Okay. What's your name?"

"Jasna."

"That's nice."

"Is it? It means bright, like light, not bright like intelligent."

John nodded. "Well, it's a lovely name either way."

"Whatever."

"You're hard to please, Jasna."

"Look, you're only saying my name's lovely because we're in this bar."

"That's not true. I'd say it if I met you in a supermarket or a carpark."

"Now you're just trying to be cute."

"Whatever," he said, pleased with himself.

"Okay, whatever," she said and walked away. He watched her go, lost in thought.

The next time she passed, he called out: "So aren't you going to ask me my name?"

She stopped and turned. "Do you want me to?"

"Not especially, but it only seems fair, in the interests of balance."

She cleared her throat and looked down at her feet. "Okay, Mr Accident, what's your name?" She glanced up and caught his gaze.

"John. Hunter. And it's Dr, not Mr, if we're being accurate." John realised he sounded pretentious. Stupid, stupid, stupid.

"Nice to meet you, Dr John," she said mockingly.

"Nice to meet you too, Jasna."

He took another swig of beer and was about to launch into another conversation but Jasna stepped back. "I'm sorry, I need to look after my other customers. I'll be back when you need another drink." She wagged a finger at him. "But don't drink too quickly, or I'll know what you are doing."

She turned and left. He sighed. When was the last time he had enjoyed a proper conversation with someone? Not since...well, he knew since when.

He took another swig and surveyed the other clients and hostesses, sweeping his eyes across the room. He froze. Sitting in a booth on the other side of the bar, with a hostess on each arm, was the Russian from the hotel. John stared as the man laughed and leered at the young women, who sparkled and writhed like fish. He looked up and saw John staring at him. He raised his glass and nodded a toast. John tamely raised his glass in return and then looked away. What is he doing here? But given he's in a strip joint with two hostesses hanging off his arm at one o'clock in the morning, it's fairly obvious what he's doing. But why does he keep turning up at significant moments? Is it just be coincidence, or is there something I'm not seeing?

He frowned at the rim of his beer bottle. Jasna appeared at his side. "Hey, Dr John. Haven't you finished that beer yet? Don't you want another?"

He took a final swig from the bottle and handed it to Jasna. "Yes please, I'm ready."

"Ready for what," Jasna asked with a cheeky grin. She grabbed the beer bottle and walked away, leaving him to gaze after her.

While Jasna was at the bar, he watched the staff, noticing

they were quiet, efficient and hardly spoke to each other. As she placed a fresh, cold bottle on his table, he asked: "Tell me Jasna, do you get many regulars in here?"

"Sometimes. We have some locals, but mostly it's people who come while they're here on holiday and then we never see them again. Why?"

"You know, you speak really good English. Have you spent any time in London?"

"Yes, I was there for a year. I worked in a bar. I knew a bit of English already, but I got much better when I was there." She paused. "Why do you ask about regulars?"

He nodded to the other side of the bar. "There's a Russian guy over there who I keep seeing everywhere I go, and now I've seen him here too. I wondered if he'd been here before."

Jasna looked over and watched him with the two cavorting hostesses. "No. Oh, actually yes. He came in last night and had a few drinks and a private dance."

"A private dance?" He looked straight at Jasna. "Do you do private dances?"

"No, I don't," she snapped and turned to go.

"Wait. I'm sorry. I didn't mean it like that." Jasna stopped and walked back to him, one eyebrow arched in indignation. He shrank back. "It was the first thing that came into my head," he said. "I wasn't asking for one."

She examined John's face. "I don't do dances." She looked over towards the Russian and then back at John. "Not everyone who works in a strip joint is a stripper, and not every stripper will let you have a private dance. Okay?"

"Yes, I'm sorry. I've only been to somewhere like this once before, many years ago. I don't know the difference."

Jasna smiled. "Believe me, you would know the difference if I was a stripper."

He took another swig. "Well, sorry. Again."

She stepped in closer. "It's okay, Dr John." She looked

over towards the Russian again. "Look, I'm just a barmaid," she said quietly. "I'm not supposed to talk so much to customers. That's for the other girls. I could get into trouble."

"I understand. I'm sorry for keeping you," he said.

"That's okay. It's been nice to meet you."

"And you."

She turned away again. "Before you go..." he called out. She glanced over her shoulder. "If I come back tomorrow night, could I steal a minute of your time again?"

"Maybe, Dr John. Maybe."

He smiled as she walked away, then regretted having said anything at all. You're a second-rate, second-hand cliché. What on earth possessed you to speak to her? She obviously saw straight through you, and she's clearly heard it all a thousand times before. He imagined her telling her friends about him, sitting around in a flat-share with the other waitresses, swapping stories and laughing over their idiot customers. He cringed. You're pathetic, John. And what, exactly, do you want out of this? To talk to her again? To meet up with her? To kiss her? To fuck her? No, you don't. And even if you did, she would only ever do any of that because she wants your money.

He looked down at the beer bottle and then at his hands. A wave of tiredness crashed over him and he wanted desperately to be outside. He checked the bills Jasna had brought with each beer. They cost twice as much as in the previous bar, although still less than in London.

He left a generous tip and pulled himself wearily out of the booth. He looked for the Russian, but neither he nor the two hostesses were anywhere to be seen. He straightened his shirt and deliberately didn't look for Jasna to say goodbye.

CHAPTER TWO

OUT IN THE COLD NIGHT AIR, HE WONDERED ABOUT finding a taxi to the hotel, but the town seemed asleep and he decided it would be more time-consuming and tedious to look for one than simply to walk back. He wasn't sure of the precise direction of the hotel, but he was confident enough to take a chance.

As he walked along the main road, he spotted a faded map of the town centre in an old display case. He saw that, if he followed the same road, he would eventually reach the long, tree-lined avenue leading down to the hotel. There were shorter, nicer routes he could follow through the narrow, winding streets of the old town but they would be harder to remember when he was so tired, and the potential to get lost was a little too great for comfort.

So he trudged on, stuffing his hands in his pockets and hunching his shoulders against the sea breeze that met him on every street corner and came sweeping across the lifeless squares. He reached a large, open space and, judging by the restaurants, offices and shops that lined each side, all now closed, and the wide roads that fed into it, he decided it must be the main square. At this hour, there was just a knot of young men standing around two scooters, deep in discussion. They watched him pass, falling silent as he approached. He smiled, and one or two nodded back.

Alone again, he turned over the events of the day. What are you up to? What did you want from this trip? What are you trying to achieve? He wasn't comfortable being on holiday. Well, he wasn't comfortable relaxing on the beach, slowly frying his brain until all that was left was a desire to eat, drink and scratch the eternal itch, before sleeping it off and repeating the cycle. Inaction had never been a life goal, and it was not going to appeal now just because he was staying in a holiday resort.

And yet. He knew he had to try to relax. The notion that he could carry on without a break was impossible. Somehow, he had to carry around the heavy weight of infinite pain and sadness until it lessened and he was able either to deal with it or to move on, at least a little. His previous solution to the problem—working ever-harder and becoming increasingly frustrated with everyone and everything around him—only served to antagonise and repel himself and other people. Everyone said they understood what he was going through, but nobody's indulgence is infinite. They need to see at some point that you're doing something to help yourself, or at least trying not to make things worse.

He stopped and looked down a narrow street that led towards the sea, listening to the silence.

A car passed on the main road.

A light in a window halfway down the street switched off.

What time is it? Two am? Three?

He didn't want to check his watch. He didn't want to take his hands out of his pockets. He was still hunching his shoulders against the sea breeze, although it had relented a little. He forced himself to relax his muscles and rotated the tops of his arms. There was nothing remarkable about the street but, all the same, John took in the small, squat buildings and power lines strung casually between the pylons and rooftops. An ancient pick-up truck and a small Fiat were the only cars to be seen. Dotted along the pavement were small piles of wood and the leftovers of several small projects.

"What do you want?" He was surprised at the sound of his own voice in the cool night air.

But what did he want? Maybe just to be free. But for now he was trapped, like a fly in a spider's web—able to see the world all around him but unable to be a part of it. And all the while the looming shadow drew ever closer.

His mind wandered to Jasna, and he started walking back to the hotel. He was angry with himself. For going on after the restaurant? No, not for that. For drinking so many beers in the first bar and then letting the demon in? No, not exactly. For following the demon to the strip joint when he knew he should have gone back to the hotel? Maybe, a bit. For staying in the strip joint once he knew what it was? Yes, definitely. For talking to her? He wanted to say he regretted it, that he was angry with himself, but he couldn't bring himself.

Obviously Jasna would think he was flirting with her. To her, he was a sad, pathetic, lonely middle-aged man who was on the lookout for whatever he could get. The thought ashamed him. He was sure he hadn't been trying to chat her up, but he was also sure that he had seen something special inside her and wanted to be near it. Yes, she was beautiful but he had met many beautiful women in his life and very few had made anything like such an impression. When she spoke, it simply confirmed what he had suspected—that she was alive in a way that reminded him of something, of someone. Of something and someone he thought had gone forever. A tornado of emotions swept through him and tears welled in his eyes. Once it had passed, he heard the echo of a generator and the revving of a far-off engine.

I am still here. I am still alive.

Time to go to bed then.

He walked on. Rounding a building, the stiff breeze returned. He shivered and goosebumps appeared on his arms and legs. He tried to ignore the sense of foreboding, and the approach of the endless storm.

CHAPTER THREE

THE HOTEL RECEPTION WAS EMPTY AND HE LISTENED TO the echo of his flip-flops as he crossed the marble floor towards the lifts. But before he could get there, Charles appeared.

"Good evening, Dr Hunter."

John started in surprised. "Good grief, you made me jump," he exclaimed.

"I do apologise. I was taught always to move quietly, and old habits die hard."

"You were a good pupil, I see." John glanced up at the clock above the reception. It was just after three. He wanted to ask why Charles was hanging around in the middle of the night, but instead said: "I did say you can call me John, by the way."

Charles nodded. "Yes, you did, and I am grateful for the familiarity, but I prefer to use your first name only when we are alone."

John frowned. "Are we not alone?"

Charles smiled enigmatically. "Have you had a relaxing day, Dr Hunter? Did you get to see some of the town?"

John reflected. "Yes, I think I saw more than I anticipated, which is not always a bad thing. I needed a relaxing
day after last night." Charles frowned quizzically. "I had a
poor night's sleep."

"I am sorry to hear that, Dr Hunter. There is nothing
amiss with your room, I trust."

John shifted closer to Charles and lowered his voice. "Not
the room itself, but there is something I wanted to talk to
you about."

Charles leaned in closer. "Yes? What is it?"

"All evening and last night, I kept being disturbed by..."

Charles turned away and said in a bright, clear voice:
"Good evening, sir. May I help you in any way?"

John spun around to see the Russian standing at
reception.

"No," the man said. "I am waiting for internet cable. I
phoned down. There is a man fetching me one now." As he
finished, a receptionist appeared from the back office and
handed over an ethernet cable. The Russian nodded at the
two men and walked away.

Charles turned back to John. "I do apologise. What were
you saying?"

John glanced at the Russian as he waited by the lifts. "It's
okay. It doesn't matter." John turned to leave.

"Before you go, Dr Hunter," Charles said.

John stopped and turned back, an eyebrow raised. "Yes?"

"Would you mind if I made a suggestion?"

"No, go ahead."

Charles cleared his throat. "I don't know if you saw it in
our hotel literature, but we own a fully functional and impec-
cably restored eighteenth-century sailing boat. A boat that is,
as we speak, moored at a private jetty just below the cliffs
here." Charles gestured towards the hotel gardens.

"No, I did not know that."

"Well," Charles continued, "for our more discerning guests, we offer a day of sumptuous luxury aboard the boat, with trips to idyllic coves and grottos well off the beaten track and stops for swimming, topped off with delicious, local food prepared by one of our chefs, all just for you."

"I see."

"Now, normally a day out on the boat costs a small fortune, of course, and I would never suggest such an outlandish expense to a man of your...principles, but it would so happen that a Japanese family staying with us have reserved the boat for tomorrow, and there remains a spare place. Would you care to join them for the day?" John looked unsure. "It would be wonderful way to take your mind off things. I think it would offer the relaxation you seek."

"Well..."

"And, of course, you would be doing the Japanese family a service, as otherwise they have to pay for the whole boat themselves."

"Um..."

"It's the chance of a lifetime to spend a day on a boat like this, Dr Hunter. There can be but a handful now in such good working order in the entire world. And although one never knows what life may bring, it is entirely conceivable that we may never pass this way again."

John smiled. "Okay."

"Excellent. I shall make all the necessary arrangements. Simply present yourself at the jetty below the hotel in time for cast-off at nine am sharp tomorrow morning."

John again glanced up at the clock over reception and calculated the number of hours of sleep available to him. "Okay," he sighed. "Thank you."

"Then I shall wish you a very good night and a wonderful trip tomorrow," Charles said, looking pleased with himself.

CHAPTER FOUR

A FACE, HER FACE, DAPPLED IN SOFT SHADOW, WITH NO EYES, melts into a vortex of falling light and forms a tree, bare in deep winter. The branches are a rib cage that explodes into a thousand dots of perfect white light. The dark spaces coalesce into lines and the face of an eyeless women, blown to dust.

A young woman, her, in a wedding dress, her unseen face turned away from you, emerges from the shadows. She stretches her bare arms towards you, her fingers crooked in pain.

You are in a boat, with a thousand demons twisting beneath you. You turn, and she lies dead in a stone corridor, her face obscured.

A beach at dawn. She runs, always just in front of you, her hand reaching back through the refracted light that flows all around you. The light falls to blackness and her hand trickles with blood.

You are in a room from long ago, the sunlight streaming in through the curtained windows. She pulls her top over her face as she undresses. You see her soft skin in the pale light and the surge of her breasts. You remember a morning when it seemed as if everything could be perfect forever. Her laughing mouth is close, and she throws her head back in joy.

You fall, sickeningly fast. Your hand holds hers and then you see her mouth, peaceful in a dust storm that falls through her eyes. In a mirror with no reflection, she walks through a winter field, her face obscured by the falling light.

You plunge into the depths of the sea and you find her, drowning. You cannot reach her. You are too late.

She shields herself from the boiling water and, above the surface, seagulls take flight in a storm.

PART FOUR

CHAPTER ONE

UNDER A CLOUDLESS SKY, A BEAUTIFULLY RESTORED eighteenth-century sailing boat was being readied by a small crew. A Japanese couple and their two young children were being shown over the boat by the captain, a tall, wiry man with a hard face. As he was pointing out the original navigational instruments, still used alongside the modern satellite communications, a crew member approached.

"We should cast-off, captain," he said. "We're already late."

The captain stared at the young sailor and elaborately shot his arm forwards to reveal his watch. "I think we can allow two more minutes." He smiled at the Japanese couple. "We don't have too many urgent engagements on this boat." The couple laughed, while their children looked bored.

John ran down the steps to the jetty and along the gangway. As he arrived, panting, he threw an embarrassed smile around the boat. "I'm so sorry I'm late."

The captain stepped forwards, smiled and extended his hand. "Not at all." The two men shook hands. "Welcome aboard, Dr Hunter. I am so glad you were able to join us." The captain turned to the crew and ordered them to cast-off while John introduced himself to the Japanese family and apologised again.

The boat, creaking and moaning, drifted slowly away from the jetty. The crew unfurled the sails and it slipped gracefully out of the small harbour and into the bay.

THEY SPENT a weightless morning sunbathing and lazing on deck, eating an endless supply of delicious snacks prepared by the chef and drinking clear, light rosé from the Côte d'Azur. The father and daughter took pictures of the breathtaking scenery, as cove after cove opened up before them like oysters revealing dark pearls within. John half-watched the man explaining to his daughter about focal lengths and the rule of thirds, and smiled at the easy comfort between them.

"Did you not bring a camera, Dr Hunter?"

John jumped and turned to find the captain standing right behind his shoulder. How did he remain so fresh-looking in that heavy uniform?

"No. No, I didn't. Actually, I forgot to bring one with me at all on this trip. I packed in a rush."

The captain smiled ruefully. "That is a shame, Dr Hunter, as we have one of the most beautiful coastlines in the Mediterranean, with a history stretching far into the ancient world."

John searched the captain's face, trying to place his accent. "I can imagine. I was looking at all those coves we've been passing. I bet they could tell a story or two of smuggling and intrigue."

The captain smiled and raised an eyebrow. "The locals tell a few old tales of pirates and lost treasure, although I can assure you that is all in the past, Dr Hunter."

John nodded. "Of course."

"While many of the coves are, in fact, inaccessible, I am

told that a few of the cliffs have stairs cut into them that lead all the way to the top. I suppose they may well have been used for smuggling in times past. Now, if you will excuse me..."

The captain drifted away, and John looked out to sea, imagining sailors trying to land flimsy boats in the middle of the night during a storm.

AFTER A LONG LUNCH, the passengers lazed once more. The sun beat down relentlessly and the day slowed to a standstill. John lay on a bench in the shade, watching the shadows move across the deck and the coastline turn like an animated diorama, presenting vista after vista of sharp, craggy rocks and trees pouring down to the sea.

The heat pulled him into a torpor and he floated in an invisible, heavy liquid, as if drowning in colourless honey. He mulled over the events of the previous evening and thought about Jasna. Her smile, her laugh, her teasing humour.

No, he didn't want to think about her. He forced his mind to focus on the banging outside his room. What on earth had been going on there? Who were they? And what about that passageway? Why did someone go to all the trouble of hiding it with a concealed door for it simply to stop in a dead end? Then he thought of Charles and some of the curious remarks he had made, seemingly layered with meaning that John did not understand. Maybe he said them to spark my curiosity? But John didn't want to play games. He hadn't gone on holiday for that. And what about the Russian? Who was he? Why did he seem to appear everywhere?

He watched a seagull float across the sky and then turn to follow the boat. The air lay heavy on his chest and he drifted away.

. . .

SEVERAL HOURS or maybe a minute later, he woke with a start. The boy from the Japanese family was standing over him, staring into his face. "Will you take our picture, please," the boy asked.

He glanced around, initially unable to remember where he was, and ran his hand over his face. "Yes, of course," he croaked, and pulled himself up straight, nauseated by the rush of blood to his head.

The boy led him to the other side of the boat, where the family were watching fish burst and dive through the surface of the water. He blinked and tried to wake himself. The rosé had gone to his head and his mouth was thick and dry. He noticed a small speedboat heading in the general direction of the boat and wondered whether it was holidaymakers out on a day trip.

As he approached, the father handed him an expensive-looking SLR. John took it carefully in his hands and told himself not to drop it as the man showed him how to use it. He lifted the camera to his face and looked through the viewfinder. He started to compose the picture but noticed that the speedboat had pulled up alongside and two men were handing over a large packet to someone inside their yacht. John shifted to get a better view and zoomed in for a close-up, but the packet had already gone and all he could see was an open hatch. Then a briefcase appeared through the hatch and was handed over. He instinctively started taking pictures.

Before he could see what happened next, a hand reached over the camera and snatched it out of John's hand. He spun around and, watched by the shocked Japanese family, tried to grab the camera back from a large, burly crew member.

"What do you think you're doing," John demanded. "Give that back." The man held the camera, the strap flapping in the breeze, out of reach with one hand and John back with the other. "Not allowed. No photo," the man said. John pointed at the family. "You're stealing their camera."

Unnoticed, the speedboat slowly slipped away. John continued to struggle with the crew member, trying to reach the camera but unable to pull the man's arm down. "What the hell is going on here," he shouted. Seeing the captain appear, he stopped and straightened his clothes. "Good, I'm glad you're here," he said. "You can sort this out."

"What is happening," the captain asked the crew member.

"He take pictures."

"And what's wrong with that," John demanded angrily.

"May I," the captain said to the crew member, who handed over the camera. When the captain started deleting the pictures, the father of the Japanese family got up and started towards the captain, but checked himself when he saw another crew member step forwards to block his path.

"What are you doing," John demanded.

"I'm sorry, Dr Hunter, but we have a very strict policy about what can be photographed on the boat. It is, unfortunately, copyrighted, and the hotel is extremely protective of its image rights."

"What on earth are you talking about? And why was he trying to stop me taking photos? Was it that speedboat that pulled up alongside? What was it doing?"

The captain finished deleting the photos and looked up at John, smiling. "I'm sorry he was a little heavy handed just now. We are all expressly told to protect the image rights of the hotel, and this boat in particular. It is the jewel in our crown."

John shook his head in amazement. "You've already told me that. But I wasn't talking about this boat. I was taking pictures of the speedboat that pulled up alongside, as you could see. What was it doing?" John gestured to the camera. "And why didn't you want me to take pictures of it?"

The captain looked out to sea, sighed and then turned back to John, staring intently into his eyes. "It is not a concern of yours, Dr Hunter." John stared back at him, noting the faint purple lines around his nose and beneath his eyes. "I suggest you go back to your holiday and forget all about speedboats." The man turned and, with a broad smile, addressed the whole of the boat. "Now we shall enjoy the rest of our day." As he passed, the captain handed the camera to the Japanese man with a flourish. "So sorry to have inconvenienced you."

John clenched and unclenched his jaw as he watched the captain disappear below deck. When he turned away, he saw the entire crew and the Japanese family staring at him. Unsure what to do, he went back to where he had been lying before the boy woke him up, and the crew slowly returned to their work.

THE LIGHTS STRUNG along the coastline switched on as the boat slowly pulled into the jetty below the hotel. The crew busied themselves with mooring the boat and lowering the gangway while the Japanese family disembarked and made their way back up the steps to the hotel.

As John stepped off, he glanced back and saw that the captain and the crew had stopped and were staring at him coldly. He turned and climbed up to the hotel, trying not to think of their eyes on his back.

CHAPTER TWO

THE LAST RAYS OF THE SUN TURNED JOHN'S GIN AND TONIC bright gold. He turned the glass in his hand, absorbed by the kaleidoscope of colours as he lounged on his balcony, his feet up on the stone wall. He finished the cold drink in one gulp and grimaced as it burned its way down. He unhooked his feet and made another from the Tanqueray gin and tonic water he had bought from the hotel bar. He'd also picked some oranges from the gardens, stolen a knife from the dining room and raided the ice box, and now, for the fourth time, made himself a strong drink.

He toasted an imaginary friend and looked out over the hotel gardens. The shadows were slowly lengthening and the temperature dropping. Music drifted up from the bar and, somewhere above him, water cascaded onto bathroom tiles.

He finished his drink in two long gulps. He pulled himself out of the chair and, grabbing the bottles, shuffled back into his room. He threw himself on the sofa and started pouring out the gin but stopped and cursed himself for leaving the oranges and ice on the balcony. He considered fetching them, but couldn't be bothered and made the gin and tonic without.

As he took the first gulp, a wave of nausea swept up his throat and he had to swallow hard to avoid vomiting. He drained the glass more slowly this time, before half-dropping it onto the table once he had finished.

He stared at the ceiling, tracing the coving and the cracks in the plaster. He rolled himself off the sofa and pulled himself upright and stood still, waiting for the rush of blood to subside.

He took the picture of the beautiful, dark-haired woman from the mantelpiece and sat down heavily. He stared intently at her and a tear rolled down his cheek. He carefully placed the frame on the coffee table and went to take another swig from his glass, only to find it empty.

Fighting back the tears and nausea, he fetched the oranges and ice and poured himself another drink. As he went to take a first sip, a thought occurred to him. He quickly downed the glass, then retched as his stomach fought against the invading alcohol. He grabbed his jacket and room key from the bed and left, slamming the door behind him.

CHAPTER THREE

He strode out of the lift and across the hotel reception. Staring straight ahead, he looked at nothing and no one. He threaded his way along the path towards the restaurant where he had eaten with Charles the previous evening. Once there, he went straight for the bar and nodded to Enrico, who was polishing glasses. Enrico carefully folded his towel and came over. John placed his hands on the bar as if preparing to leap over the gleaming surface.

"Good evening, Dr Hunter. What may I get you?"

He drummed his fingers, an impish smile on his face. "A rum and coke," he heard the demon say. Enrico turned and picked out a tumbler. "Make it a double." Without turning around, Enrico switched the glass for a high ball.

"Right away."

The demon glanced around the bar. It grinned at two businessmen on shiny bar stools. They nodded politely, then turned away. The demon spotted two tanned, expensively dressed women sitting at a nearby table. It thought about taking them back to the room and tearing their clothes off in a frenzy. Instead, it grabbed a stool and sat down, folding its arms on the cool bar top.

Enrico carefully placed the drink on a leather coaster emblazoned with the hotel logo. "May I charge it to your room, Dr Hunter?"

The demon inspected the glass, admiring the dark, rich liquid and the fresh, bright green of the lime. "Yes, two-three-five," it said. It picked up the glass and held it up to the light. Bubbles ran along the edges of the ice cubes, then shot up to the surface.

I could drown in this.

I will drown in this.

The demon smiled and drained the glass in one go. It carefully placed the now-empty glass to the coaster. It stared straight at Enrico, who raised his eyebrows and smirked. "Another, I think."

CHAPTER FOUR

HOURS OR DAYS LATER, JOHN WAS DRUNK, DRUNK AND swaying as he tried to tell a joke to a small group of hotel guests gathered around him. One was laughing at him with the amused detachment of someone regarding a dancing bear in a circus. Enrico placed another rum and coke on the bar by John's elbow and smiled darkly. John turned and grabbed at the glass. Trying to take a swig, he spilled the fragrant liquid on the floor and across his trousers. Some of the audience stepped back instinctively. Others tittered and pointed. John gave up on the drink and clumsily put the glass back on the bar, spilling it again.

Where was I? Ah, yes... "So," he said, licking the sticky traces from his lips. "So, the horse says to the man..." He shook his head. "No, no, that wasn't it." He looked down at the floor to steady his eyes, which had begun to flicker. Talking more to himself, he added: "Or was the man saying it to the horse?"

Someone piped up: "Either way, I think they were both drunk," at which point everyone in the circle laughed as much in relief at having the tension broken as in amusement at the comment.

John's face hardened in anger. "Who the fuck are you," he demanded. "I don't see you telling a joke."

"And I don't see you telling one either," the guest shot back.

John flashed forwards to hit the man, but he stumbled and, before he could get there, Charles appeared and expertly restrained him. John struggled but, once he saw who was holding him back, collapsed into the older man's arms and turned his face away in shame.

"Perhaps our guests have lost their appetite for humour, Dr Hunter," Charles said, as the small crowd drifted away.

"Perhaps," John said quietly.

Enrico came around the bar, and he and Charles helped John into an empty chair. Charles sighed and narrowed his eyes as he inspected John's face. "Or maybe it's just the way you tell 'em," he said. He turned to Enrico. "Perhaps we have been a little too generous with our measures this evening," he said sternly. "It may amuse you to allow him to get like this, but we have a duty to look after our guests, especially when they can't look after themselves."

"Yes. I'm sorry," Enrico said, chastened.

John tried to look at the two men, but he couldn't focus his eyes, so he let his head fall and roll from side to side. "No, it was my fault," John slurred. "I insisted. In fact, I'm going to insist again," he said, brightening up. "Another double, my dear Enrico, and go easy on the coke this time."

Charles arched an eyebrow. "Now, Dr Hunter, I really think..."

"No, I really think," John said in mock seriousness. "What was that joke I was telling," he asked, trying to cast his mind back.

"Was it the one about the hotel guest who'd become a

drunken bore but realised that it was time to go to bed," Charles asked.

John glanced up at Charles. "I can never remember the punchline to that one," he said quietly.

Charles nodded and smiled. "I'll remind you of it on our walk back to the hotel. Do you think you can stand up?"

John rolled his eyes in annoyance at the question but nevertheless pushed against the floor to test his legs. "Yes, I'm fine." Turning to Enrico, he added: "I'm so terribly sorry about my behaviour this evening," he said mock seriously. "I shall leave you all in peace now."

The two men pulled John up to his feet by his armpits. John steadied himself and straightened his jacket. "Thank you, gentlemen. I think I can take it from here."

Charles stared at John, whose empty eyes resembled those of a dead fish. "Are you sure?"

"Yes, thank you. I'm sure I'm sure."

Charles and Enrico stood together watching John stumble out of the restaurant, then Enrico returned to the bar.

AT THE POOL, John stopped and contemplated the slowly undulating water, turned electric blue by the evening lights. He involuntarily stepped towards the water's edge and then back again, as if dancing to an imaginary tune. The bright surface stung John's eyes and brought back his nausea. He breathed in deeply and tried to steady himself. A swarm of emotions flew through him and John's face crumpled as the tears flowed.

"Dr Hunter," Charles said softly.

John spun around and stared hard at Charles. His face was wet with tears and his eyes were bloodshot. "Have you come to have a laugh, eh? At a man in tears, making a disgrace of himself in a place he doesn't belong?"

Charles sighed. "Not at all," he said gently. "You seemed agitated and I wanted to make sure you were okay."

John laughed sardonically. "Well, clearly I'm not. So gawp away while you can. I'm sure it makes a change from the usual gossip around here."

Charles gazed calmly back at John. "Not as much as you'd think. All life is here, for better or worse."

John frowned and turned back to the pool.

Charles cleared his throat. "I understand that you have suffered a loss."

John spun around. "How did you know about that? I have told no one here. No one."

"I'm sorry. I read about it the newspapers. I'm terribly sorry about what happened. It must have been awful to lose your wife that way, more than words can express."

John looked away. "I didn't want anyone to know about it here. I just wanted to get away from it all, at least for a while. I just wanted to escape." John stared at the water and swayed back and forth, seemingly readying himself to dive in. Charles clasped his hands in front of his paunch and regarded the younger man.

"I failed her, Charles," John said eventually. "I couldn't do anything to save her."

The two men stood in silence. Charles listened to the faint hum of the hotel air conditioning, audible now in the late evening, and the slow crashing of the waves against the cliffs below the hotel.

"I'm a doctor," John said, turning back to the older man. "I of all people should have been able to save her. But I couldn't, and she died. And I'll never get her back." John swayed as he stared at Charles, desperation in his eyes.

"I'm so sorry, John. Sometimes, events are taken out of our hands and, despite our strongest and most desperate wishes, we cannot do anything to help."

John contemplated the older man's face and saw for the first time the kindness behind the professional sheen.

"If you ever need to talk, John, I'm here, not as an employee of the hotel but from one human being to another. I can only imagine how hard all this is for you, but I've had some experiences in recent years that allow me to make an educated guess." John nodded and straightened himself up. "And if I may be so bold," Charles said, "perhaps the best thing for you now would be to go to bed and get some rest."

"You're right." John held out his hand and Charles folded it in his. "Thank you. And I'm sorry about earlier. I made an idiot of myself."

"Please, don't mention it."

Charles let go of John's hand and the younger man walked unsteadily back to the hotel.

CHAPTER FIVE

JOHN PACED HIS ROOM LIKE A CAGED TIGER. THE ALCOHOL was wearing off and he was bright and agitated. At almost every pass of the mantelpiece, he stopped and stared at the photograph. Eventually, he stopped and addressed it directly.

"I can't stand it." He frowned, then laughed bitterly. "This is stupid."

He turned away and walked over to the balcony. He clenched and unclenched his jaw as he stared out over the gardens and to sea. He strode back into the middle of the room. He wanted to throw something. He picked up the gin bottle and swung it behind his head, ready to launch it at the far corner of the room. But then he thought of the broken glass and the alcohol soaking into the carpet, of having to clear it up or, worse, having to explain it to Charles. He put the bottle down and picked up an orange. He was ready to hurl that too before he thought of the fruit stain on the wall, and the carcass sliding down to the floor. He let out an animal roar. "What the fuck is wrong with you," he shouted. "You can't even throw a fucking orange without thinking about the consequences."

He clenched his fists and squeezed the fruit in his hand until the juice and oil seeped out between his fingers. He caught sight of the photo. "I'm sorry."

He dropped the orange on the glass table, then stared up at the ceiling before falling back on the sofa, sighing in exasperation. "You can't stay cooped up in here."

He went to put his head in his hands but realised they were covered in orange juice. Angry again, he wanted to smash something, anything, but most of all himself. He raised his fists to hit the glass table but, thinking of the first aid he would have to perform if he cut himself, slowly lowered his hands. "You can't even do that. You are so wrapped up, so constrained, you can't even smash a glass table." But what would it achieve? Nothing. Absolutely nothing.

Instead, he poured himself a generous gin and tonic and downed half of it, luxuriating in the burning down his throat and the warmth growing within him. He breathed deeply and sat up, staring straight ahead. Then the demon rose up and swept through him.

CHAPTER SIX

As he reached the old town, he dived into the narrow, twisting lanes and slowed his pace. He pulled his hands out of his pockets and loosened his shoulders. He looked up for the first time since he had left the hotel and noticed the stars dusting the night sky above the ancient rooftops. He knew where he was going, but he wanted to be lost, to take his time, perhaps not arrive at all.

At each corner, he took a turn that led him further into the labyrinth and paid no attention to the street names and shop signs, hoping he might arrive at a small square and have no idea of how to get back to his route. He passed countless restaurants, bars, souvenir shops, jewellers and emporia, all shiny and unfamiliar. Yet there was a calm, solitary voice that told him he knew where he was going and his destination would be waiting for him, no matter how long he tried to put it off.

He found the lost square he was seeking and stopped in the middle, looking all around, examining every window, every door, every crack in the walls. There was no one and all was silent. The emptiness was oppressive. A bolt slid back and a large wooden door opened with a creak. A small man in a brown suit stepped out and locked the door. Without looking in John's direction, he walked along the far wall of the square, keeping his head down and hands in his pockets. John watched the small, smartly dressed man until he was no longer in sight.

No sense in putting it off any longer.

He walked back up towards the main road, then turned in the now-familiar direction, passing the bar from the previous evening. He smiled at the memory of the intensely debating women and the father and son sharing a moment.

Once he reached the discreet door in the wall, he knocked firmly and fidgeted impatiently while the doorman checked his face on the CCTV. After a few seconds, the door unlocked and swung open.

"Good evening, sir," the thick-necked bouncer said flatly. "Welcome back."

John smiled uncomfortably at the recognition and stepped along the narrow, dark corridor to the gaudy, charmless bar. There were strippers performing tonight, and there were many more clients and hostesses. He instantly regretted coming, and regretted even more having hoped to see Jasna.

The girls gyrating mechanically on the tiny dance floor crushed any tender desire for warm company. Instead, the scene drove home the ugly sense he had frequented a brothel masquerading as a bar. Even the demon didn't want that. And it certainly didn't want anything that was on offer.

He was still idling in the entrance when a pneumatic hostess came up to him and asked him in a bored voice if he wanted a drink. He came to his senses and breathed deeply. Yes, he would like a drink, thank you. No, not a beer; a double rum and coke on the rocks. No, he would not like a private dance, although thank you for asking. Could he sit in a booth? He pointed to the one he had sat in when he first met Jasna, but it was taken. His stomach sank. What the hell am I doing here? Why don't I just cancel the order and leave? Jasna isn't here and she wouldn't talk to me even if she was. And you don't want to be in a strip club gawping at poor women you'd rather help than leave being exploited for money.

But the hostess had already pointed him to a free booth on the other side of the bar and gone to collect his order. He sighed and told himself he would stay just for one drink. He pulled himself into the booth as the hostess was putting his drink on the table. He stared at the bubbles rising up the glass and bursting, occasionally displacing an ice cube on their way up.

He thought again about the father and son in the other bar and how they had cupped their drinks. A jealousy rose up in him. But jealousy of what? Did he miss the company? A little. Did he wish he could share a drink with his own father? Not really and, anyway, they were never close. So what was it? Why was he jealous? Oh, that's it. I'll never get to have a son with my wife.

He shook his head free of the thought. He stared at the glass and then downed it. As his hostess was passing, he ordered another.

He barely looked up when she placed the next one in front of him. He was too busy listening to the blend of Euro house music and incomprehensible chatter, that low, male drone punctuated by the tinkle of forced female laughter. Forced, but so well-practised that it almost sounded like the real thing. He wasn't used to being in such a masculine environment, and he could smell the heavy mist of unresolved testosterone hanging in the air.

He took a sip of his drink. The ice cubes were melting and he could taste the tap water cutting through the alcohol and cheap coke. He examined his hands as he contemplated what to do next. I could stay here and try to get drunk. But you've already been drunk, far too drunk, this evening.

He was starting to sober up. The lights were harsh neon now, rather than beacons of exotic mystery. The furniture looked what it was—cheap, wipe-clean and functional, with a garnish of second-rate luxury. He saw that the floors weren't too clean, and wondered what the other customers did for a living. The 'magic' was gone. He could no longer participate in the fiction that anyone was there to do anything other than transact money for female submission.

He sighed, then laughed at himself. He picked up his glass and inspected it. The ice cubes were nearly gone. He didn't want to drink it but, at the price he was paying, he wasn't going to let it go to waste. He was about to put the glass to his lips when he sensed a presence beside him. He turned slightly, his drink still in the air, and was surprised to see Jasna, her hands on her hips and a smirk on her face.

"When did you get here," she demanded.

John put down his glass and gathered himself. "Oh, I don't know," he said, clearing his throat. "Maybe half an hour ago? An hour?"

She peered at him. "You didn't come and say hello." John opened his mouth to speak, but she carried on. "And what are you doing hiding from me on this side of the bar? Are you trying to avoid me?"

"No, not at all," John said, embarrassed. "There weren't any free places on that side and the hostess put me here. I tried looking for you, but I couldn't see you." She frowned at him. "I was hoping to run into you," he said. "It's nice to see you," he added, although he instantly regretted saying it.

"That's very sweet, Dr John," she said, smiling. "I'm kidding, you know." She peered into his glass and turned her nose up. "That's finished."

John shrugged. "Yeah, I left it too long."

Jasna grabbed the glass. "That's okay, I'll get you a new one. I'll just tell the barman I spilled this one. He'll put it on the house."

Before John could say anything, she was gone. Part of him was elated, too elated, to see her, and he cursed that he was so fragile that his mental state seemed to rest on whether or not someone working in a strip joint paid him attention. You should go. He glanced at the door. But he didn't want to leave now she had turned up. In any case, the demon wanted to see what would happen next.

A few minutes later, Jasna returned with a fresh rum and coke, sparkling with bubbles and possibility. "Here you go," she said as she put it down carefully in front of him. "Do you mind if I ask you something, Dr John."

"No, not at all."

"Why are you on holiday on your own. No wife? No girl-friend? Are you here on business?"

"No, it's just me, on my own," he said, trying to act casual. "I'm here on holiday." He watched a drunk man trying to clamber out of a booth and almost fall flat on his face. "I came here to get away from everything."

"From what?"

John turned back to her and smiled wryly. "Everything, absolutely everything."

"Did you manage it?"

"Not exactly. It's funny. Even if you leave everything behind, you are still there waiting for yourself when you get there."

Jasna nodded thoughtfully. "I'm sorry," she said. "I have to go back to work. Enjoy your drink." She turned to go.

"Wait," John heard himself say, unsure what he was going to say next. She turned back. "When do you finish tonight," his voice asked. "I was thinking maybe...maybe we could meet up later and have a proper conversation. Away from all this."

John cast his arm and looked around the bar, wondering what on earth he was doing.

Jasna frowned. "I don't think..."

"No. No, it's not like that," he said quickly. "I think you're...interesting. I like you, as a person. You're the first person I've met since I got here who I'd like to get to know, like two normal people." He studied her face for a reaction, but lost himself in the delicate beauty of her profile. "Like friends," he added quietly.

Shut the fuck up. You sound like a complete idiot, and a desperate one at that.

He waited for Jasna to give him another withering put down and turn on her heel. Instead, she breathed deeply and looked around, a trace of nervousness in her eyes. "I can't talk like this with a client."

He leaned forwards. "I know this is a terrible place to meet someone and tell them you want to be their friend, but I don't have any choice, unfortunately."

A smile flickered across Jasna's face, quickly suppressed. "I finish in an hour. But I can't be seen meeting you. I'll meet you in the square overlooking the harbour."

"Th..." he went to say something, but he didn't know what and, by the time he'd thought of something, she was gone.

What on earth is happening to me?

John watched her talking to other clients, a stab of jealousy piercing his stomach and his heart. You're just doing this to distract yourself from your real emotions, from the nightmares. You're just trying not to grieve, to drown everything out. You're using this woman to help you forget. A woman you don't even know. It's stupid, and you have to stop it.

Resolved to leave, he drank down his rum and coke in two swift gulps. He calculated how much he owed and folded the correct money, plus tip, under his glass, still wet with condensation. He wanted to look around, to see her, but he didn't want to attract any attention.

As he made his way towards the exit, something caught his his eye. There, sitting in a booth near the door, with a hostess on each arm, was the Russian. John stopped in surprise and stared at him. Before he could tear himself away, the man, who was only a few feet away, noticed and looked up. He smiled and slowly raised his glass in a toast. Embarrassed, John half-smiled and rushed away.

Outside, he caught his breath and revelled in the cool, fresh night air. He looked around the small car park and wondered who owned the expensive vehicles on display. He thought back to the Russian. "We really must stop meeting like this," he said out loud, and walked away.

CHAPTER SEVEN

JOHN SAT ON THE LOW WALL OVERLOOKING THE HARBOUR and wondered why, exactly, he was there. Not just there on the wall, but anywhere. Why was he alive? What was he still trapped on this wretched earth, staring at the sky?

The moon hung large and bright, a disc more white and luminescent than he remembered seeing in England. Maybe I never really looked before. He became aware of the sharp stones of the parapet and the film of dust on the ground as he moved his foot back and forth over the cobbles. Yes, he was aware. Too aware. Every sense and sensation was magnified a thousand-fold. His skin was electric, every touch an intense burst that made him want to cocoon himself and go in to hibernation. His eyes saw further, more clearly, and he could hear the faintest betrayal of humanity echoing from all across the town.

Revellers in a nearby street laughed and shouted. Surely he should be one of them. He had drunk enough; a lot, in fact. How many gin and tonics? How many rum and cokes? At any other time, he would be completely drunk. No, he had been drunk. Very drunk. Offensively drunk, and he'd had to be saved. But saved from what? From that other hotel guest, who he surely would have punched in the face? Saved from himself? Yes, from himself.

Perhaps it would've been better if he had punched me in the face. At least I would have suffered the consequences of my drunkenness. He paused. But aren't I already suffering? Haven't I been suffering, day after day, everything that has happened to me? He closed his eyes and the memories clawed at his insides and pulled him down into the darkness. I should have just stayed in my room and sweated it out, like an addict battling his demons.

He knew he shouldn't be sitting there waiting for her. He knew he should have gone straight back to his hotel. Actually, he should never have gone back to the strip club. And why on earth did he persuade her to meet him, when they both knew instinctively that it was wrong? She'd hesitated, she'd wanted to say no. Error compounding error.

He looked out to sea. I'm far too unstable to have a holiday on my own, given the state I'm in. And here I am, waiting for hostess from a strip joint who wants to meet in secret. What are you doing, man?

He thought of trying to describe the situation to colleagues in the neon-lit sterility of the hospital staffroom, to his friends in the corner bar of the pub, or to his mother in the still quiet of the family room. He almost laughed at the absurdity of it all, then was nearly sick as the reality of his situation dawned on him. He was trapped in a cycle of unbearable pain, one he was making worse with his own actions.

He gazed at the stars, then looked down at the harbour and beach below. People sitting on deckchairs, drinking and laughing. He stared with curiosity, as if examining ants. He slipped slightly and had to grab the rough-hewn stone to steady himself. What if I fell? A middle-aged couple walked past him, hand in hand. What if that man pushed me off? He looked out to the slowly rolling waves, made silver in the moonlight. I could jump. I could end it all now. At least it would stop the howling storm inside my head and the churning, sickening pain.

I could end it all now.

He stared at the silver-edged water and then back down at the beach.

I could jump off, and that would be it.

Directly below him, a large rock stuck out of the cliff. Perhaps I'd smash my head on my way down. I'd be dead before I hit the ground. Simple as that. It'd all be over. Nothing more. Everything, finally finished. And then you'd be reunited with her, after she was torn away from you...Oh, no, of course you wouldn't. You don't believe in an afterlife, remember?

He tried to estimate where he would land if he jumped off and hit the rock on the way down. Just by those people having a drink on the deckchairs. And how would they feel, witnessing that? They would be horrified, traumatised. It wouldn't be fair on them.

Maybe I could swim out to sea and drown.

He watched a gull as it drifted across the sky. Tears welled up and he scrunched up his face in pain.

You could swim out to sea and drown.

He could almost taste the infinite sea that awaited him... No, don't think about that. Don't think about any of it. It wouldn't achieve anything. Nothing at all.

He tried thinking again about jumping off the low stone wall and the sweet taste of death in his mouth, but the moment had passed. Instead he sighed, swung his leg over the stone parapet and stood up, stretching. Unsure what to do, he glanced around and spotted a bar on the opposite side of the square that seemed to be open.

"Tonight," he said to himself, "death can wait."

PART FIVE

CHAPTER ONE

THE BAR WAS SMALL AND BASIC AND THERE WERE ONLY A few customers lost in the dark corners. John pulled himself onto a stool and planted his elbows on the old wooden bar. He caught the barman's eye, who slowly pulled himself off his stool and ambled over, straightening his dishevelled clothes as he went.

"I'm sorry to ask, but do you speak English?" The barman nodded slowly and John couldn't tell whether he took it as self-evident that he spoke English or that he was bored with having to serve yet another foreigner.

"A beer, please."

"Large or small?"

John glanced at the taps. It seemed like it was the same choice of beer as practically every other place. "Large, please."

The barman shuffled away and busied himself with pouring a watery looking pint. While he waited, John glanced around the bar again, but saw little to recommend it. Just another anonymous dive that was nothing without its customers, and there were precious few of those.

He sipped slowly at his drunk, unsure whether he really wanted it. He contemplated ordering a whisky chaser but decided he had been drunk enough already that evening without starting all over again. He examined the half-empty refrigerators behind the bar and tried to think of nothing. He sipped at his beer slowly but soon finished it. He ordered another and, as he watched the barman, realised how glad he was that he hadn't waited on the harbour wall for Jasna.

Of course he should have gone straight back to the hotel rather than hanging about waiting for her. Better still, he should have just stayed in his room after Charles and Enrico had rescued him but at least here he wouldn't end up meeting her—an idea that was beyond stupid.

That was assuming, of course, that she would bother turning up. After all, what on earth possessed him to think, when she agreed to meet him, that she was doing anything other than trying not to make a scene? There you go, that asinine male arrogance again. That caveman logic. Why is it so believable that a woman is telling the truth when she says she is happy to meet you, but so unbelievable when she rejects you? What an idiot. How many times must she have given out fake numbers, agreed to plans she knew she would never keep, or shown interest towards someone simply to get out of a situation, to end a conversation, to leave without causing offence? And you, John Hunter, are just another in a long line of sad and emotionally vulnerable middle-aged losers who are overly susceptible to the minutest sign of encouragement from a woman. She thinks you are a pathetic prick who falls for every slightest intimation that she might, just might, be interested in you as anything other than a walking wallet. This, of course, from someone who should never have been in the strip joint in the first place, let alone talking to her. Idiot.

"Hello, Dr John, I thought I might find you here."

John nearly knocked over his drink. He spun around and

there she was, her head titled to one side and a grin on her face. She was dressed casually, loosely, with just the merest trace of make-up and a hint of lip gloss. To John, she was more beautiful than ever, and his delight at seeing her ashamed him.

"Hello. How lovely to see you."

She narrowed her eyes. "I should have known you wouldn't wait for me and go to the nearest bar. Did you think I wouldn't come?"

"Well, I..."

"What are you drinking?" Jasna took a sip of his beer and sneered. "It's okay, but I'll have a vodka and lime." She nodded to the barman and ordered a double before pulling over a stool and planting herself next to John. She studied his face. "Why are you unhappy? What happened?"

He was surprised. Not her directness but her ability to see straight through him. He looked down and watched her feet moving on the rungs of her stool. "How did you know?" He looked up into her eyes. "When did you know?"

She shrugged and took a sip of her drink. Then she put her glass down carefully on the bar and turned to face him straight on. Her coat fell slightly from her shoulders, and he distracted himself from the impending gravity of the moment by imagining her in a different place and different time.

"Dr John," she said. "I've been thinking." She took another quick sip. "Tell me this." She held out a long pause, during which a knot tightened around his stomach. "When was the last time you went to a strip club? Before here, I mean."

He cleared his throat. "Um, fifteen years ago, in London, for a friend's stag do."

"And you are not on a stag do now?"

"No."

"You are a doctor, in England, yes?"

"Yes."

"You are paid well?"

He reflected. "Yes, I suppose so, relatively speaking."

"And you have friends who you can get drunk with when you need to?"

He smiled at her question and nodded. "From time to time, yes. There's a small group of us leftover from university."

She frowned. "But you wait fifteen years to go to a strip club." He looked down at the floor. "And you wait until you are on holiday alone, away from your family and friends." She tilted her head. "When did you get divorced, Dr John?"

He stared at the door and tried to hold back the tears. "I'm not divorced." Jasna raised her eyebrows. "My wife...she died."

"Oh, I'm so sorry," Jasna blurted out. "I didn't mean to—"

He held up his hand. "No. It's fine, really. Don't be sorry. Please. There's no way you could have known."

Jasna took a long sip and studied his face.

"I know you don't believe me," he said, "but I genuinely didn't know that your bar was a strip club. I admit I wanted to get drunk. I admit I wanted some company, and I wanted to forget, ideally by meeting someone to talk to, to distract me, you know?" Jasna started to speak but John carried on. "And if the person I met was a woman and we harmlessly flirted with each other...well, I knew it wasn't the best thing I could do, and I knew I should have gone back to my hotel and gone to bed rather than staying out into the small hours, but I needed a moment like that. I know it sounds stupid, but I needed to get a bit drunk and get out of my head, just for a bit." Jasna took another sip. "And then I met you."

She smiled. "And here I am." She put her glass down on the bar. "I'm sorry. I thought I would come and tease you, especially after you hid in here. But instead I reminded you about your wife. It must be painful."

He nodded and downed the rest of his beer. "Yes, it is painful," he said, surprised to hear himself articulate something he had not acknowledged out loud before. "It's very painful. But there's nothing I can do about it. I just have to carry it around with me until it lessens and I can start to live again."

Jasna thought for a moment. "But you are living now."

They lapsed into silence, John lost in his thoughts, Jasna wondering what to say next. The barman, who was watching them, shifted on his stool. Jasna studied John's face, and he could sense her eyes on him. "I want to be outside," she said at last. "Will you come and walk with me?"

He frowned, not sure whether he wanted to laugh or cry. Instead, he meekly said: "Yes."

Jasna paid for the drinks. He watched her as if he was having an out-of-body experience and, when she pulled her coat fully over her shoulders and got off her stool to leave, he turned and followed her like a lost schoolboy.

Outside, she walked briskly ahead. He inspected the stone cobbles in between them as they walked, trying to think of nothing. In that moment, he was empty, weightless. He had no idea of what he was doing or where he was going. He had relinquished all responsibility and was contentedly following her wherever she led. When they reached the middle of the square, Jasna turned abruptly to face him. He straightened up and looked at her in surprise.

"There isn't much to do here at this time of night," she announced.

He shrugged. "I don't care. It's a warm evening. Why don't we just sit on the harbour wall, like we were supposed to?"

"Okay," she said, spinning on her heel and resuming her purposeful walk.

When she got to the other side of the square, she swung a leg over the wall and sat astride it. He stood next to her and looked out over the sea. She patted the stone in front of her. "Why don't you sit down?"

He glanced down and frowned. "I think I'd prefer to stand. Do you mind?"

Jasna shook her head. "No. I've been running around fetching drinks for you guys, so I'm going to sit down."

He watched the sea rolling into the shore, the moon shining brightly on the crests of the waves. He realised that, for the first time since he had got there...no, for the first time in a long time...he was relaxed. He wasn't sure whether it was Jasna, the alcohol, the holiday, or that he had finally started to express himself. Or maybe it was all of those things. He glanced at her. She was rolling a cigarette. "Tell me about you. I don't know anything about you or your life."

She carried on rolling the cigarette and, as she lifted it to her mouth to run her tongue along the glued edge of the paper, she caught John's eye. She finished rolling and pulled a lighter out of her pocket. She looked out to sea and, lighting the cigarette, took a long, deep drag. He wondered whether to ask her again, or whether her silence was a sign that she didn't want to tell him anything about herself. Was he being stupid in believing there was a connection between them? Perhaps. Should I just walk away and go back to my hotel? She obviously wouldn't come after me, and at least then I could stop feeling guilty. A breeze came up off the sea and he shivered. No, don't go now. You'd regret it later.

She leaned back and looked John up and down. "What do you want to know?"

He shrugged. "I don't know, the usual stuff that people tell each other when they meet? Where they come from?

How they got to where they are today? What they want from life?"

She shifted on the wall, adjusting her legs. "Isn't that all just boring," she asked. "Who cares about all that stuff? I come from there, you come from somewhere else. I live here, you live there. And in a few days, you'll be gone and we'll forget about each other. What difference does it make to know anything about me, or me about you?"

He considered for a moment. "If you really thought that," he said, "then what are you doing here sitting there on that wall and talking to me?" He folded his arms. "Admit it. You are at least a little curious about me. Enough to say yes when I asked you to meet me."

"Maybe I was sorry for you and I met you because I wanted you to be less lonely and sad," she retorted.

He laughed. "You? You would never do that, I'm sure. I may not know much about you, but I know that you definitely wouldn't do something just to make someone else feel better." She frowned and looked out to sea. "Frankly, it's normal for two people to exchange information about each other when they meet."

"I don't want normal," she said, staring at him. "It's boring, all that stupid information. And for what? What would you or I do with all that stuff, all those details?"

He sighed and scratched his head. "You know what I'm talking about, even if you don't want to admit it." She narrowed her eyes. "Maybe it's been such a long time since you met someone in a normal way that you've forgotten what it's like."

She looked back out to sea. "Maybe. Or maybe I just don't have anything interesting to say. Maybe I'm just a boring girl from a boring part of Eastern Europe and that's all there is to know." She turned back to him. "Maybe I'm not as interesting as you think, Dr John. I'm just another girl serving drinks in a

bar. I haven't done anything with my life, not like you. I'm
not a doctor. I don't have a degree or qualifications. What use
am I to anyone? Who cares about me or my life? If someone
else comes along and works in that place instead of me, no
one will remember I was there. No one will care. I'm just
another girl, another nobody, with nothing interesting to say."
She jabbed her cigarette towards John. "Do you really want to
know something about me?" He nodded. "Okay, I'll tell you
this—my life, it's all been a waste. A waste. I have nothing to
show for it. Nothing. Okay? Is that what you wanted to
know?"

She turned away and took another drag on her cigarette,
but it had gone out. She tried to light it again but her hands
were shaking. Eventually, she controlled herself enough to get
it going and took a long drag.

He waited until she had calmed down. "Jasna, I don't
believe at all that you aren't interesting, or that you have
nothing interesting to say. No one on earth is like that.
Everyone has had a life, no matter how trivial it seems to
them, and we can all learn and grow from each other and our
experiences." She looked at him out of the corner of her eye.
"Okay, have it your way," he said. "No more questions about
your life."

They fell into silence. How can she have such a low
opinion of herself? Who told her that her emotions and
thoughts were not worth listening to? Who poisoned her
mind like that?

She turned over her hand and examined her palm and the
end of the cigarette that stuck through her fingers. You
should stop smoking. But what would be the point? There's
so much else that could kill you. It wouldn't be worth the
effort. Besides, smoking was the only pleasure that was
entirely her own, that only she could experience. Her mind
wandered to her tiny flat and her flatmate. When would she

get back tonight? And what state would she be in? Poor thing.

"Can I ask you a question?"

He smiled. "Yes, of course."

"How did your wife die?"

He should have known the question was coming, but it still shot a bolt of pain through him. He focused on the horizon and tried to think about the moonlight and the rolling sea, but it couldn't stop the memories overwhelming him.

"I'm sorry to ask you," she said quietly. "I didn't mean to upset you. You don't have to talk about it if you don't want to." She almost reached her hand out to his, but checked herself. Instead, she watched him struggle to stop himself from breaking down. She wanted to say something kind, something that would make him feel better, but she just repeated: "I'm sorry. I didn't mean to..."

He looked down at her, his eyes bright with tears. "It's okay," he said softly. He folded his arms and looked back out to the sea, still rolling in the dark silver light. "She died in a car accident. She was killed by a police car."

Jasna frowned, wondering if she had heard him correctly. She wanted to know her name, but couldn't bring herself to ask.

"They were chasing a stolen car. The police driver lost control at a junction and skidded. We were out for an afternoon walk. We'd just had lunch with some friends in a pub and she wanted to find a throw for the sofa, and some candles." John paused and frowned. "She was texting someone I think. She'd fallen behind me. I didn't notice. I was watching some jugglers practising in the park. When the police car hit the pavement, there was a huge crash. I turned and saw it had flipped and was skidding towards us. I shouted to her to move, and tried to grab her. It was all in slow motion, you know?" John glanced at Jasna. "She was frozen to the spot. Fear, I guess. I tried to reach her but I was too late. She turned towards the police car and she put her hands over her face. And then it hit her."

Jasna was transfixed by the tumult of emotions on his face. She wanted to stop him having to be like this. She wanted to hold him tight and rock him in her arms. She almost reached out for his hand again.

The tears rolled freely down his face. He glanced at her and their eyes connected. He smiled a warm, intimate smile and a line was strung between them. Her heart jumped.

John looked back out to sea. "She spent a week in that hospital room, hanging onto life. But she never woke up. We never spoke to each other again. I held her hand." He turned to Jasna. "I held her hand for days and nights. I waited...no, I longed for her hand to squeeze mine, just once. Just to show she knew I was there and she wasn't alone in the darkness. But she never did squeeze my hand. Not once." He screwed his eyes up in silent pain.

Jasna remained fixed to the wall but an ocean flowed through her. She wanted to leave, to stay, to hold him, to run away, to touch his skin and have the electricity flow through them, to kiss him, to push him away, to turn and run and never see him again. The breath shook in her lungs and she shivered. This is the moment. This is us, now. Reach out and show him you can see it, that you can sense it. You can have this moment, now. He has shown you his soul. Show him yours too. Get up, Jasna, take his hand, hold him, kiss him, be with him.

But she stayed on the wall, her hands shaking, tears gathering in her eyes. After a few moments, John stopped crying, and she merely whispered: "I'm so sorry, John."

"I know," he said. "I'm sorry I cried."

She shook her head. "It's normal."

"This is the first time since she died that I've really been able to talk about her. Thank you for listening."

Jasna smiled awkwardly. They fell into silence and she watched him look out over the rolling waves. After a while, she shifted on the wall and pulled her coat around her. "Where are you staying," she asked.

John gave a start. "Sorry. What did you say?"

"Your hotel, what is it?"

He told her and she screwed up her mouth in disappointment. He laughed. "What's wrong with that? Don't you think it's a good hotel? It seems okay to me, although it's not at all where I'd normally go. It's not at all my kind of place."

She shook her head. "No, it's fine. It's just too far away." He smiled. "Hey, don't get any ideas, Dr John," she said, wagging her finger. "I was only thinking about getting another drink. It's cold, but there's nowhere open now apart from hotel bars. And you definitely can't come back to my place." She wondered if her flatmate would have burned herself out by now and fallen asleep. "Do you want to meet me tomorrow," she asked abruptly. "For lunch?"

John stared at Jasna in surprise. "Are you sure?"

"Yes, of course. Why not?"

"No, nothing, it's just..."

"Do you want to meet me here," she said, pointing at the stone wall between her legs, "at midday? I can take you to a nice place, where only locals go. No tourists. It's very good."

"Yes, absolutely, that'd be great," he said. "I'd like that very much."

"Good."

With that, she swung herself over the wall and stood up, stretching her legs, made stiff in the cool sea breeze. She put her hands on her hips and gave John a cheeky grin. "See you tomorrow, Dr John, and don't think about me too much."

She turned and walked away. "I'll try not to," John called

after her, but she was already halfway across the square and out of earshot.

HE WATCHED her until she disappeared around a corner and then laughed to himself. Shaking his head, he set off back to his hotel. The weather was almost identical to the night before, but he was completely different. This evening, he was not tortured but light and airy, like a room with its windows flung open on a fresh, spring day, the wind blowing in life and possibility. And guilt. Guilt that he was betraying the memory of the only woman...no, the only person he had ever loved.

But I've been honest with Jasna, he told himself as he retraced his steps through the old town. I've not pretended that I'm something I'm not. After all, this is just a friendship, complicated by the confusion that arises between men and women. We're conditioned to believe it has to have a deeper meaning when we like each other, but this thing between us is simple affection.

A sliver of doubt pushed its way into his mind like a shard of broken glass, and he tried to ignore it as it sliced through him. But doubt about what, exactly? Her? Him? His desires? If so, what desires? Physical? Emotional? The desire to have a friend is not wrong. But you can still have sex with a friend, the demon whispered in his ear. John turned away from himself and focused on silencing the demon. You always try to find the worst in me. He pushed his hands further into his pockets and quickened his pace.

CHAPTER TWO

You are walking through a moonlit winter forest, the swell of a black ocean steadily rolling towards you. A bird flies high in the dark sky and you turn to find blood seeping through the walls of a stone passageway.

Her head is thrown back in agony or ecstasy, but she is gone and you are staring at a decayed door overgrown with death. Behind you, a stone wing, cold and hard, beats through the air. You follow, and a flock of seagulls searches the waves of a black lake. She holds a bird to her chest, lifeless both, and you turn to chase her shadow as it disappears from view at the end of the passageway.

You fall, and the pain rips through you. The light dances in the raindrops perpetually falling on water, and you know you will drown. Candles illuminate a shattered pane of glass and, in the reflected light, she reaches up from the water, her face hidden beneath the still, dark surface.

You dive in for her, but she is falling. You try to grab her, and she catches the light as she unfolds her wings and flies away.

You lie on the floor and watch the curtains moving slowly, silently in the breeze through the open window. The rain is falling endlessly but you make out the silhouettes of birds as they fly through the gloom of approaching night.

She wades into the dark water that embraces and pulls you in. She wades further out, the veil of her wedding dress trailing on the water. The last thing you see before you slip beneath the surface is her eyes turned towards you and the mist-laden mountains stretching off into infinite darkness.

IN THE UNKNOWABLE hour between night and day, John was woken by loud banging and whispering outside his door. He lay with his eyes shut, knowing he should investigate but, still drunk and disorientated, he lay still.

The banging and whispering went on and on, then stopped abruptly. Then whispering became urgent. There was a final bang and then a click, and all fell silent.

CHAPTER THREE

JOHN WOKE UP ON HIS BED STILL FULLY DRESSED, THE FULL light of day streaming into his room. He moved to get up, but a headache slammed through the back of his skull and he lay down again. He stared at the ceiling and the plaster decorations that lined the edges. What is that called? Cornicing. That's it. It's called cornicing.

He pondered for a moment. How long, realistically, can I lie here? I'm on holiday, so technically as long as I want. I could lie here all day, in fact. Although you haven't put the Do Not Disturb sign on the door. He shifted slightly and instantly regretted it. His headache was much worse when he moved. It was at least manageable as long as he lay still. But I need a shower. I can't be trapped here all day by a headache.

He lay there a while longer, thinking of what he could eat for breakfast and trying not to dwell on the events of the night before.

Hold on, that's it.

FIVE MINUTES LATER, he dived head-first into the fresh,

cleansing blue of the hotel pool. The coolness of the water instantly refreshed his body and drained away his headache. He pushed himself to swim as many lengths as possible before the dregs of half-processed alcohol seized up his muscles and stiffened his joints. Once he could continue no longer, he trod water at the deep end, panting heavily and waiting for the lactic acid to subside.

He examined the hotel building. It was a beautiful old palace, and he tried to imagine life there when it was still a family home. What money they must have they had to build something like that? The upkeep costs alone must be ruinous. He spotted his balcony, and thought about the oranges and knife he had taken from the hotel restaurant. They must still be sitting outside on the table. What would the maid say when she found them? Would she mention it to someone, or simply take them back? He wondered how many people 'borrowed' things, and whether everyone who did it thought they were the only ones. Or maybe he was the only one who cared what anyone thought of him.

He was hungry and recalled his breakfast the previous morning. Was Charles watching him now, making notes so he could talk about his morning swim in front of everyone?

He didn't like the stiff formality of the hotel breakfast ritual: the gossipy curiosity; the sly mentions of late-night returns; the clumsy attempts at cross-examining. To him, the whole purpose of going away on holiday was precisely not to have to deal with meaningless enquiries and fake friendships and be isolated as much as possible from real life. That a hotel is run by human beings and not mute robots is an unfortunate necessity. He wondered if he'd prefer to stay in a robot hotel but decided he wanted human contact to be available, but only on his terms. How ridiculously English. The islander-prisoner mentality all over.

He watched the ripples of a breeze run across the pool

and two pairs of feet walking along a path behind a hedge.

He became aware of the cooling water and pulled himself out in a single, fluid movement. He dried his hair slowly, methodically, lost in thought, beneath the shade of a palm tree. He thought he was being watched, but there was no one there when he spun around. The hotel was eerily quiet and the loneliness of holidaying alone crept into him.

BACK IN HIS ROOM, he sat on the edge of his bed, dressed in a white cotton shirt and loose trousers, contemplating the room-service menu but not really taking it in. His head was spinning slightly and, after running through all the various options, decided that he must still be a little drunk. What's wrong with you, man? What are you doing getting so drunk at your age. It's pathetic. No, it's not pathetic, it's called grief. But getting drunk like that, in public, it has consequences. You know that. You've got to get a hold of yourself. And when, exactly, was getting drunk ever a solution for grief?

He read through the menu again, then rang down for a bowl of fruit and strong black coffee. He thought of asking for scrambled eggs on thick toast with lots of butter, but he was already hot and the heaviness of bread and eggs was not appealing. Besides, the alcohol from the night before had left stomach his delicate and churning constantly. Most of all, he was thirsty and he rang down again to add a litre of lightly sparkling mineral water.

He sat back his elbows and gazed at the photograph of the beautiful dark-haired woman on the mantelpiece. He tilted his head and smiled, trying to imagine her smiling back. "I think you'd like her," he heard himself say out loud. How stupid. You can't talk to a photograph like that. But there's no one here, and what's so wrong with it anyway.

"I think you'd like her. Jasna, I mean. Actually, I'm sure

you would. She's smart and funny, and she's a thinker, like you. When she's not sure what to say, she doesn't say anything. Wasn't that your father's definition of a wise man?"

He paused and looked out through the balcony doors. He watched a gull gliding across the sky, and the slowly waving treetops in the gathering breeze. He got up and walked over to the glass doors.

"I'm glad he wasn't still alive when all that happened. It would have crushed him to see you like that. He couldn't have coped. It was bad enough for your mum, but at least she had her sisters around her." He turned back to the picture. "They were such a help, you know. Not so much for me personally, but just to know that they were taking care of your mum, so I didn't have to worry about that as well." He sat back down and picked at the bedding with his fingernails. "I mean, whose daughter, whose wife, dies like that, at 36?" He scrunched up his face in pain and then glanced up at his wife. "We all miss you so much. You do know that, don't you? I hope you do anyway," he added quietly.

He stared up at the ceiling. "It's been tough, without you." He laughed ironically. "Everyone said it must be so difficult. They said they understood my pain, that they sympathise. But they had no idea. It was like someone had torn my heart right out of my body, right through my chest." He tapped his rib cage. "I know it was you who died, and that you're the one who's no longer here, but I die for you all the time, my love. I die for you every day. Every day my heart is ripped out and I die all over again." He stared at the picture. "I miss you so much." He turned away, trying not to cry again.

A FEW MINUTES LATER, he got up and paced around the room. He glanced at the picture each time he passed and nodded. Eventually, he said: "I think I want to tell you about

Jasna." He paced some more. "If you were still here, I would tell you about her." He carried on walking. "It's just that, well, I'm a bit worried that people will get the wrong end of the stick, that they won't understand what's happening." He paused and frowned. "Maybe I'm worried I'm getting the wrong end of the stick."

He started walking again. "The thing is...Well, yes, it's true, she's young, she's beautiful and she's got a great figure. She's sexy, I suppose. But so what? I've met loads of beautiful women, and it doesn't mean I want them or that something is going to happen. She's just a friend, a good friend...I mean, it's ridiculous. I'm a grown man, an adult, and I've never once messed around."

He paused and then carried on walking. "No, the thing is that, well, she's the first person I've had any kind of connection with since...since..." He glanced at the photo. "Well, you."

Before he could continue, there was a soft knock at the door, followed by a bright, cheery voice announcing: "Room service."

He sighed. "Dammit." He opened the door and a small waitress he recognised from breakfast the previous morning walked briskly into the room with a tray and went straight over to the low table by the balcony, throwing a cheerful "good morning" over her shoulder as she passed. John felt a lurch of guilt when he saw the half-empty gin bottle and tonic water standing where he had left them. The waitress carefully placed the tray on the table, pushing the bottles out of the way with its edge.

She smiled warmly at John as she passed on her way out again. "Bon appétit," she called out brightly as she left and closed the door behind her.

John stared at the breakfast waiting for him on the table and wasn't sure if he was still hungry. He poured himself a cup of coffee and stared at the black liquid. He thought about the scene at breakfast the previous morning and the gull staring back at him. He turned back to the photograph.

"I hope you don't mind," he said, taking his cup and resuming pacing back and forth. "You know, that I'm talking to her. I hope you understand. I don't think anyone else would if they knew but you are the most understanding and thoughtful person I ever met. Even though you laughed every time I said that."

He took a sip of coffee. "I mean, who else could I talk to, if it wasn't someone like Jasna? Men don't open up with their emotions, at least not until you've been drunk with them. If I was going to talk to anyone properly, openly while I'm here, it'd have to be with a woman."

He looked out over the hotel gardens and took another sip. "It'd be easier in America. People there are more open. Maybe even in England, if we were both smashed." He turned back to the photograph. "But here? The locals don't speak enough English, and holidaymakers don't want to listen to my tales of grief."

He stared sadly at the picture. "I haven't really been able to talk to my friends. I was such a mess after the funeral. They were so kind and patient. I didn't want to burden them any more." He frowned and looked down into his cup. "I suppose I should see someone, a professional, and talk it all through. Maybe I'll sort that out when I get back. There's someone good at the hospital."

He paced around the room again before stopping to refill his cup and eat some grapes. The zingy, bright flavour of the fruit contrasted badly with the dark bitterness of the coffee and he grimaced.

"The thing is...and I know how this sounds, but she works in a...well, a strip joint. She says she's just a barmaid, but if I didn't know better I'd wonder if she's at least a dancer, if not a prostitute." He shook his head in disbelief. "I know, I know. It all sounds so stupid."

He stared out over the balcony, watching the clouds darken the sky into an undulating mass of silver grey and the sea harden in the falling light. He thought about the waves crashing against the cliffs beneath the hotel and guessed that the sailing boat had not gone out that morning.

He turned back to the photograph. "I'm confused. I can't pretend otherwise. But there is something so innocent about her, and about whatever there is between us. She seems to understand that there's nothing more to it than friendship."

He took another sip of coffee but it was tepid. "You know, I really do think you'd like her," he said while refilling his cup. "In fact, she kind of reminds me of you when we first met." He checked himself and stared hard at the floor, frowning. He looked up and noticed the time. "I'd better go."

OUT IN THE CORRIDOR, his stomach jumped when he saw that the entrance to the stone passageway was slightly ajar. He looked around to see if anyone was watching, then glanced up at the CCTV camera, wondering whether he should forget all about it and walk away. But he remembered the banging and whispering from the night before, and his guilt at having done nothing. The more he thought about it, the more his curiosity got the better of him. As quickly and as quietly as he could, he pulled the door open and stepped inside. He tried to put it back in the same position he'd found it, all the while praying it wouldn't click shut and trap him inside.

The passageway was cold and dark, and he had to use the torch on his phone to see where he was going. This time, he saw that, rather than it being simply a corridor, there were several doors along one side. He tried the first two, but they were firmly shut. The third opened after a small shove, and he found himself in a windowless, crumbling room that could have been a prison cell in a former era. As he flashed the light around, he spotted a stack of cardboard boxes in a corner, each one emblazoned the name and logo of an international office-supply company. Given the dampness in the room and their pristine condition, he guessed they must have been there no more than a day or two.

Inspecting the boxes, he saw the top one was not completely sealed and opened it carefully. He recoiled in horror when he saw what was inside, and hurriedly checked that there was no one else around. Once he was convinced he was alone, he checked it again. There they were, nestling in shredded paper—two handguns and several cartridges of ammunition. His stomach sank. He wished he'd never given into his curiosity. Oh fuck, oh fuck, he said quietly to himself over and over again. He breathed deeply and glanced around, trying to calm himself down.

What are you going to do now, eh? He stared at the guns and thought of a hundred things he could, or should, do. But if you call the police, they'll never believe you just found them. And what about Charles? Well, the first thing he'd ask you is what the hell you thought you were doing in the passageway in the first place. You are such an idiot. Well done.

He stared a little longer, then, unsure whether his finger-prints could be picked up from cardboard, he carefully, gingerly closed the box, wishing he'd paid more attention to how it was arranged.

Checking constantly as he went, he picked his way care-fully back along the passageway, and was extremely grateful to step into the safety of the hotel corridor. He pulled the door to as best he could and, with a nameless fear rising up inside him, hurried to the lift.

CHAPTER FOUR

JOHN TURNED HIS NAPKIN OVER AND OVER WHILE HE watched an old woman struggling with several bags of heavy shopping. The sun was blazing down after a short, intense rain shower, and he thought she must be incredibly hot inside her dark clothes. He wanted to go over and help her but he remembered that wouldn't be able to speak to her and, besides, he didn't know how far away she lived. What if it took half an hour, or even longer, to carry her bags home and get back to the restaurant?

Not that it would matter.

He impatiently grabbed at his glass of over-sweet white wine and took a big gulp, finishing it down. It's not as if Jasna has anything to say today, even if she does come back from the bathroom, or wherever she is. Besides, it might be more interesting to carry shopping for an old woman than to pretend to enjoy lunch with someone who'd clearly rather be anywhere else.

He glanced around the square, now shaded by the passing clouds. The old lady was gone, so he picked at his napkin again.

He just didn't understand it. Jasna was waiting for him by the stone wall in the square as planned. Although she initially seemed pleased to see him and chatty, he had the distinct impression she was going through the motions and was, in fact, entirely absent. It occurred to him, as they wended their way through endless narrow streets that took them further and further away from the town, that they weren't actually conversing. Instead, she was simply responding to his statements and questions with one-word answers, if she said anything at all.

At one point, he had tried an experiment and stopped talking. As anticipated, they lapsed immediately into silence, broken only by their shoes crunching on the crumbling pavements. In those unfamiliar streets, following this now-unfamiliar woman, he was lonely. He thought of stopping or turning back, or taking the next corner and seeing what happened. But he didn't want to get lost and, anyway, he didn't want to give up on her just like that.

He wouldn't have minded being silent if it had been companionable, but there was a palpable tension emanating from her that permeated the air around her. Not wanting to endure any more awkward silences but also sensing it was not the moment to ask what was going on, he started speaking again, externalising the first piece of nonsense that came into his head. Her response was so minimal that by the time they reached the small, ugly square, lined on one side by an unprepossessing and distinctly unpromising restaurant, and she said "we're here," he had almost forgotten that they were together.

Once they sat down, she had busied herself with either the menu or checking her phone and sending texts. He had been about to say something when she abruptly got up and went inside, presumably to go the toilet. But given how long she had been away, he wasn't so sure anymore.

Having run out of ideas as to what to do, he had fallen to staring at passers-by. He was so engrossed in every minute detail of life in this tiny corner of the world that he jumped when, for a second time, the waiter come back and asked if he wanted to order. For a second time, he had to signal that he wanted to wait for his companion. Out of sympathy for the waiter and because he wanted something to do other than just sit idly waiting, he ordered another glass of wine, choosing randomly once more from the indecipherable menu.

While he waited for his second glass, he watched two young men talking next to a moped, one with a helmet in his hand, the other smoking a cigarette. They seemed to be not exactly friends but at least to know each other well. How many years had they been talking together like that? Had they started as boys around a bicycle and graduated to the scooter when they became adults? While he watched, they stopped talking and stared in his direction. He shrank back into his cheap plastic chair.

When the waiter came back with a new glass of wine, he gratefully took a long gulp, relishing its freshness in the growing heat of the day and happy that, this time, he had accidentally chosen a dry wine. He made a mental note not to get too drunk. Again.

He was taking his second large sip when Jasna reappeared and sat down in a hurry, not really looking at him and immediately picking up her menu. "Sorry, I had to make a phone call," she said quickly, clearly hoping that he would simply accept the explanation and forget all about it.

He stared at her bowed face. She was making a show of reading the first page of the menu with great intensity. He wasn't sure what exactly to say, although he wanted to say something. Clearly things were not the same as before. In any case, she was simply being rude now. But he didn't want to provoke her into a reaction or, worse, an argument.

He sat back and took a small sip of his wine, examining her hair, which seemed limp and flat today. "Are you okay," he asked softly.

"What do you mean," Jasna shot back. She looked up, full of challenge.

He smiled calmly. "You seem a little agitated." He looked straight in the eye. "Is anything wrong?"

She paused and took a deep breath. The anger melted a little. Then she sighed, sat back in her chair and threw her menu onto the table. "No." She looked at the square. "No, nothing's wrong."

He cleared his throat. "Would you prefer if we didn't do this? The lunch, I mean. It's okay if you'd rather not. I'd understand. We don't have to do anything we don't want to, even if it's something we'd planned."

She turned back. "No, no. I do want to do this." He waited, and her expression crumpled. "I'm sorry. I want to have lunch. It's just..."

He frowned. "Just what?"

"It's just...you and I are so different. We have such different lives. How can we ever be friends? What for? What's the point? Why do you even want to talk to someone like me?" She shrugged her shoulders dismissively and looked away.

He smiled. "But how will you...how will we ever know if we don't try and find out?" Before Jasna could respond, the waiter returned and John picked up his menu, trying to find what he had chosen. He could sense her eyes on him, and she half-smiled when he looked up. She ordered for both of them, choosing local dishes. By the time the waiter had gone, she had softened up. He was relieved, although he had been trying to retrace their route from the square, in case she stormed off and he needed to make his way back alone.

Instead, she launched into a long history of her life,

explaining how she had grown up in a small village in Romania and was brought up by her mother and older sisters. When she reached puberty, she was picked up by a local man more than twice her age who promised her the world, but in reality sold her to a massage parlour in the nearest city. When it became obvious that giving massages was only the start of what was expected of her she ran away, initially back home, but then joining one of her sisters in Prague when she heard that the gang running the parlour were going to take her back by force.

A forged passport and a few dollars got her out of the country, and it took her a week of hitchhiking and sleeping rough before she eventually got to Prague. Her sister looked after her for a night but made it clear that she didn't want Jasna to stay with her, so she stole five hundred euros from her sister's flatmate and made her way to London. She'd heard it was easy to find work there and wanted to improve her English. After working in bars and clubs for tips for a couple of years and failing to make ends meet, she decided to move closer to home. She wanted to see her mother and her sisters, if the chance came, and to have some Mediterranean sun. Since then, she said, she'd been working as a barmaid in the strip club, living with a girl from the bar and trying to save up enough money for a fresh start.

John was initially impressed with how she'd managed to evade the usual pitfalls of so many young girls growing up in rural southeastern Europe, several of whom he'd met as patients at the hospital, but began to wonder if it was all too good to be true. By this time, they'd finished eating and were having a last glass of the wine.

"So, how much money are you trying to save up for your fresh start?" John turned his glass between his fingers, trying not to betray the doubts rising in his mind. "Has it been easy to put money by?"

Jasna curled up the corner of her mouth. "It's been okay." She looked out across the square. "The thing is I have to pay off my debt with the club."

John frowned. "What do you mean? Did you borrow money from them?"

"No, not exactly." John waited for her to continue, watching her eyes, narrowed against the sun. "To get a job at the bar, you have to buy a contract," she said causally.

"I'm sorry? What did you say?"

"If you want to work there, you have to buy your contract. You can't just work there for free."

John stared at her. "What? You are telling me that if you want to work there you have to pay them?"

Jasna glanced around to make sure no one was listening. "Yes," she said softly. "They make you buy your job. They do it to everyone working there." She leaned in closer. "They take your passport and only give it back to you once you've paid off the debt."

"What? That's crazy. And how much did you have to pay?"

"Well, if you're a foreigner, it's is a bit more expensive."

"How much?"

Jasna screwed up her face. "For a Romanian like me, it's five thousand euros."

"Seriously? You're telling me you have to pay them five thousand euros? You're kidding me?" Jasna shook her head.

John thought for a moment and then frowned. "Hold on, you mean they don't pay you at all, nothing, until you've paid off the money? How can you afford to live?"

"No, no, it's not like that. They pay you normally, but you have some money taken out of your wages until you've paid them back. And they take all your tips as well."

John sat back, amazed. "I see. And why on earth would you agree to do that?"

"I couldn't get work anywhere else."

"What do you mean? What about all the hotels? You could work in any of those with your English. What about the one where I'm staying?"

Jasna shook her head. "You don't understand. They wouldn't employ someone like me."

"What do you mean 'someone like me'? What's wrong with you?"

She shrugged her shoulders. "For someone where I come from...they think we're no better than whores, and they don't want us working in smart places like your hotel." John stared at her, unsure what to say. "Look, it's fine about the debt," she continued. "I'll have it paid off soon. And I don't have to pay for my apartment. It's owned by the club and they use it just for us girls. I'm doing fine," she added, "honestly."

"Jasna, can I ask you a question?" She nodded as she took a sip of wine. "Are you a prostitute?"

Jasna's face hardened instantly. "No, of course I'm not," she said at the top of her voice. "What do you think I am? You," she spat, jabbing her finger at him, "are just like all the rest. You think us Romanians are just here to be the whores of Europe." She folded her arms and stared out over the square.

John watched as she fought back the tears. He shifted in his seat and cleared his throat. "I'm sorry, Jasna. I didn't mean to offend you, and I certainly don't think that all women from Romania are sex workers. It's just that I work in a very busy hospital in central London, and we see a lot of young women who have been trafficked from Romania to London to work as prostitutes. Your story is very similar to a lot that I've heard over the years. I'm sorry, but I had to ask. I couldn't not." He sighed. "But clearly I was wrong."

Jasna didn't respond and continued staring at the square. He inspected her face for any signs of emotion or thoughts betrayed, but she completely ignored him.

She must know I'm watching her.

Why am I still sitting there? If you're being completely rational, you're trying to have a friendship with a young woman you met in a strip joint two nights ago; a woman who may or may not be a prostitute, who, at the very least, is clearly emotionally damaged and fragile, and who is inhabiting a world that you don't understand and don't want to be a part of. Who is she, anyway? Will I ever know? Maybe I'll never know truly know her, or whether or not I can even trust her.

And yet.

To John, she was a puzzle, an enigma. More, she was an enigma that wanted to be solved. She clearly wanted to break out of her life and her apparent destiny. Otherwise she wouldn't be sitting there with him, no matter how much she tried to resist the cold light of scrutiny. There was something locked in the centre of her and he wanted to find it and bring it out before their eyes. He also wanted to hold her hand and reassure her, but he knew he couldn't trust himself enough to do that. He was seduced by the situation and by the demon as much as by her.

He cleared his throat. "Would you like to go for a walk with me?"

No response.

"You don't have to talk to me or even look at me, if you don't want. You can just walk beside me, in silence."

A small smile crept across her face that she quickly suppressed.

"Or not. It's up to you."

She sighed and turned to him, her eyes softer now. "Yes, Dr John. I'd like to have a walk with you."

She beckoned over the waiter and he paid the bill.

CHAPTER FIVE

HE WASN'T SURE WHETHER THEY WENT THE SAME WAY down the narrow, winding streets towards the old town. They had a view of the sea, rather than the endless stone walls that had hemmed them in as they'd climbed up to the square. Besides, this time Jasna was doing the talking, and she told him about her sister in Prague and how she had been like a second mother to her when she was young, especially when their mother went abroad to Norway each summer to pick strawberries. At that time, she and her sister had been inseparable and shared everything. But by the time Jasna got to Prague she found her sister cold and remote, and all that they had shared as children had gone. She also spoke of her apartment near the strip club and the problems her flatmate was having with drugs.

She was open and relaxed, not guarded and anxious like before. She was not even the sassy, confident, woman of the world she'd been in the strip club. This was a new Jasna, one who didn't strike a pose but who spoke from the heart. Her voice rose and fell with emotion. Her limbs were looser and more flowing, her steps light. At times, she seemed almost to be skipping as she told him her stories. John watched her arms, lithe and tanned, swing with the beat of her walk, and she caught him looking at her. She smiled at him, warmly, like a friend, a confidante. He was elated, and relieved. For the first time since he had met her, he wasn't questioning what was happening. For the first time, she was being the way her eyes had always suggested she could be, if only she trusted the world, and herself, enough to open up.

She smiled and they locked eyes. She stopped talking about herself and started asking John questions. She wanted to know about his upbringing, his family, his school, why he'd become a doctor and how he met his wife. Recounting his life in such detail was awkward. It had been a long while since he had talked about himself. In any case, his life had not been his own since his wife's death. Even when people took an interest in him it was only in relation to that all-consuming, overwhelming tsunami. Consequently, John Hunter, a man with a past, present and future, was beside the point.

Now, when he recounted tales from his childhood and early adulthood, it struck him as almost odd to hear his own voice saying those things out loud. In that moment, those tired old anecdotes from his boring, familiar life seemed fresh and new. However, he was also acutely aware that he was describing events and situations, and a thousand unconscious privileges, that must have seemed like something from another planet to Jasna. The more he spoke, the more he saw that their notions of existence and what it meant to enjoy life were poles apart.

And yet.

There were things, subtle sometimes, that they held in common. When you stripped away the surface there lay a kinship, a chiming between their characters and outlooks that pulled them in. She was, underneath it all and despite her protestations, an optimist and open to the world. She had adventure in her soul, even if life had tried to beat it out of her.

As they crossed a street, he made a joke, as he would have done with any of his friends, and she laughed, happily, unself-consciously. He caught the moment and wanted it to last forever.

It started spitting with rain as they got closer to the old town. He inspected the dark, lowering clouds and realised this would be no quick tempest. "Do you want to go for a drink," he asked. She stopped and turned. "To get out of the rain," he added, glancing up to the sky.

She followed his gaze and frowned, then looked back at him. "Yes, that'd be nice, John," she said quietly, a smile in her voice. His heart lifted a metre, and he knew they were in a different place now. Without any warning the rain lashed down, and they ran down a side street far from anywhere that he knew. She spotted a small bar and they dived inside.

It was small and intimate, dark and cocooned against the world, and almost empty. As the rain beat down outside and the wind lashed the trees, they knocked back glasses of wine and snacked on small plates of delicious local food that came with every round. They talked and talked, about everything and nothing, and they laughed as if they had known each other all their lives. And between them, a glowing light grew.

BY SEVEN O'CLOCK, John was tipsy and, when Jasna disappeared to the bathroom, he found himself staring out at the slow majesty of the falling day. The rain had gone now, and the sunset spread itself against the sky, stretching out into evening. He smiled when he recalled their tiff during lunch and wondered whether it had been a necessary step so they could be so free with each other now.

He thought back to his dinner two nights before, when he

had sat outside the trattoria behind the young German couple. Were people watching him and Jasna now smiling as indulgently, as warmly, as they had for them, seeing the same intimacy? The difference was that the two young Germans were the same age and from the same place, with the same possibilities ahead of them. For him and Jasna, it was more than obvious that they lived at least one world and one generation apart.

When she returned and slid onto the stool beside him, he looked at her curiously, inquisitively. She took a sip of wine but put her glass down when she noticed he was staring at her. "What," she demanded. "What is in your head?"

"Nothing." He paused. "Well, there is something actually."

She narrowed her eyes. "What?"

"I was just wondering what people would think of us if they saw us here together in this bar."

She regarded him for a moment. "You think too much, John."

"No, no, I don't" he protested. "Well, yes, I do actually. You're right. But, really..."

"Really what?"

"What do you think people think about us, when they see us?"

She shrugged. "Maybe that you're my sugar daddy and you're taking me out for a drink so you'll get a blowjob later?" She looked him straight in the eye and he looked away, nodding his head.

She frowned. "What? It was a joke." He looked back at her and wrinkled his mouth. "Who cares what anyone thinks," she said defiantly. "We're not doing anything wrong. And how can you know what people think anyway? So what if you're older or we're from different backgrounds? I don't give a fuck." John laughed. "What now," she demanded. He carried on chuckling. "What is it? What have I said?"

"Nothing, it's...it's just funny."

"What is?"

"The way you say 'fuck'. You make it sound so...sweet." He laughed again and she raised an eyebrow.

"I'm glad someone finds me sweet." She looked out of the door at the sunset. "Are you really bothered about what people think of us together?"

"Yes, I suppose. A bit."

"Is it because you are guilty about your wife?" He nodded. "You know you can't live with that hanging over you forever, John."

"Yes, I know. But it's not long since she died. It all seems a bit wrong, like I haven't grieved for long enough."

"There is no right length of time, and we can't help who we meet and when." She took a sip of wine. "Besides, nothing has happened between us. We're just friends, remember? Having a nice time."

He smiled and nodded. "You're right. But, you know, even forgetting about all that, I can't help thinking about what other people think. I don't want to look like one of those old sleazebags with loads of money who doesn't care how they get their hands on some hot piece of ass, as long as they get their hands on it.'

She narrowed her eyes. "Number one, you have no idea how hot my ass is, because you haven't seen it. Number two, I don't give compliments but no one is going to think you are that kind of person. Ever."

He raised his eyebrows and looked at the ceiling. "Oh yes," he asked doubtfully.

"Yes." Jasna finished her glass and put it down determinedly on the bar. "You are one of the nicest, kindest people I have ever met, John, and you make me feel like a real person, like you actually care about me."

He looked straight at her. "I do, Jasna. I do care about you."

"Well, that's good." She reflected. "Do you want to celebrate something?"

"Yes, what?"

"I don't know. We'll think of something." She gave him a cheeky grin and winked.

He laughed. "Okay, that sounds good to me. How do you want to celebrate?"

"I have an idea." She beckoned over the barman and ordered another round of wine plus two shots of rakija. "You don't mind doing shots, do you? You're not too old for that?"

He laughed. "No, not yet."

"Good."

The shots, one after another, swirled around the evening, folding the two of them into their own, private space of happiness. Shot after shot, wine after wine. They forgot about having dinner, about the other people in the bar, about their earlier conversations, and about any doubts they might have had over each other or what was happening between them. They saw only one another, and the outside world was there simply to adorn and illuminate the personal stage show they were laying on for each other. John made wisecracks and word plays and told dirty jokes, while she pulled him this way and that with her endless, intricate teases.

Soon, the flowing shots slowed their wits and they talked no more. The barman played music over the PA and an apparent dance floor classic that was way after John's time had Jasna turning and spinning, swaying her hips to the beat. She sparkled in his eyes and he followed her into the cloud of music. They danced together, energetically at first, and then slower and closer until he grabbed her hand, and they pulled each other in, holding and separating, spinning and locking, all the while staring into each other's eyes.

The music changed, and a romantic ballad reached around them. They slow-danced, John holding Jasna close. She said something that was lost in the music, and he pulled her closer in to hear what she had said. Her face was next to his and her eyes became still, motionless. The loud, drunken bar was no more and, in the silence of the moment, they kissed delicately, tentatively. He found the warmth of her mouth strange after so many months without intimacy, and he pulled back when he remembered where he was and what he was doing. He looked at the floor and then turned away and grabbed his drink. Putting his glass down again without taking a sip, he leaned on the bar and put his head in his hands. She watched him, unsure what to do. Eventually, she stepped forwards to grab her coat and leave, but he turned on his elbow and stared straight at her. She stopped and half-smiled.

"What are we doing, Jasna," he asked imploringly.

"I don't know, John. What do you want to do?"

He frowned and shook his head. "No, I don't mean now. I mean generally. We hardly know each other. I'm grieving for my wife and in no fit state to make any judgement about my emotions. What are we doing, here, right now?"

She shrugged and smiled, lost for words. John looked at her curiously and he swayed slightly. "I know all of this is ridiculous and stupid, and there are a thousand reasons why I am being a self-indulgent, blind, male chauvinist pig who is pretending that something is happening simply to excuse my actions. And there are a thousand reasons why you are either secretly laughing at me or quietly taking whatever it is you want from me before I go away again." He stared into her eyes. "But..." Jasna's blood ran cold and the thoughts stopped in her head. "I know, despite all that...that nonsense, I know I feel something for you, and it might be the most stupid, ludicrous and inconvenient thing to say right now, but I think you are special, Jasna, and I want you in my life."

She stared back at him, her eyes wide. She was frozen to the spot and no longer sure whether it was real or she was trapped in a movie. She started to panic. Once she had controlled her breathing, she stepped forwards and they melted into each other. He pulled back and looked into her eyes. "Will you come back to my hotel with me," he asked softly.

"Yes, of course."

CHAPTER SIX

THEY DIDN'T SAY ANOTHER WORD AS HE PAID FOR THE drinks and she stood watching him. He slowly pulled on his jacket and adjusted his sleeves. When he turned and saw she was waiting for him with her coat on and her hands clasped shyly in front of her, he smiled.

They said nothing as they walked along the still-drying streets and dodged the puddles that had formed between the old cobblestones. As they rounded a corner, he saw a taxi and grabbed her hand as he darted forwards to hail it, yanking her with him. In the taxi, they looked ahead or out of the window but not at each other. Yet they were still holding hands, between each other's thighs, calmly, simply.

As the taxi pulled into the hotel forecourt, she said softly: "I think it's better if we're not seeing walking into together. I'll meet you at your room."

He stared at her in surprise. The driver had already turned around to ask for his money, and he glanced back and forth between his passengers.

"I'll explain when we get outside," she said self-consciously.

Saying nothing, John paid while Jasna clambered out of the car. She fumbled with her tobacco and papers as she stared nervously at the hotel, lost in thought. He watched her, puzzled. Once the taxi had left the hotel forecourt, he asked: "Why do you want to meet me in my room?"

She turned to him, wide-eyed, with fear in her eyes. "It's just better that way," she said. He frowned. "It's fine," she added, trying to sound calm. "I'll see you in your room."

"But why?"

"I'll explain when I get there."

He sighed. "Okay, whatever you want."

He started to walk towards the hotel but stopped and turned back. "Are you sure you're okay?"

"Yes, I'm fine. I'll tell you everything when I see you."

"Okay. See you there." He started walking again.

"Wait," she called after him. He turned back again. "I don't know your room number." She smiled awkwardly.

He raised an eyebrow. "That would help, I suppose. It's two-three-five."

He walked away and she called after him: "See you soon." But he was almost inside and didn't hear her, or pretended not to, and she went back to making her cigarette, all the while staring at the hotel entrance.

In the quiet of his room, John realised he was drunk. He paced up and down, stopping at the picture of his wife and glancing at her each time he passed. He thought about turning her face down, or putting her away in his suitcase. Then he thought it would be better to leave her where she was, as anything else would just seem wrong. Maybe Jasna wouldn't even notice her. If she came at all.

"Christ, this is all so stupid," he said out loud. "She isn't going to come up here, and even if she does she probably won't notice you." He gazed at his wife's picture. "And if she does, what's the problem with that? What have we got to hide? I've already told her about you."

He paced up and down again, then stopped, realising in a flood of acrid emotion that it was his wife seeing Jasna that he had wanted to avoid, not the other way around. It was his relationship with Jasna that was the inconvenient, undeniable truth he wanted to hide, not his marriage, and he wanted to hide it not only from his wife but also from himself. He stood clenching and unclenching his jaw. He wanted to run away, to escape. But it was too late for all that now. John checked the time. How long had he been back in his room? Ten minutes? Fifteen? Twenty? He had no idea, but it seemed like an eternity. Jasna wasn't coming, that much was certain. Clearly she had decided when they were holding hands in the taxi that it had all gone too far and it was time to get away from him and his stupidity.

He was about to mix the remains of the gin and tonic when there was a soft knock on the door. John spun around in surprise and had to catch the gin bottle from falling. He opened the door a crack. There, with a soft smile and down-turned eyes, was Jasna. All his fears and concerns fell away, despite the dull throb of guilt over his wife's picture.

He opened the door wide and Jasna stepped in. "Oh, very nice, John," she said as she looked around the room, swishing the bottom of her coat as if she was in a ballgown. He closed the door quietly, checking that the corridor was empty. He turned around and his stomach fell to see Jasna holding his wife's picture and staring at it intently. "Is this your wife," she asked.

He sighed. "Yes, it is."

"She is beautiful. You must miss her very much."

He didn't know what to say and put his hands in his pockets for something to do. Jasna glanced up. Seeing his expression, she added: "It must be hard to talk about her with me." He shrugged and looked away. She put the picture frame down and walked over to him. She placed her hands on his shoulders and looked him in the eyes. "It's okay."

He swallowed uncomfortably. "What is," he asked, his voice breaking.

"This is." She kissed him softly, delicately on the lips. She tasted of cigarettes, but he forgot about that as their mouths flowed into each other. He reached for her waist and pulled her to him. She leaned back to break the kiss and smiled. "Shall we put on some music?" He nodded. Glancing down at the bottles on the coffee table, she said: "I'll put some radio on the TV. Can you make us a drink?"

"Yes, of course."

While she fiddled with the remote, he made them gin and tonics. She found a radio station playing electro chill and turned it up loud enough to drown out any nagging doubts. He held out a glass to her, and she danced over to him and grabbed it, taking a quick sip in an easy, fluid movement. She then put her glass down and took his drink, carefully placing it next to hers. She found his awkward hands and placed them on her hips, leading him into a slow dance. They swayed together and stared silently into each other's eyes.

They kissed, slowly at first and then more passionately. Then they stopped swaying and simply kissed, exploring each other with their hands, each movement more insistent than the last until they were tearing at each other's clothes in a frenzy. Soon, his shirt was pulled from his shoulders, and he yanked at her top until it sprang from her body. He barely had a second to register her sensual beauty before they were kissing again.

He revelled in the delicious, intoxicating thrill of a woman's body against his and a thousand electric shocks pulsed through his neglected skin. He grabbed her and pulled her hard into him. She forced her hands between them to undo his trousers, fumbling her way into the waistband. She pulled back to concentrate and laughed at how complicated his buttons were to unfasten. He simply stared at her, bending down in front of him half-naked, her tanned, smooth skin glowing in the half-light of the room.

He was scared. Not of her, but of himself and the volcano of emotion that was brimming inside him. He had a fiery animal passion for her, and he wanted her. He wanted to explode inside her, to unite them in their desire for each other. He wanted it, all of it, but it revulsed him in equal measure. He didn't want to want this thing that he desired with every fibre, every molecule, every last drop of lava that burned red hot within him.

He wanted to step back and end it right there, just to talk to her. But she finally prized open his trousers, yanked down his pants and took his hardening cock into her wet, warm mouth. He rolled his eyes to the ceiling and hoped that somewhere, somebody would forgive him, even if it wasn't him. She gently sucked and licked him, and ran her fingernails over his body. When she reached his stomach, he involuntarily convulsed, his skin having not been touched for months. She started with surprise and gave a muffled laugh as she wrapped her tongue around him.

After a moment of bliss he had thought he would never experience again and had not realised just how much he missed, he stepped back from her mouth and pulled her up, kissing her deeply. He pushed down her stretch jeans and lace knickers, and they fell together onto the bed, rolling back and forth, fighting for supremacy, until she pushed him back and straddled his groin.

She fell forwards and kissed him passionately while she reached around and guided him into her. She sat back up and, in an instant, his cock was thrust deep inside her. She rolled her hips back and forth and stretched up her arms and, as he reached his zenith within her, a wave of pleasure and excitement overcame her. She tipped her head back in ecstasy, closing her eyes in beautiful agony, dissolving into nothing.

He was overwhelmed, swept away by her and the moment. But as he watched her and involuntarily thrusted deep into her, cherished, perfect, crystalline memories of his wife surged up through him. Snatched souvenirs of exquisite bliss jostled for his attention and, as he sank further into tortured recollection, he started to panic, fighting for breath as he drowned in his own mind. He tried to rationalise, to hold himself together, to focus on the moment, to hold back the flood, but nausea overcame him and his heart pounded in his ears. Crushed and almost tearful, he twisted and pushed Jasna away, shocking her out of her sexual reverie, apologising endlessly as he turned over and buried himself in the bedclothes.

He lay, turned away from her and she sat with her legs half pushed apart, the electricity still flowing through her and the blood pulsing in her clitoris and vagina, now empty and wanting. She touched her glowing nipples and watched him, unsure what to do next.

After a few moments, he turned back to her. "I'm sorry," he said quietly.

Still in the same awkward position, she frowned. "What happened?"

He sighed deeply. "I don't know. Actually, I do know. Memories of my wife came back to me a huge rush, and I couldn't stop it. I couldn't control it, and it overwhelmed me. I'm sorry, Jasna, but I couldn't carry on."

She said nothing, just carried on frowning.

"It's not you," he continued, uncomfortable with her silence. "I think you're amazing and I wanted, I really wanted to but I...couldn't. I'm sorry." He looked at the drinks, untouched on the coffee table, while she stared at the bedclothes, smoothing them absentmindedly with her hand.

She pulled the sheet over her thighs and stomach and rearranged herself. "I wanted it too, John. Very much." He reached out and took her hand in his. He noticed the music from the television and turned it off, and they held hands in silence.

AFTER A FEW MOMENTS, he sat up and let go of her hand. He pulled his shirt from the floor and dragged it over himself, his nakedness now seeming ridiculous, and pulled on his trousers. "You must think I'm crazy," he said as he did up the buttons.

She shook her head sadly. "No, John, I don't think that. I don't think you're crazy. I think you're very unhappy because your wife died. It's normal. I wish things were different for you, and for me, and that we had met in a different way, but that's the way it is. You are here because your wife died; otherwise I would never have met you."

She stared into his eyes. She wanted to lean forwards and kiss him. She wanted to tell him how much he meant to her, how he made her feel special, how she would leave everything behind to follow him, wherever he went, for the rest of her life. She wanted it all with him so much that her body ached. She imagined a life with him—simple, kind, shared. But she knew it was not meant to be. Women like her, thrown against the wall of life by brutal, callous men and traded like meat? No, women like her were not meant to meet kind, sensitive men who treated them like real people and not like dogs tied to a post, fending for scraps, cowering from the lazy swing of a stick. She couldn't have a simple life with a man who loved her. For a moment, she almost hated him for awakening all that was best left dead inside her. She looked down at the bed, lost in thought, and sighed deeply.

He watched her. "What happened before, when we arrived at the hotel?"

"What do you mean?"

"When we came here in the taxi, and you didn't want to be seen walking in here with me?"

She hesitated before answering. "It's not a safe place for me to be, this hotel."

"What do you mean," he asked, sitting down beside her and taking her hand in his. "Why?"

She picked at the bed clothes. "The men who run the strip club also run this hotel, and I'm not supposed to come here without their permission."

"What do you mean? The owners of the hotel? The staff working here?"

"No, the gang behind the strip club. They control all the drugs coming in and out of the hotel, and all the girls working here."

"What on earth do you mean? Do you mean there are prostitutes working in this hotel?"

"Yes, all the time."

"And people are bringing drugs here as well?"

"Yes, it's famous for it."

He frowned. "All that right under the nose of the hotel owners, the staff, the guests?" She nodded. "But don't they... Hold on, maybe that explains..." he said, his voice trailing away as he thought back to the yacht and the captain deleting the photos of the speedboat.

"Explains what?"

"What? Oh, nothing." He frowned. "But that means that Charles must know a..."

"Who is Charles?"

He shook his head. "It doesn't matter. Look, I don't understand. What difference does it make if the people who run the strip club know that you're here with me?"

She cleared her throat. "Girls who work at the strip club are not allowed here. There are certain girls who are allowed come here, and they don't work at the club. They're kept separate from us. If I get caught here, I'll been trouble."

"What sort of trouble?"

"If they catch me here, they'll expect money, and if I can't give it to them..."

He narrowed his eyes. "Why would they expect money from you?"

"Because they'd assume I must've been here to see a client and would have got paid for it. I'm not allowed to come here, and I'm certainly not allowed to meet a client here, but they might let me off with a small punishment so long as they get their cut."

"What's a small punishment?"

"They cut you, give you a scar. Nothing visible when you're dressed. It's meant to be a reminder, so you remember your place."

He stared at her. "Charming. And what do they do to you if you don't have any money?"

She swallowed and looked away. "I don't know, but I've heard stories."

"But you aren't a prostitute. Why would they expect money from you? Can't you just be visiting me in your time off?"

She laughed. "They don't care whether I'm a prostitute or not, and as far as they're concerned I don't have time off. In their eyes, they own me. It doesn't matter to them what I am or what I do. Like I said, if they catch me here, they'll want a cut, whether I've got the money or not. And if I haven't got the money, then they assume I've been acting on my own and they'll punish me for it."

"So why did you come here tonight at all, if it was so risky?"

"Because I want to be with you, John, and any risk is worth that." She stared into his eyes and then looked away.

He watched her face, trying to discern what lay within her mind, and then picked up her hand and kissed it. "Then you'll need some money."

"No, no, definitely not. I don't want your money," she protested. "I came here because I wanted to, because I want to be with you. Anyway, I'm sure I can avoid them if I'm careful."

"Look, Jasna, it's not worth taking the risk. I want you here too, more than anything, but I don't want anything to happen to you, especially not because of that. I have money, plenty of it, and I don't care about it. But what I do care about is you. If they think you're here to see a client and they want a cut, just give them my money. You're worth more to me than any money."

She said nothing as he got up from the bed and picked his jacket up off the floor. He fished out his wallet and handed her a thick fold of notes. "Here, take it. I can get more tomorrow, any time, but there's only one of you and I don't want anything to happen to you."

She stared at the notes, tears filling her eyes, and reluctantly took them from him. "I didn't tell you all this to get your money."

"I know, Jasna," he said, sitting back down on the bed. "If I had thought for a second you were telling me all that to get money out of me, I wouldn't have given you a penny." He took her hand in his. "I know you are a good person, Jasna, and I want to help you." She looked at their hands, their fingers entwined, and sensed the warmth flowing between them. She didn't know what to say or what to think, but her heart burned. She placed her hands on his cheeks and kissed him.

. . .

OVER THE NEXT HOURS, John talked about his life in England and how everything he had assumed had been thrown to the wind by his wife dying. His wife was always the more positive and outgoing of them, and she'd always seen adventure in the unfamiliar. He knew, had she been there, she would be counselling anyone in his position to grieve but also to make sure they looked forwards, and outwards. Of course, neither of them wanted any of what had happened. "But what can I do about any of it, Jasna? I can't change any of it. She won't come back, no matter how much I wish it. I will never hear her voice again or see her, except in my imagination. It's awful and I hate every second of it, but nothing about that will change. The only thing I can do is live, so we don't both end up dying because of the accident."

Jasna watched his face intently as he spoke, following the waves of emotion that took hold of him. She wanted to say something that would make him better, to say something useful or wise, but she couldn't think of anything. She was empty and hopeless, and it hurt her to realise how unfamiliar a moment like this was to her. He squeezed her hand and turned it on the bedclothes. "You know, it's so wonderful that I can talk about this with you, that you can listen to all my stupid thoughts. Do you mind? It helps me so much just to be able to say all these things out loud."

She smiled weakly and the tears welled up. "Of course, John, I want to hear everything," she said quietly.

He lay back on the bed and told her he would like to take her away from all this, to England, and help her find a new life. Not with any expectations for anything in return, but because he wanted to help her become all that she could be, to fulfil her potential. She was surprised and happy to hear the words but how could they possibly apply to her? After all, she was a prisoner and would never be free. He was standing outside the bars of her cell window, showing her a light that would never warm her skin.

While he talked, he drifted gently, almost imperceptibly, to sleep. She watched him with tenderness and smiled sadly at their small, short-lived escape from her life and destiny.

Once his breathing was deep and regular and she knew she would not wake him, she pulled herself carefully from the bed and dressed as quickly and quietly as she could.

When she picked her jeans up from the floor, she found the money that he had given her. She stood, holding it, staring at the crisp bills, turning it over and back again. Eventually, she put them on the bedside table.

While pulling up her jeans and jumping up and down quietly to get them into place, she spotted a writing set on the bureau. Checking that he was still asleep, she went over to the desk. She hesitated and then sat down, writing a two-page note in large, untidy handwriting. She folded it carefully and placed it in an envelope. She looked across the room, deep in thought. Then, spotting the money on the bedside table, she placed the envelope underneath the bills.

Finally dressed, she stood in the middle of the room, watching him sleep. Holding back tears, she blew him a kiss and left, closing the door gently behind her.

PART SIX

CHAPTER ONE

THROUGH THE BECKONING LIGHT, SHE IS LYING IN THE WAVES, *her wings outstretched in the bleaching surf. You gaze at the perfection of her slender back in the morning light and dive into the water after her. Through the dark shadows you find her in the bedroom, waiting for you. The birds circle overhead and she shields her eyes, bloodshot and empty.*

She swims away under the surface of the river, her shadows mingling with the reflected branches and fallen leaves. Ivy envelopes her milky, naked skin and she is pulled beneath the earth, worms forcing their way into her eyes and mouth. You reach up to the sky in a silent scream and the birds lead you to the edge of a vast lake, where blinking eyes stare at you from the treetops. Her naked form, perfect, falls through the shadows, and you fall too.

The light bursts and the birds swoop down, an endless rain on the surface of the lake. She turns her blind eyes from you, but her hand reaches back, pulling you through the water and into the vortex. Her head tilts back in agony or ecstasy.

Dawn is coming. She is in the window, the curtains billowing around her. All you have to do is reach out, beyond the curtain, and step with her into the light that obscures her face.

She disappears into the glistening reflections and the churning light that flows all around you. There is a gap in the clouds. You dry her tears and hold her in the blinding light that is coming for you both.

JOHN WOKE WITH A START. Disorientated, he looked around in a panic. Jasna was gone. He saw the money on the bedside table and his heart sank. He heard a muffled banging and he froze, listening intently. There was an angry, incomprehensible exchange and a muffled scream that he knew instantly was her. He flung himself out of the bed and, grabbing his phone, pulled open the bedroom door. The entrance to the stone passageway was ajar and, yanking it open, he ran in. As the door clicked shut behind him, he stopped, listening. There was no sound. In the distance was a faint light that he hadn't seen before.

He inched his way along the passageway, the sharp stones digging into his bare feet. Instead of the wall at the end, he found another passageway that sloped downwards and towards the light. He stood, unsure what to do or where to go. Somewhere in the distance was a shout and a splash. He started running, speeding up when he heard an outboard motor being started.

Halfway along, he tripped over something and fell heavily. He picked himself up and, without looking back, ran on. Arriving at a stone jetty far beneath the hotel, he saw the speedboat that made the delivery to the yacht powering across the bay with two men onboard, bouncing over the waves as it disappeared into the distance. Angry at having missed them, he inspected the jetty for clues. He spotted a piece of torn packaging with the same logo as the cardboard boxes in the storeroom and threw it into the water in frustration.

He massaged his painful feet and inspected the cuts on his hands from where he had fallen. He then walked disconsolately back up the stone passageway, wondering where the scream had come from and whether he was mistaken in thinking it had been Jasna.

He stumbled again over the obstacle that had tripped him on his way down. He fished his phone out of his pocket and switched on the torch. There, illuminated in the cold, harsh light was Jasna, covered in blood, her face twisted in silent agony. Trying to keep calm, he inspected her, finding stab wound after stab wound, too many to stem the flow of blood. The tears flowed from him and he cried as he rocked her in his arms. He sensed a twitch and pushed the blood-soaked hair from her face, desperate for any sign she could be alive. She half swallowed and then choked, coughing up blood that ran down her chin and throat and onto her chest. He sobbed and kissed her forehead, his lips slipping on her blood-soaked skin and the taste of iron invading his mouth. She half-opened her eyes, searching aimlessly until she could focus. She saw his face and smiled, before choking again.

"Don't try to move," he whispered urgently. "I'll get an ambulance. Don't die. Please don't die."

She reached up to his face and stroked him with her blood-stained hand. "John," she said softly.

His face crumpled and his body shook. "Please don't die," he implored.

"John." She gazed up at him calmly, peacefully. "I love you."

Then her eyes glazed over and the life drained from her. He howled, pressing her to him and rocking back and forth. "Oh, god, no," he cried out into the semi-darkness, the tears pouring down his cheeks.

After a moment he recovered himself, and carefully laid her down. He ran back down to the stone jetty, hurriedly dialling the emergency services on the way. The phone rang endlessly and he panicked, wondering if they would ever pick up.

"Hello, hello? Yes, yes, emergency. Do you speak...Okay, I need an ambulance...ambulanza? Quickly."

He frantically tried to explain where he was, what had happened, that a woman was dying, that it was very, very urgent. Once he was convinced someone was on their way, he ran back to Jasna, cradling her in his arms and sobbing as the last traces of warmth leached away.

CHAPTER TWO

JOHN SHIFTED ON THE UNCOMFORTABLE PLASTIC CHAIR AND gripped the edge of the table to steady himself, trying to fight off the dizziness and panic. His eyes darted back and forth at the assortment of police officers, secretaries and clerks who were milling around, chatting, disappearing, reappearing, staring at John, ignoring him completely, urgently whispering into a colleague's ear, sharing a joke, popping their head around the door to look for someone and passing sheaves of paper from one hand to another.

In the middle of this ever-changing melée stood a slim man in his late thirties or early forties with dark eyebrows and half-asleep eyes, who lounged on one hip while regarding John like an animal in a zoo. He seemed apart from the crowd of comers and goers, but also at its centre. He watched as John searched every face for someone, anyone, who could help him, becoming increasingly frustrated with every passing minute.

Eventually, the slim man pulled himself off his hip and, scraping a chair noisily across the floor, sat down across the table. He leaned back and a hand appeared over his shoulder to place a folder, slender from its lack of contents, on the table in front of him. John watched this little piece of theatre with barely concealed contempt and stared directly into the man's eyes, waiting for him to speak, all the while clenching and unclenching his jaw.

"Good afternoon, Dr Hunter," the man said with a heavy accent. "I am David. I am a policeman." John continued staring at him, saying nothing. "I believe you would call me a detective. I have been assigned to your case."

Noting John's lack of response with a raised eyebrow, David leaned forwards and flipped the folder open. Inside was a sheet of paper, which was clearly a form setting out the details of the case, such as they were. David moved the piece of paper aside to reveal a photo of Jasna's lifeless, bloody face staring out at them. John shuddered. David went back to the form, slowly, deliberately reading it. He nodded as he finished and pushed the folder away from him.

Finally losing patience, John demanded: "Why am I here?" The slim man looked up at John and gazed at him without expression. "I said: Why am I here?" The man carried on staring blankly. "Are you even listening to me?"

David breathed deeply before sighing. "I am listening to you," he said.

"So why won't you answer my question," John barked back.

"I think, Dr Hunter, you know why you are here. Someone is dead and you were the last person to see her alive. The question I have for you is: Why would you brutally murder this young woman?" David gestured at the photograph in the folder.

John screwed up his face in disgust. "I have already told you told you people at least five times already that I did not murder Jasna." John raised his voice as he said her name and banged his fist on the table. Everyone in the room stopped and stared.

David sat back in his chair. "I think, Dr Hunter, that calmness would be your friend right now."

"Why on earth would I kill Jasna," John hissed between his teeth. "She...I..." The emotion welled up inside him. He didn't want to cry, but he wasn't sure he could stop himself. "She was my friend," he said quietly. A tear rolled down his cheek.

The slim man regarded John and then turned to a colleague who had just walked into the room. They talked for what seemed like an eternity, with the comers and goers glancing at them as they spoke, although John couldn't understand a word they said. The colleague backed out of the room and then walked briskly away. With their closed body language, John could not even guess at what had passed between them.

David turned back to John. "I'm sorry, Dr Hunter. I hope you will forgive me, but I am a simple man with no imagination." John held his breath, knowing what would come next. "If you will permit me, I would like to go back to the beginning and for you to tell me everything from the start. Why did you come to our town?"

John sighed and looked around the room. "Look, I have already told at least one of your officers the whole story. Why should I repeat myself?"

"I do apologise. However, as I am sure you are aware, life is full of inconveniences. My colleague cannot find his notes from your discussion, and I am keen to hear everything from your mouth."

John shook his head in bewilderment. "Okay, have it your way."

"I appreciate that."

John sat back. "I came here because I wanted a holiday.

It's as simple as that. I needed a break, and someone suggested I should come here. They said I would be able to get away from it all, to escape," he added bitterly.

"Sadly, not even your friend is able to see into the future, Dr Hunter, much as we would all like to." John frowned. David consulted the folder again. "You will be aware that we searched your hotel room this morning," he said without looking up. John bristled at the thought of careless policemen invading his room, the space he had shared with Jasna. "We found some interesting things, Dr Hunter." David looked up. "We found money. A lot of it." John sighed. "And we found a picture. Of a woman."

"I want that back," John said angrily.

"Do not worry. You will get it back eventually." John swallowed hard. "Who is she, Dr Hunter?"

"She is my wife," he said quietly.

"I see. But I understand that you are, if I am using the correct word, a widower?"

John nodded his head slowly. "Yes, I am."

"Did you murder her too?"

John flew forwards from his chair with all the force he could muster and tried to grab David by the throat. The detective sprang back and two burly policemen who had been watching the scene grabbed John by the shoulders, slamming him into the wall in one, fluid movement. John hung in their grip, gathering his breath. David stepped slowly around the table and walked up to John, close enough that he could see the thin red veins in the yellow whites of the policeman's eyes.

"Fuck you," John spat out at him.

David sighed. "I am only asking you a question, Dr Hunter."

"Fuck you."

David regarded John with curiosity. "It is always sad to watch a man who does not know how to help himself."

"Why don't you ask me a proper question, instead of trying to provoke me?"

David thought for a moment and then said something to the officers. They loosened their grip and David walked slowly back around the table to his chair while John rotated his shoulders and stared at the detective. The two officers stood back.

David motioned to John to sit down, and they resumed their seats. "How did your wife die, Dr Hunter?"

"She was killed. By a policeman." David sat back in his chair and placed his hands carefully behind his head. The room fell silent. "We were walking down a busy street in London and a policeman who was chasing a stolen van lost control of his car and crashed. My wife got in the way and she died of her injuries in hospital." John stared at David. "Are you happy now?"

David unlaced his fingers from behind his head and placed his palms flat on the table. "I am sorry, Dr Hunter."

"Look, I'm just a doctor who came here to get over the death of my wife, and I became friends with Jasna. She was helping me come to terms with my loss. Why would I want to kill her?"

David looked down at the table. "I understand, Dr Hunter," he said, closing the folder. "But a young woman is dead and, as I mentioned before, you were unfortunately the last person to see her alive. We know from the closed circuit television outside your room that she spent the night with you..."

John's face lit up. "Of course, the CCTV. So you will have seen her leave, and me go after her down the stone passageway."

David shook his head. "Again, unfortunately for you, Dr

Hunter, the recording from after she entered your room and until the morning is corrupted and the images are not available. No further video has been registered." John's face fell. "I'm afraid that we have nothing and no one to corroborate your story."

John swallowed and shifted on his chair. "What about the speedboat that I saw leaving the jetty? What happened to that? I told you people, it's the same one I saw when we were out in the Mediterranean, on that yacht the hotel owns."

"There is no trace of any such speedboat, either this morning, or on the day of your sailing trip, Dr Hunter."

"What? But that can't be..."

"In the absence of any other evidence or leads to follow, and with you the last person to see her alive and found covered in her blood, what other choice do I have than to question the only suspect?"

John crumpled in his chair and David returned to the single piece of paper in the folder. "I should also tell you," he said without looking up, "that there is no trace of a Jasna, not at the strip club, not in our system, not anywhere. No passport, nothing. There is not even a record of someone with her name and description entering the country. We cannot even be sure that Jasna is her real name. In short, Dr Hunter, she does not officially exist." John swallowed again. He became dizzy and a thousand thoughts crowded his mind. "So, you can see why I am interested in making sure that I have all the facts. A wealthy European doctor coming to our country on holiday, apparently hiring a prostitute from a local strip club and murdering her when he has finished with her? It would not be difficult to persuade the judge that we could secure a conviction, don't you think?"

John froze. He thought of his wife, his family, his mother, and what the papers would make of it. He composed a dozen lurid headlines and his heart sank. He knew his career was over, that all the kindness, the patience, the understanding that had been afforded him would evaporate the second the story became public. And he cursed himself for leading Jasna to her death. Yet again, he had failed someone he cared for deeply. Yet again, someone he could have saved died in his arms. Again, again, again. John rocked back and forth on his chair and stared blankly at the corner of the table.

The policeman studied him and frowned. He went to speak but at that moment a female assistant in a tight uniform and too much make-up walked into the room. Everyone aside from John and David turned to inspect her like farmers regarding a cow. She glanced at John while she leaned in to David and whispered in his ear. Shocked, David turned and looked into her eyes. She repeated everything and David turned slowly back to John. The assistant left, her heels clacking down the hall, echoing in the silence of the interview room. David watched John, who was still rocking back and forth. "It seems, Dr Hunter, that you have friends in high places."

John looked up. "What? What did you say?"

"It seems that all investigations into your involvement with Jasna's murder are at an end."

"What? What do you mean?"

David sat back in his chair. "You are free to go."

"But why?"

David smiled. "I do not understand you, Dr Hunter," he said. "First you want me to let you go because you say you are innocent, and now you do not want to leave when I say you can go. I think that you need to make up your mind about what you want from this situation."

John stared at David suspiciously. "So, I am free to go?"

"Yes."

"I can get up from this chair and just walk out of the police station?"

David gestured towards the door. "There is no one here who shall stop you."

John got up slowly from his chair. "Okay."

The two officers who had pinned him against the wall stood back and John made his way out of the room, all the while staring at David, who regarded the doctor with an inscrutable smile.

CHAPTER THREE

ONCE JOHN HAD COLLECTED HIS THINGS FROM THE FRONT desk and checked his wife's picture for damage, he stumbled out of the police station and stood at the top of the steps blinking in the bright afternoon light. He gathered himself and shook his head in puzzlement. He wiped his gritty eyes and ran his finger along his shirt collar. It was greasy and loose, and he shuddered in his day-old clothes.

He walked slowly down the steps and stood on the pavement, unsure of where to go. As he was looking up and down the busy road, which teemed with cars, scooters, buses and people threading their way along the narrow, dusty pavements and between the slow-moving lines of traffic, a taxi pulled up next to him. He stepped back, assuming it was for someone else, then thinking, as the electric window slid open, that the driver must be lost.

The man leaned over and looked up at him. "Dr Hunter?"

"Yes," John said, surprised.

"Taxi to your hotel. With compliments."

John frowned. "Compliments? Of whom?" The taxi driver

shrugged his shoulders and smiled. John hesitated, unsure whether he could trust the man enough to get into his car.

"It's okay," the driver said. "I take you only to hotel."

John sighed. He was too tired to argue, and he didn't have anywhere else to go.

Once in the car, he watched the streets roll by. He examined the back of the driver's head, and thought of his ride from the airport on the day he arrived. The driver checked him in the rear-view mirror, looking away when John caught his eye.

John sat back and stared at the roof of the car. His mouth was sticky and dry. They had given him a terrible coffee in the police station, and now he had a metallic taste in his mouth and his stomach was churning. His mind kept trying to flicker back to the stone passageway and Jasna's face as she lay dying in his arms, but he pushed it away, forcing the memory into the farthest recesses.

He sank further into his seat. Sleep swept over him and he fell instantly into an abyss filled with horrific images that seared his mind. He tried to force himself awake and concentrate on the passing cars and blurred trees but he didn't have the strength and his head lolled as he battled the nightmares.

The taxi pulled into the hotel courtyard and the adrenaline rose up within him. He walked into the reception and stood staring at the reflections and shadows on the marble floor, unsure where to go and acutely aware of looking out of place in his blood-stained clothes. He didn't want to go back to his room, but where else could he go? He ached to be at home, to close the curtains, to get into his own bed and let it all drain away, not to be trapped here in a gilded cage.

He stared at the other guests milling about, politely ignoring him as they passed. Look at them with their normal lives, on holiday, relaxing, their only care being where to go sunbathing or what to eat for dinner. As he watched a tanned, content and expensively dressed couple pass, it dawned on him that, whatever had just happened at the police station, he remained the only suspect in Jasna's murder. He swallowed and looked at his dirty fingernails. He recalled the warmth of her body draining away, her blood on his hands, her matted hair as he pushed it back to kiss her one last time, the tears running down his cheeks and the echo of his wailing into the darkness.

"I love you." He wished with all his heart that he'd said it too. Rage flashed up inside him. He couldn't leave it like that. Not with her dead and her murderers still walking around. I can't let her die like that and do nothing. They can't get away with it. He wanted to do something, to ring someone, to fix something, to find out who was behind it all. But what? What could he do? Who was he? Just another doctor on holiday who'd got himself into trouble with a girl working in a strip joint.

"Good afternoon, Dr Hunter." John spun around to see Charles standing beside him, smiling calmly, his hands knitted in front of his paunch. "You look a little tired. Would you care to join me in my office for a refreshing cup of English tea."

"Um, well," John stammered.

"I have it sent over especially from Fortnum and Mason. Only the finest Earl Grey."

John frowned, jolted by the reference to home. "That sounds..." he said.

"Excellent," the older man declared. "Would you care to follow me?"

Charles bustled off to a door in the corner of the lobby, with John following mechanically behind him, happy to inhabit the distraction of thinking about Piccadilly and the riot of colour, sounds and smells of the food hall at Fortnum and Mason. He transported himself to the road outside, gazing at the Royal Academy, wondering about the Summer Exhibition. Perhaps I could manage to go this year, maybe even think about buying something, for once.

If I'm not in jail.

Inside Charles's office, John slumped into an immaculate armchair, instantly exhausted. Charles gently closed the door and turned to face John, his face animated with worry and tension.

"Are you okay, John?"

John looked up through half-closed eyes. "In what sense?"

Charles raised an eyebrow and turned to a sideboard ranged along a wall, busying himself with kettle and cups. John watched the tea ceremony and sighed, trying to hold back the wall of emotion that lay behind his eyes.

"Did they treat you badly at the police station?"

"No. No, they didn't." John tried to take in the chaotic jumble of Charles's desk, but registered nothing. "They were fine," he said, his voice trailing off to nothing.

Charles turned back from the tea things and perched on the edge of the sideboard, examining John's face. "It must have been awful." He paused. "What happened last night? Who was the girl? How did she die?"

John looked out of the window and swallowed. He breathed in and out, slowly, deliberately. "She was a...a friend, I suppose." He buried his head in his hands. "Charles, I've got myself into a terrible mess," he said through his fingers. He looked up. "I didn't kill her. I tried to save her. Someone..." He looked away. "Some animal murdered her, stabbed her to death, and they want to frame me for it."

Charles was about to respond, but the kettle boiled and clicked off. "Nothing a nice cup of tea can't sort out," he said cheerily. John laughed in spite of himself. "Do you take milk? Or lemon, perhaps?" John shook his head. Charles handed him a china cup, filled to the brim with delicate, near-golden tea, and saucer. "Here you go."

John took a sip and revelled in the comforting taste. He placed the cup carefully on Charles's desk. "Thank you, I needed that."

Taking his own cup, Charles sat down and listened patiently as John explained from the beginning how he had met Jasna and what had happened between them, and about his reservations over her. He described their last evening, and her fears over coming to the hotel. Charles nodded in comprehension, and sighed when John said he had offered her money so she would have something to give if she got caught, but that she hadn't taken it. John saw how stupid it all sounded, that he was just another desperate and lonely fool who got caught up in a scandal, another face to be plastered all over the newspapers and the internet when the vice closed around him.

He took s sip of tea, waiting for Charles to tell him that he had made a mess of everything and he shouldn't be surprised to be in trouble. But the older man said nothing and waited for John to carry on. So he explained how he had woken up suddenly to find her gone, and heard the noises from the stone passageway. And then the scream. Charles nodded again, increasingly concerned as John described how he had run down the second passageway, only to see the speedboat race from the jetty, and then found Jasna, alone and dying.

The police hadn't even paused for a moment before arresting him for Jasna's murder and had stomped all over the scene without taking any evidence or calling forensics. They made no effort, he said, to look for anyone else before they had hauled him into the back of the van. He sat alone in the metal cage as they sped across town, unsure whether he would ever be free again, wondering whether his life was over.

He had then spent hours waiting in a cold stone cell, his belt taken from him in case he tried to commit suicide, before he was called into the interview room and finally met David. "And then I was released, just like that," John said, clicking his fingers. "No explanation, no nothing. I was free to go. And then, when I got outside, there was even a taxi waiting for me, to take me here." John narrowed his eyes. "Was that you," he asked. "Did you get me out of there?"

Charles spread his palms across his desk and cleared his throat. "I would like to be able to claim that I was so well connected that I'd managed to retrieve you from the clutches of the police, but I'm afraid that I don't wield that kind of power. However, when I heard that you had been hauled away, I did ask one of our regular taxi drivers to wait outside the station and to bring you back to the hotel, once they'd let you out."

Taking another sip of his tea, John frowned. "And how did you know I would be released?"

"The police here may be careless and always on the lookout for a quick resolution to their cases, but they are not stupid. They would be aware that holding a foreign national from Western Europe without charge would become problematic, and even their bosses might get a little suspicious if they were able to fit you up for murder so easily. I guessed that they would have to release you eventually, even if it was only temporarily."

"Well, I'm glad you were right. And thank you for the taxi. However, I'm beginning to think that my problems are only just starting."

"How so?"

"Well, I'm still the only suspect in Jasna's murder."

"But I thought you just said they dropped the charges."

"For now, yes. But Jasna is still dead, and they'll have to pin it on somebody eventually, and that somebody is surely going to be me. If they do fit me up for it, that means that her real killers will have got away with it. I just can't let that happen. When I was in the station, they told me they have no record of her, not in the bar where she worked, not registered at her flat—nothing. She doesn't exist, as far as they're concerned. They're not going to bother finding anyone else."

Charles frowned and went to speak, but John cut him off. "Look, even if the police don't go after me anymore, once that story gets out it won't matter whether or not I killed her. My name will be mud. I'll be all over the papers, everywhere. My life, my reputation, my friends, my family. It's all over for me."

"John, I really think—"

"Charles, do you know what? My life's over anyway. My life finished the day my wife died. Since then, I've just been existing, nothing more. It doesn't matter what happened to me, but I can't let Jasna die like that. I got her into this mess. It was me that brought her here, to this hotel. I persuaded her it would be okay. I gave her the promise of another life, away from the strip clubs and drugs and violence. And now she's dead. That's me, Charles, that's my fault. It's me that did that." John stared hard at Charles. "You know what, the police are right. It was me that killed her."

Charles shook his head. "No. No, John. You didn't kill her. You can't say that."

"Why not? She'd be alive now if she hadn't met me." John's face crumpled and he started to cry.

"Don't do that to yourself, John. Please. Jasna came back to the hotel with you, despite her reservations, because she wanted to be with you. That was her choice. And she chose to leave in the middle of the night because she didn't want you to be involved in all this, and she didn't take your money because she respected you too much. She thought she would be able to get out of the hotel without anyone finding out. It's her terrible bad luck that she got caught. But it was her choice to take those risks, not yours. You tried to stop her, and you must remember that."

John wiped away his tears. He went to take another sip of his tea, but it was nearly cold. "Let me make you another cup," Charles said.

John shook his head. "No, it's okay. I think I need to get some rest. I'm so tired." He pulled himself awkwardly out of the chair and shuffled to the door.

"Before you go, John."

He straightened up and turned back. "Yes?"

"I might be able to help you find who killed Jasna." John frowned and stared at the older man. Charles's voice had hardened and the jovial Englishman abroad had vanished.

"What do you mean," John asked.

"Meet me for dinner, tonight, in the hotel restaurant. I'll explain everything."

"Okay," John said, puzzled. "What time?"

"Nine."

John searched Charles's face for clues but found nothing. He then stepped out of the office and back into the gentile bustle of the hotel reception, closing the door softly behind him.

CHAPTER FOUR

JOHN LAY NAKED ON THE BED, THE BREEZE FROM THE OPEN balcony doors wafting across his bare skin. His eyes were closed, but he was awake. He wanted so badly to shut off the endless, deafening horrors of the last twenty-four hours, which turned over and over inside his mind in an endless loop, but he couldn't. Each time he thought that he had tamed his mind, the sensation of Jasna's blood on his hands and the dying light in her eyes seized him whole. The searing pain of her death became unbearable as it mixed with memories of his wife. He tried to visualise his wife's smiling face but could only see Jasna.

A thought crept through his mind. He had given Jasna the money but she hadn't taken it. She'd left it behind and instead taken her chances with the gang. Why would she do that? Why did she take the risk? Maybe she wanted to die. Why? What for?

His eyes sprung open and his breath held in his chest. The note. He hadn't even read it. There hadn't been time before he was arrested and dragged off to the police station. He sat up and stared at the bedside table, his heart pounding. The note wasn't there. His heart sank. Hold on, they'd talked about the money at the police station but no one had mentioned the note. What if it's still here? He scrambled over to the bedside table and pulled open the draw. Nothing. He looked around on the floor but there was nothing either. Where else could it be? Ah, maybe…He dropped onto his hands and knees and pulled up the bed covers. There, under the bed near the middle was a crumpled envelope.

He had to lay on the floor and push himself right under the bed, but eventually he grabbed it and, sitting down on the floor, tore it open. His stomach rising with fear and anticipa- tion, he carefully unfolded it and read her final words to him. But his mind was racing so much that he couldn't take it in. Once he'd calmed down a little, he read the note again, then again, and again. When he could take it no more, he scrunched it up and let it drop to the floor. He stared into the middle distance, then fell back against bed and covered his face with his hands as wave after wave of sobs wracked his body.

CHAPTER FIVE

HE LAY IN SILENCE, LISTENING TO EXCITED CHILDREN playing by the hotel pool and a lazy game of tennis in the court below his window.

A scooter started up and drove away.

The warm midday breeze wafted over his skin, now tight and uncomfortable. He thought about taking a shower, but he didn't want to stay in his hotel room any longer. It had been at least five minutes since he had thought about everything, and he needed something to distract him.

He pulled himself off the bed and stood up. Momentarily confused, he stared at the floor, frowning and wondering what on earth it was he had just decided to do. He saw the scrunched-up note and picked it up. He thought about straightening it out and keeping it, maybe putting it in the photo frame behind his wife's picture, but he just threw it in the bin.

HE WALKED UP to the edge of the hotel pool and around. Families and couples were ranged along the sides, lying on sun loungers, chatting, ordering drinks, painting nails, massaging in sun cream. They were in the same space as him, but separate somehow, in another dimension, partitioned behind a transparent wall through which he could see and hear, and even touch, but could not connect. They're in a fish bowl, staring out. Or is it me? Am I the one who's trapped and can't get out?

After staring blankly for a few seconds, he found an empty lounger slightly apart from the rest and sat down heavily. He realised instantly why it had been left unoccupied as it was in the full, brutal sunshine and had no umbrella. He thought about moving the lounger to a shadier spot or leaving all together, but he didn't really care what he did. If he stayed, he could always flop into the pool if he got too hot. Anyway, he wanted to be burned by the searing light. He wanted to live the pain. Anything to remind him he was alive and not dying alone inside his head.

For a while, he watched the children running around and diving in the pool, each splash greeted with a shriek. He inspected the couples, mostly lying in silence, the slow, deliberate swimmers pacing back and forth and the posers constantly checking whether they were being looked at.

Everything fell away into an empty, dead quiet, and his mind drifted into nothing. The white, burning sunlight filled his eyes and the heat stifled his breath. His head throbbed and he could hear nothing but the uneasy beat of his heart. He stared at a cloud; white, lonely, delicate against the strident blue. The drone of cicadas mixed with the woozy beat of his heart and he became entranced by the slow shifting of the white mass in the sky. Everything slowed. A fly zipped past his ear. Then another. The drops of water churned up by the children were held in suspension and all he could hear was the pulsating saw of the cicadas. Another fly, closer this time. The iridescent blue of the sky burned onto his retina and everything became inverted. The cloud seemed to pulsate, then break apart, shattering in slow motion. He panicked, and sweat poured down his back. He tried to tear himself away and became aware of laughter. Are they laughing at me?

HE STARED AT THE POOL, curious at how he had got to be sitting there. He inspected the glistening, sweaty lines on his palms; the dazzling, shimmering blue of the water; the slim arms of the children turning through the light as they splashed in delight; and the oiled, tanned skin of nameless bodies lazing in near-naked submission to the heat, the curves of their thighs arcing into stretched Lycra.

Jasna, his wife; they invaded his thoughts, drifting across the water with the breeze that rippled its heavy surface. Jasna had shown him there was still some meaning to his life, that there was a way through the unending grief. And now she was gone. Maybe she didn't believe she deserved a happy ending. He had hoped, naively, that she could get away from her brutal life, that she could find a crack in the wall large enough to slip through and join him on the other side. But she seemed to have been poisoned against happiness, against hope.

He shuddered. She was crawling under his skin, calling him. He looked up at his balcony, praying that she would be there. He imagined her smiling down and waving, even though she never had. But her face became his wife's and, with a lurch in his stomach, he turned away.

He glanced over to the waiter and caught his eye. He ordered a rum and coke, although he knew he should have water. I don't even like rum and coke, he mumbled to himself as the waiter departed. But it was the only thing he could think of in the moment and, anyway, they're all the same. Just a flavoured means to an end.

He looked up at the treetops swaying gently and the bright blue sky beyond. I could fall, he thought, into the water and drown. Then it would all be over.

The waiter brought the drink and John watched the ice slowly moving, the ripples of heavier liquid snaking around the cubes, throwing out clear, bright light. Soon the ice will melt and the moment will be lost. He thought back to Jasna bringing him a fresh drink on the house the last time he had been at the strip joint. He screwed his eyes shut to hold back the memory and drank the rum and coke down in one. It will numb the pain, if only temporarily.

He placed the glass down and the cold liquid surged through his body. He caught the waiter's eye and ordered another.

CHAPTER SIX

HOURS LATER, ALTHOUGH IT COULD HAVE BEEN DAYS, JOHN walked unsteadily to the restaurant at the end of the hotel gardens and stood gazing emptily at the waiters flitting between the tables and chairs like finches. The diners reminded him of an animal he had seen in a documentary. Something large and hairy, endlessly chewing as it lay in the water while tiny birds picked insects from its hide.

I must still be drunk. That's good. If I stay drunk maybe it'll all drift away and I can be lost here, floating on an invisible ocean whilst they carry on living in the space beyond.

What the hell am I doing here? He checked his watch. It was eight-thirty in the evening. The sun was setting somewhere in the distance, staining the darkening sky in gold and blue ink. Concentrate, damn you. Why are you standing there? Why would you come to the restaurant at this time? What for? He breathed deeply and coughed. Nothing came to mind, so he decided he would go to the bar and order another drink. That's never a bad idea.

"Thank you for coming." John spun around to see Charles standing next to him, a concerned expression on his face.

Everything, every detail he was trying to insulate himself against, came back to him in a flash. "No problem. Happy to," he lied, swallowing down the nausea.

Charles set off and John followed him to an isolated table in a far corner of the restaurant. They sat down and looked at each other. A day's worth of alcohol burned through John's stomach and into his soul. His kidneys were aching and his body was heavy. He wished he had been sharper for this moment.

"How are you," Charles asked in a tone that suggested he expected response to be "awful."

"I'm okay," John said slowly. He glanced out over the sea to the falling sky. "Actually, I'm not okay, but you probably guessed that already."

Charles nodded and looked down at his hands. A waiter came over and asked them what they would like. Charles ordered something from the menu for both of them, but John stopped him when he added a bottle of Italian red. Instead, he asked for lightly sparkling mineral water and a large lime and soda, with slices of lime on the side. Frowning, Charles changed his order to a single glass of the same red.

The two men made small talk until their drinks arrived, and then Charles asked John for a second time whether he was okay. This time, he didn't hold back. He spoke about his life before his wife's death, his guilt at not being able to save her, and why he had gone on holiday to this rich resort, despite his misgivings. He told Charles of how badly he was coping with the grief, and how vulnerable and lonely he had been when he had gone out for a drink and ended up in the strip club; how he had told Jasna about everything, and how much she had helped him.

Charles said nothing as John talked. He listened quietly, patiently, taking occasional sips of his wine. When John finished, Charles let the silence grow between them. John drifted into his thoughts, until the slow crashing of the waves against the cliffs below the hotel forced its way into his mind and he could think of nothing else. He watched a seagull gliding across the darkening sky. Another day gone. He made a quick calculation and realised he must have been at the resort for five days. Two left to go. He almost laughed at the ridiculousness of it all.

The waiter brought their food and explained what each dish contained, where the ingredients had come from and how they had been prepared. John knew he should listen, that that was the kind of thing he would ordinarily do, but he couldn't bring himself to care. Once the waiter had hone, John stared at his plate, unsure whether he wanted to eat anything.

"I understand." Charles said. John looked up and stared at him. "Of course, I don't understand entirely because I have never been married, so I have not lost a wife, but I do understand what it is like to lose someone you love more than life itself, and to be entirely powerless to save them."

John swallowed and stared at the older man, wondering what was coming next.

Charles carefully moved his glass an inch and rearranged his knife and fork. "I have...I had a granddaughter, John." Charles glanced up and looked John straight in the eye. "Many years ago, more than I care to remember, I had a daughter. I thought I wanted that kind of life, but I soon realised that, well, it wasn't for me. I didn't stay with her mother for long and, being the era that it was, I didn't have much contact with my daughter either. I thought that it was okay, at the time. I was nineteen, and I wanted to live my life. I didn't want anything, or anyone, holding me back. I suppose you could say I was selfish." Charles paused and looked down at his plate. "And I suppose you'd be right."

Charles took a sip of his wine. "Anyway, it was not the

easiest of times to be a man like me in London. I joined the hotel trade to go abroad and enjoy more, let's say, freedom. And I did. I found freedom." Charles looked straight at John. "But there was always a sense of regret, deep regret if I'm being honest, that I didn't see my daughter growing up. There were years when I didn't see her at all. It was not so easy to travel then, of course. There were no low-cost flights or any of that sort of thing."

John shifted in his seat and took a sip of his lime and soda, welcoming its freshness.

"But that's all excuses. If I'd have wanted to spend more time with my daughter, I am sure I could have done." Charles contemplated his dinner but didn't start eating. "The long and the short of it is that when my daughter turned up at the hotel in Geneva where I was working, twenty-something and pregnant, I leapt at the chance to have her back in my life. I got her set up in a tiny apartment and, between the two of us, we looked after my beautiful, bonny granddaughter. I changed Erin's nappies, I fed her, I read her stories, I looked after her between my shifts when my daughter needed to go to work. In short, I was the father to my granddaughter that I had never been to my daughter." Charles smiled to himself. "I was given a second chance, John, and I took it. And when my daughter moved back to England, I followed them, finding a job as a manager in a nearby hotel and doing my best to be a part of their lives. After a while, I got an offer that was too good to turn down, and I moved abroad again. But, by then, Erin and I were very close. She would phone me practically every day, she'd spend her holidays with me. And we talked and talked and talked. We shared everything. It was the most profound relationship of my life."

Charles paused and started eating his dinner. "Mustn't let it get cold," he said, trying to sound jolly. John followed suit, slowly munching at his tepid dish, imagining how much better it would have tasted when it arrived.

"So what happened," John asked after a few mouthfuls. Charles stopped eating and lay down his knife and fork.

"Because of her international upbringing, living all around Europe with her mother and grandfather, Erin grew up to be an outgoing, confident, curious and free-spirited young lady, who loved adventure and had no fear about pretty much anything life could throw at her. When she decided she wanted to do something, she did it. Not out of sheer bloody mindedness, but from an unshakeable self-belief, a knowledge that there was nothing to worry about, that everything would turn out fine." John decided he had finished eating and carefully placed his cutlery on his plate. "So I wasn't particularly concerned when she told me she'd taken a summer season job in a resort I'd never heard of. She told me it sounded great, that it was a nice place, with some good hotels, that she'd meet lots of new people and would have a fabulous summer. I asked around and everyone said the place was up and coming, and had a couple of luxury five-star hotels with a good reputation, and a history as long as your arm. So I trusted her instinct and decided not to worry. Not at first."

John took another sip of his drink, watching the dark clouds gather on the older man's face.

"Everything went well at the beginning, just as Erin described. She had a nice job, she worked hard, and there was a good crowd her own age. She was having lots of fun." Charles took another sip of his wine. "Then she started calling a little less often. Which was okay. She was a grown woman, living an adventure. She didn't have to call her grand-pappy every five minutes, or even every day. But then, when she did call, she sounded distant and not herself. The care-free, relaxed swing in her voice was gone, and she sounded tired and listless, and irritated when I brought it up. And then the calls stopped all together." Charles stared at John. "For a week, I waited patiently. Then I called her mother. She hadn't heard from her either and was beginning to worry. So we called the local police, who were useless. We called everyone we could think of. Until, a few weeks after that, I got a phone call."

Charles stopped and swallowed hard. His eyes started to glisten. "They said she had been found. Dead. Actually, she had been murdered. They'd done horrible things to her, John. She must have suffered terribly. My poor baby, my angel..."

The older man looked away and cried. John didn't know what to say and simply watched his suffering. Once he had got hold of himself, Charles dried his eyes and smiled in embarrassment. "It's okay," John said quietly, "I understand."

"Of course," Charles took another sip of wine and resumed his story. "You know, her mother and I tried everything we could to help the police, to help find out what happened and track down her killers. But nothing. They got nowhere. After a while, I realised I was going to have to take matters into my own hands and track them down myself." John raised his eyebrows. "Yes, I know I'm an old man, John, way past his prime."

"No, no, I didn't mean—"

"It's okay. I wondered what the hell I was doing too, but what was I supposed to do? Just sit there and let whoever murdered my beautiful angel get away with it while the authorities did nothing? I'm sure you, of all people, understand that." John nodded. "So I did the only thing I knew how, which was to take a job in a five-star hotel in the resort where she was working. This hotel, in fact," he said, spreading his arms, "and gather as much evidence as I could to find Erin's killers and bring them to justice."

"This was the resort where she was killed," John asked in surprise.

"Yes. Think about it, John. Is it really such a shock, given everything you've learned?" John frowned. "That's two savage murders of young women that you and I know of. And that's not all. It turns out there's been a whole string of unsolved murders all along this coast in the last few years, all young women, all with a verdict of accidental death. No trace of any weapon or clues leading to the killers, yet all of them brutally murdered. Don't you think that's all just a little strange?"

John nodded thoughtfully.

"When I first got here, I started asking around discreetly about things I could maybe procure for my guests, all with the aim of providing the best possible service, of course, but really so I could understand how things operated. It turned out this entire place is effectively run by a gang, running drugs and girls, and providing whatever people want, at a price. It even includes political influence and having the police turn a blind eye when things turn ugly. And these guys are rough. They started off fighting in the Balkan war, but when it was over and they had nothing else to do they turned to every vice you can think of. Their one-time loyal soldiers in war became their enforcers in a battle for supremacy in the region."

John took a sip of his drink, watching the anger build on the older man's face.

"And now they have everyone...politicians, the police, local businesses, hotels, strip joints, bars, shops, restaurants— literally everyone, in their pockets. Really, they're the ones that run this place," Charles said, jabbing his finger onto the table cloth. "I don't run this hotel. Not me, and certainly not the owners. Aside from booking hotel guests and choosing the menus, it's the gang who decides who comes and goes. They bring in the drugs, the prostitutes, and they run the 'parties' that we have to hush up and sort out when someone gets hurt or has an overdose."

John raised his eyebrows. "It sounds like something from the movies."

"Indeed. And your little incident with Jasna is pretty much run of the mill around here. It's just that, normally, someone rings down to me in a panic rather than calling the police. But then you're not the kind of run of the mill person that we get staying here."

John shifted uncomfortably. "So you think your granddaughter's death is part of all this?"

Charles shook his head. "I can't say for sure, John, not one hundred per cent. But I suspect it is, and everything tells me it is. I've heard she was mixed up with the gang in some way, but I don't have any proof. All I have is some sketchy details I managed to get out of the police and a couple of addresses. On the other hand, what I do have is proof of everything else I have told you this evening."

"What do you mean?"

"I have records. Of pretty much everything that's happened since I got here. All the comings and goings in and out of the hotel. Names, places, dates, what was brought in, what was smuggled out. Drugs, prostitutes, the lot. And all backed up by recordings from every CCTV camera in the hotel. Everything from the last two years."

"Even from the camera pointing at my room when Jasna died," John asked hopefully.

"No, not that, I'm afraid. I only have what the system records, and someone must've tampered with that feed before I could get to it. Maybe they switched the camera itself off." John sighed. "But what I do have is a trail, and a very rich one, showing just how far the corruption goes in this place. It could put away a lot of people for a very long time. Some very important people."

"So what are we waiting for? Let's get it to the police and

start the ball rolling. We can get these people behind bars," John said enthusiastically.

Charles smiled. "You mean the same police who tried to frame you for Jasna's murder this morning because they couldn't be bothered to look for the usual suspects? The same police who couldn't find a scrap of evidence in Erin's murder, even though she was dumped on a backstreet in the old town in broad daylight?"

"I see what you mean," John said. "So what can we do?"

"I have a friend at the British Consulate. He can't help us in an official capacity, of course, and he certainly doesn't want to be seen to be interfering in a local police matter. However..."

"Yes?"

"However, if we can link Erin's murder—and Jasna's, for that matter—to the evidence showing what's been going on in the hotel, enough to make a solid case, he can make sure it gets into the right hands."

John thought for a moment. "But how does he know whose are the right hands? We could end up back where we started if the wrong person gets hold of all this. Maybe even worse."

Charles nodded thoughtfully. "Yes, that's a possibility, but my contact has a friend who is an ambitious young judge with an eye on running for office on an anti-corruption ticket. He needs to land a big, public case to show that he's serious and can take on the gangs and beat them. The problem for him is that no one from the police is willing to bring him the cases he needs, so he's stuck with nothing concrete to work on. If we can oblige him with something solid, something big, he'd jump at it, even if that means circumventing the police and striking out on his own."

"Interesting," John said. "So what have we got to work on? I guess the sooner we can get something together for him, the sooner we can link it to Erin and Jasna and bring their murderers to justice."

"Yes, but all I have on Erin's death, apart from what the autopsy said, is the place where she was found and the address of some rather unsavoury character she was supposed to know. I wanted to speak to him myself, but I just couldn't bring myself to do it. The pain of Erin's death was too raw and I wasn't safe as an old man poking around in that world."

"Why don't you give me the addresses and I can take a look and see if I can find anything?"

"Okay, but what good it would do? Any leads must have gone dry by now."

"Maybe, but it's all we've got, and we've got to start somewhere. You never know. Maybe someone will remember something, or maybe tell me something they wouldn't tell the police. Who knows until we try?"

Charles reflected. "Yes, you're right." He paused. "Okay, let's do it. I'll get the addresses to you by the morning."

"Thanks. And maybe I could have a photo of your granddaughter? To jog people's memories?"

"Yes, I'll dig one out," the older man said, getting ready to leave.

"One more thing," John said.

"Yes?"

"What about this Russian man? The one who told you off for mentioning Stalin on my first night, when we were having dinner."

Charles frowned. "Oh yes, I remember that. That was a rather awkward moment, wasn't it. What about him?"

"He's not mixed up in all this, is he?"

Charles pondered. "No. No, I don't think so. I think he's just a guest who's overly proud of his nation. Why?"

"It's just I keep seeing him everywhere I go. He was in the strip club both times I was there, and he seems to be right in front of my face every time I turn around. I'm not normally paranoid, but it keeps happening, all the time."

The older man smiled. "I think you may be overthinking this one."

"How so?"

"He's on holiday, just like you?"

"Yes."

"What else is he going to do, other than see the sights, hang around in the hotel and look for...pleasures?"

John sighed. "Okay, maybe," he said, fiddling with his glass.

"Look, I have to get back to work. I'll have the addresses and the photo sent up to you, and let's keep in close contact."

"Okay."

The older man paused. "John, please take care of yourself, and make sure you trust no one. No one at all."

John searched the older man's face, wondering whether he included himself in that advice, but it was too late for such concerns. Whether Charles was trustworthy or not, he was the only person who could help him find Jasna's killers. So he simply said: "Of course, and you too."

Charles walked away, leaving John to contemplate the growing night and the hushed chatter of the other diners.

After a while, he got up and looked around. He noticed out of the corner of his eye a man in a dark suit sitting on his own, who appeared to be watching him. He wondered if there was anything significant in it but then remembered what Charles had said about the Russian. It's probably nothing. You're just being paranoid. John shrugged his shoulders and walked away.

PART SEVEN

CHAPTER ONE

JOHN WOKE WITH A START. THE TRACES OF A NIGHTMARE drifted from his mind and slowly he came to his senses. He was wet with sweat and he yanked off the bedsheet, glad of the fresh morning air on his skin. He lay staring at the ceiling, listening to the day begin.

For the first time since his wife's death, he was truly alone. No, not just that. He was lonely. Was that what attracted me to Jasna in the first place, to stop feeling lonely? Maybe, but I could never have known how much she would mean to me.

He heard her dying breath once more and saw her bloodied face, twisted in agony. He sat up, breathing heavily. He stared out of the open balcony doors, then buried his head in his hands. The pain rolled through him in wave after wave. He wanted to cry, to howl, to let it all out, but the tears didn't come and he made no sound.

How strange that I'm still alive. He stared at the carpet and waggled his toes. How strange that I am still functioning, that I am not insane or wasting away in a prison cell. He stared out of the window again.

A seagull drifted across the sky.

I am alive, and the world continues.

He thought about going for a swim to wash the residue of fever from his skin, but he didn't really want to. Instead, he got up and walked over to the mantlepiece. He stared at the picture of his wife and ran his finger along the frame. She was remote now. He couldn't get back to their memories, to the space they had occupied together. He knew why. He had to solve the murders and connect them to the gang. Otherwise, he would never be able to lay Jasna to rest and find his way back home.

HE SHOWERED AND DRESSED SLOWLY, lost in thought, contemplating what Charles had told him the previous evening. He wondered whether he would find anything on his search, or whether it would end up being a wild goose chase, with him just killing time to escape the vast, aching cauldron of emotion boiling within him.

As he was buttoning his cufflinks, he heard a soft knock on the door. He listened carefully before gently opening it a crack. There, waiting patiently, was the maid who had brought him his breakfast the other morning. Relieved, he opened the door wide. However, she was not cheerful this time and there was fear in her eyes.

"Mr Charles asked me to bring you this." John glanced down and took the plain envelope. It was thick and heavy, in a perfect ivory white. John watched the light fall across its textured surface as he turned it over in his hand. Before waiting for a reply, the maid walked quickly away. A little concerned by her demeanour, he watched her disappear down the corridor and then gently closed the door.

Five minutes later, he stepped into the corridor. He pulled the door to his room firmly shut and hung the Do Not

Disturb sign on the handle. He looked up, remembering the CCTV camera pointing at him. He inspected the entrance to the stone passageway, barely visible against the smooth corridor walls. It was as if nothing had happened.

He stared, transfixed by his memories. Then he swallowed hard and walked quickly to the lifts.

CHAPTER TWO

THE SUN WAS BRIGHT AND HARSH, AND HE CURSED HIMSELF for leaving his sunglasses in his room. By the time he reached the old harbour he was too hot in his jacket and had had to take it off.

Halfway along the waterfront, he stopped and pulled out the hotel compliments slip on which was written, in Charles's large hand, the address where Erin was found. He could see it from where he stood: a narrow, shaded alleyway where the bins for the neighbouring restaurants were stored.

When John caught up with him at the bar, Charles had told him that Erin was dumped behind one of the bins, half-naked and clearly having been tortured. There were burns on her body and needle marks on her arms. The postmortem report said she had been raped by numerous men. Her right ankle was broken and her jaw was fractured before she died, and she had multiple bruises that suggested she had struggled violently against her captors, although the fractures in her left arm and leg and the compression fracture on her skull had all happened later. The coroner had concluded that the cause of death was strangulation and that she was already dead when she was thrown behind bins the from the street above, presumably from a stopped car.

John looked up and traced the line of the road as it wound around the cliffs, passing above the alleyway on its way down to the harbour. He imagined a fast car pulling up and men getting out, bundling Erin's body over the side of the cold metal railing and not even waiting to see her land before getting back in and speeding away.

The postmortem had also revealed that some of her fingernails had been ripped out. It was assumed that her torturers had been trying to get information or money out of her and, when they either got what they wanted or had given up trying, they had drugged and raped her, abusing her like an animal until they had had enough, at which point they killed her and dumped her body, in full view of the world, to warn any others who might wish to cross the gang.

Charles had been remote and efficient when he described the coroner's report, and John wondered if this was his way of keeping his emotions in check just enough to finish giving all the details. All the way through the story, John said nothing and merely nodded his head when Charles had finished, but he cried when he was back in his room. He cried for his wife, for Jasna, for Erin, and for being unable to stop all this death and torment.

JOHN STOOD at the entrance to the alleyway, staring at the bins and the roadway above, transfixed by the horror of the story Charles had told him and the banality of where Erin had been dumped. Although no witnesses had come forward, John and Charles both thought that it was next to impossible that no one had seen anything. What kind of hold did the gang have over the locals if they could dump a body in broad daylight, knowing for certain that not one person would say something?

John pulled the photo of Erin from his jacket pocket and contemplated her confident and open face. He tried not to imagine her as the coroner's report had described her but rather as the fun, outgoing young woman Charles had talked about over dinner. He put the photo back in his pocket and looked all around the bins, pulling them out and opening each one in turn. All the while, he sensed he looked slightly stupid and imagined that he was being watched. He hoped that the locals would think he must have lost something.

Once he was satisfied he wasn't going to find anything, he went back to the waterfront and wondered what to do next. He was a doctor, not a detective, and had no idea what he was doing. He tried to think of what a detective on the television would do. Well, they would go into each of the shops along the waterfront, show them Erin's picture and ask them what they knew, that much was obvious.

But he was nervous and he hesitated, glancing up and down the harbour, unsure whether he could go through with it. On television, it would be clear that someone was hiding something. But here? He'd be relying on people being able to speak English for a start. But what else could he do? He didn't have any other options. He looked up and down a couple of times more, gathered himself and walked over to the nearest shop. Not expecting much, he initially admired the tourist trinkets and local lace before plucking up the courage to show Erin's picture to the shopkeeper. The old man running the shop shook his head and then called over a young woman who was working there with him. They had no idea who Erin was and suggested he try the next place along.

Slightly disheartened but emboldened by having at least

successfully explained what he wanted, he walked straight up to the shopkeeper in the next shop and showed him the picture. But it was the same story, again and again in every place. Even if the locals understood enough English for him to explain what he was looking for, no one seemed to recognise her. If he mentioned that she had died and he was trying to find some information, no one wanted to talk at all.

At the fourth or fifth rebuff, he became frustrated and made a scene in a cramped shop specialising in terracotta pots and a local aquavit. They asked him to leave and threatened to call the police, and he found himself standing back on the waterfront, disconsolate and wondering what to do next.

After a bout of self-recrimination and soul searching, he spotted a café further along the harbour where the waiter was setting out the tables and chairs. He checked his watch. Only 10 am and already a failure. Hoping the waiter wouldn't have seen his humiliation, he decided to take a break from his abortive attempt at amateur sleuthing.

The waiter welcomed him with a warm smile and a gestured for him to sit where he liked. He thanked him and sat despondently at a still-drying table near the water's edge. While the young man busied himself with finishing laying out the tables, John stared out at the boats tied to their moorings in neat rows, bobbing gently in the slow roll of the sea. The water was a pure, light blue and the sun's rays reflected a warm glow that made the water seem like a bolt of silk being rolled out in slow motion. Further out, a car ferry passed, throwing the nearby yachts and pleasure boats into sharp relief.

The waiter came and took John's order before walking briskly back inside. He sighed as he saw just how much of a Sisyphean task he and Charles had set themselves to try to link the gangs to the murders. Who were they, the two of them? An old man in his seventies desperate over the death of his granddaughter and a grieving doctor, both fish completely out of water. He tried not to think about it, otherwise he might give up. Instead, he focused on the boats in the harbour. They were quiet now as they waited for the next catch. Had they been out already that day? He imagined old fishermen with sea-lined faces offloading heavy poly-styrene crates laden with fresh-caught fish, their every move watched by seagulls. He thought of the decks and pontoons teeming with rubber boots, drumming in the new day and marching out a line stretching back to ancient mariners. And what am I, he asked himself. What am I fishing for? Too many things to count.

He looked up as the waiter placed a coffee next to his elbow. He saw his smile, but could not bring himself to respond. He stared at the cup, a torpor coming over him as the sunlight warmed his chest.

A couple, clearly tourists, held hands as they wandered along the waterfront. They said nothing and didn't even look at each other, but when they reached a decorative tile embedded in the wall of an old counting house they turned in synchrony, without hesitation, as if responding to an inaudible instruction. John wanted to smile, but desire and memory clawed at him and he turned away. Instead he watched a small boat chug across the harbour. Finally, he tasted his coffee. It was strong and rich and, thankfully, still warm. Today will be too hot for me, he reflected, regretting having brought his jacket.

A seagull, unseen, called out into the deep blue sky.

He heard footsteps approaching and, thinking it was the returning waiter, turned, ready to offer his compliments. Instead David pull a chair from another table and swiftly sit down. He stared at the policeman, unsure what to say.

David smiled. "Good morning, Dr Hunter. How are you today?" John recovered his composure but said nothing. "I can see that I have caused you some surprise. I do apologise."

"No, not at all," John said.

"If I may ask, Dr Hunter, what brings you to the old harbour at this time of day? I would have expected to find a tourist like you on one of our beaches, or perhaps exploring the old town. This place," he said, motioning around him, "is, what would you say? Dead?"

John straightened up. "I'm taking an interest in the local culture."

"I see," the other man said seriously.

"Although I must say that the local culture doesn't seem very interested in me," John added ruefully, taking a sip of his coffee.

"Please don't take it personally, Dr Hunter. People here can be very closed-minded." David took a packet of cigarettes from his jacket pocket and, producing an old Zippo lighter, lit up and took a deep drag. "May I offer you a piece of advice," he asked, blowing out a thick cloud of smoke.

"If you wish."

David considered John's face while he took another drag. "Do not allow yourself to become mixed up in things that you do not understand."

"I see," John said.

"There is something far more complex and dangerous happening here than you can comprehend, Dr Hunter."

John stared at the detective. He cleared his throat. "As I said, I am just a tourist taking an interest in the local culture." He looked away and watched a vaguely familiar man in a dark suit sit down at another café and place a notebook on the table.

David smiled. "Tourists do not usually carry pictures of dead young women in their pockets, or look down alleyways behind garbage bins." John's face fell. "It is clear to me, Dr Hunter, that you are an honest man, and a moral man. These are important qualities. However, they are best saved for your patients in the hospital, where they can do the most good." The policeman paused and took another drag of his cigarette. "Out here, such values are of less relevance and could get you into trouble."

"Look, two girls are dead, and you are doing nothing about it," John said angrily.

David stared hard at John. "As I said, Dr Hunter, there is much here that you do not understand. Helping a man to find his granddaughter's killers? Why are you doing this? There is so much that you can do for people who are still alive. Everyday, in your work, you can help people, Dr Hunter. Go home. Do your job."

John looked away. "Thank you for the advice."

"Becoming mixed up in this is not going to help anyone, me and yourself included. And certainly not Jasna, or Erin. It is too late for them." David watched John's face for any sign of change, but saw nothing. The policeman smiled. "I don't think you are going to take my advice, are you?"

John glanced at David and then went back to staring at the harbour. David sighed and stood up. "I must be going," the policeman said, holding out his hand. John took it, shaking it slowly. "Please do take care of yourself."

John caught his eye. "Thank you," he said quietly.

David turned to leave, but stopped himself. "I do hope that no one else tries to change your mind, Dr Hunter. I am afraid that they may not be as...civilised as I am."

"I do appreciate your concern, detective," John said, "but I'm sure I'll be fine."

David nodded. "Very well then." The policeman turned and left.

John waited until he was out of sight before taking Erin's

photograph out of his jacket pocket. He then took out the
hotel compliments slip and stared at the second address
written in Charles's scrawl.

In the distance, the man in the dark suit took a sip of
coffee and made a note in his book.

CHAPTER THREE

An hour later, John looked around a small, dirty square in a part of the town he didn't recognise. He read the address on the piece of paper again and checked it against the map on his phone. It just didn't make sense. Where could it be? The old men in the café on the opposite side of the square were staring at him. He smiled but they carried on staring blankly, as if he was on television. An old mangy dog came up to him and sniffed at his legs and his shoes, before deciding that the stranger was of no use and moving on.

He gazed at a dilapidated and shambolic block of flats, with the detritus of marginalised lives filling the balconies. The pockmarked building jostled for space between forgotten shops and run-down villas. Not one street sign. No indication of where he should go. It was hot, and the sweat was trickling down his back. He wanted to take off his jacket but he didn't want the inevitable sweat patches on his shirt to make it even more obvious that he was a tourist who was out of his depth and had no idea where he was going.

"Hello, Dr Hunter."

John spun around to see a man who he didn't initially

recognise standing next to him, beaming. "It's me," the man said. "Enrico. From the hotel."

John nodded. "Of course, of course. I'm sorry I didn't recognise you straight away. You surprised me. How are you?"

Enrico laughed. "That's okay. The last time you saw me it was the evening and you were drunk. Maybe I look different in the daytime and with sober eyes."

John smiled uncomfortably at the memory. "Maybe."

Enrico frowned and glanced at the piece of paper in John's hand. "What are you doing here, Dr Hunter?"

John hesitated. He didn't want to confide in Enrico, but he realised that he was never going to find the place without his help. "I'm looking for this place," he said, handing over the piece of paper, "but I can't seem to find it."

Enrico read the address and looked at John with a concerned expression. "This is not somewhere for you. Why are you looking for it?"

John looked at the floor. "Well, I got a bit lonely. You know how it is. And I was told I wouldn't be so lonely if I went there," he added, pointing at the piece of paper.

Enrico nodded, and handed it back. "I understand. But next time, if you are lonely, you should have your friend come to see you in your room at the hotel. It's safer than coming to visit her here."

John frowned. "But how would she get into my room? Surely the staff wouldn't let her in?"

Enrico laughed and laid his hand on John's shoulder. "My friend, it is so common for young ladies to help our guests overcome their loneliness, they even have their own entrance, away from the main reception." John raised his eyebrows. "There is a discreet door behind the hotel, where no one can see them come and go."

"Really?"

"Yes, Dr Hunter. This door leads to stairs and secret

passageways than run in parallel to the main corridors, with
an entrance on each floor. That way, the girls can come and
go as they please, and no one need ever know. It's ingenious,
Dr Hunter."

"Indeed."

"It was all built when it was still a monastery. I don't know
what the monks would have needed them for, but now they
help our guests do what they want without being detected."

"Does everyone know about this?"

"Oh no, not at all. It is not a secret for everyone to know."

"I see."

"But you and I are friends, Dr Hunter, so it's okay. I assure
you, your secrets are safe with me," he added, winking
conspiratorially.

"Thank you," John said, lost in thought.

Enrico regarded John. "I am going back to the hotel now,
Dr Hunter. Would you like to join me? I could make you a
rum and coke at the bar," he said, smiling.

The thought of another drink made John's stomach turn.
"No. No, thank you. Tempting though it is to make a fool of
myself in front of the other guests again, I think I'll pass and
visit my friend after all." John waved the piece of paper.

"If you are sure," Enrico said, taking the paper and
reading the address again. He looked across the square and
gestured. "You go up there," he said, "turn at the first right,
and then it will be on your left. It is the big blue and yellow
block in front of you. You cannot miss it."

John took the piece of paper back. "Thank you."

"Piacere," Enrico said and turned away. "Good luck, Dr
Hunter."

John watched the barman disappear before following his
directions. Once he was outside the block of flats Enrico had
described, he checked the piece of paper to make sure he was
in the right place. He stared at the windows and recessed

balconies, wondering which one was his destination, or if the apartment he was heading for would be on the other side of the building. He checked the address again and realised he must be nervous. He folded the piece of paper and put it back in his jacket. He thrust his hands deep into his trouser pockets and kicked at the dust, imagining a thousand different scenarios when he knocked on the door, each one worse and more violent than the last.

"Maybe he won't even be in," John said out loud. He looked around to see if anyone had heard him, and then laughed at himself. "Oh, pull yourself together, man," he mumbled, "you're never going to get anywhere standing around out here." He shook his head and walked up to the building, hesitating before pushing open the double doors and stepping inside.

CHAPTER FOUR

JOHN STOOD NERVOUSLY IN FRONT OF THE LIFT, WATCHING the numbers slowly descend as it approached. The doors opened and he stepped into a bare, metallic, half-mirrored box that was covered in graffiti and stank of old urine. He instinctively held his breath and narrowed his eyes against the acrid air. He pressed the button for the fifth floor and willed the doors to close quickly so that the journey could be over and done with. Instead, it rose slowly and, creaking and groaning all the way, the numbers drifting up one-by-one. His stomach twisted with fear with each passing floor, and he prayed that, whatever happened, he could handle it.

The lift jolted to a halt and the doors scraped open. He contemplated pressing the button for the ground floor and running away. But he thought of Jasna and Erin and all he had discussed with Charles and tried to steel himself against his fear. Before he stepped fully out of the lift, he checked the corridor and listened carefully. All was quiet.

In front of a dirty, anonymous door, he hesitated for a moment before knocking firmly on the cheap wooden surface. After a few seconds, he heard movement from inside the apartment. The door opened a touch to reveal a thin strip of unkempt face and a bloodshot eye staring out at him from behind the latch chain.

"Who are you," the man demanded in an American accent. "What do you want?"

John swallowed. "I was sent here by a friend. He said you could help me."

The man narrowed his eyes. "Oh yeah? I'm not a charity. Go away." He started shutting the door.

"No," John said urgently. "No, of course, I realise that." The door stopped closing. "I, um, was told that you could help me get hold of some things that I want. You know?"

Without opening or closing the door any further, the man looked John up and down. "I don't know what you're talking about."

"Look, don't mess me about," John hissed. "You know what I'm here for." The man carried on staring at John without responding. A door opened further down the corridor and a woman pushed a pram out into the narrow hallway, having to shift the wheels twice to turn it properly. "I don't want to talk about it out here," John said in a whisper. "Just let me in."

The man considered him for a moment and then closed the door. John was about to bang on it or shout in protest, but he heard the latch chain being drawn slowly back. The woman approached with the pram and he became nervous. He would have preferred not to be seen there at all, let alone having to move awkwardly out of the way in a corridor far too small for the both of them. He pressed himself flat against the wall as the woman got closer and tried to engage her with a smile as she pushed the pram past, but she ignored him. Once she was further down the corridor and almost at the lift, the door of the apartment opened just wide enough for him to enter, closing softly behind him once he was inside.

He was greeted by a untidy, rancid bedsit, with an unmade bed rammed into one corner and a stained sofa, bursting at the seams, pushed underneath the window. There were old takeaway trays and plastic plates piled up on the floor and a table by the bed, and old newspapers and rubbish scattered all around. A beetle scuttled from the safety of a mound of dirty washing towards a half-eaten cheeseburger on the other side of the room.

The man, dressed in an old Nirvana t-shirt and a pair of stained grey sweatpants, pushed past John and threw himself on the bed. He watched his tall, well-dressed visitor clenching and unclenching his jaw and smiled. "Why don't you take a seat," he drawled, motioning towards the sofa.

John looked disdainfully at the stained sofa and then out of the window. "Thanks, but I'd rather stand."

"Suit yourself," the American said as he started rolling a spliff.

John stared at him and frowned. "Are you Conrad?"

The man sighed and, without looking up, said: "Look, it doesn't matter who I am. Just tell me what you want and then we can all get on with our lives. What is it to be? Weed? Coke? H?"

"No. I. For information."

Conrad stopped rolling the spliff and stared at John. "Oh, great, another one. That's all I seem to get nowadays: middle-aged guys who want to know something. What happened to you people? What happened to all those broken-but-wealthy losers, hanging on to life by a thread, getting by with a little trip to the dark side when the siren call couldn't be ignored any longer? I made a good living off of those guys. And now I'm stuck with people like you," he said, waving his hand contemptuously before returning to rolling his spliff. "Just angry men with a stick up their ass who want to know things."

John watched Conrad turning the giant Rizla in his hands, making sure that he caught every speck of weed, every thread of tobacco, with each pass.

"Okay," Conrad said eventually. "What are you? You aren't police, that's for sure. A husband? A lover?" He looked up, an excited expression growing over his face. "That's it. I've got it." He stopped rolling the spliff, pausing with it held between his fingers, ready for the finish. "You know who you remind me of?" John shook his head and shifted on his feet, unsure what to say. "Harrison Ford, in *Frantic*. That's it," he exclaimed. "Harrison, man. You've seen Harrison's films, right? He's so good at playing scared. You know, all those white dudes who get into shit way above their heads. It's so far above their heads, they're trapped, lost. There's no way out." He carefully put down the unfinished spliff and bounced on his bed in excitement. "They're tied to a chair and the room's on fire," he said, "or, or they're in a plane and about to be shot down." Conrad pulled a face and then laughed. "And he has this look. A look like he's literally shitting his pants, 'cos he knows there's no way out."

Conrad picked up the spliff and, turning it tight one more time, lifted it to his mouth. He ran his tongue along the glue side and rolled it shut. Satisfied, he turned the finished spliff in his fingers and pointed it at John. "That's who you remind me of. A scared Harrison Ford, who's beginning to realise that he's so lost that he's in way, way over his head." Conrad laughed hard. "Oh, man, you have no idea what you're doing, do you? You're, what? Asking for information? Is that it?" He waggled the spliff. "Don't tell me, don't tell me. I want to guess." Conrad picked up a lighter and lit the spliff. He took in a deep puff and held the smoke in his lungs before exhaling slowly. "You're looking for someone, right," he said slowly. John said nothing, trying not to react. "Yeah, that's it. Who was it? Your wife, your daughter? What happened? Your precious little baby got lost on her trip down the dark side of the Med did she? And now you're clutching at straws, visiting small-time drug dealers in some vain attempt to find her, when you know for a fact the police gave up a long time ago because the case will never be solved. Am I getting warm?"

John sighed. "She is a daughter, but not mine. She's a friend's granddaughter, in fact, and he wants to know what happened to her."

Conrad narrowed his eyes at John and took another long drag of his spliff. John took Erin's picture out of his jacket pocket and handed it to Conrad. The American examined her face closely and then turned over the picture. There was nothing on the other side.

"Do you know her," John asked.

Conrad handed back the picture and nodded. "Yeah, I know her. It's a shame. Erin was a nice girl."

John carefully placed the picture back in his pocket. "What happened to her?"

"The usual."

John frowned. "What's the usual?"

Conrad sighed and took another long drag. "Are you sure you don't want to sit down? You look uncomfortable."

John looked out around the room. "I'm not sure I'd be more relaxed if I did sit down, to be honest." He walked over to the window and gazed out over the townscape, his eyes drifting along the tops of the buildings and down to the sea. He looked down at the patch of grass below the apartment block and watched a group of children playing in the late afternoon sun. He turned away from the window and stared at Conrad. "So, what about Erin?"

Conrad took a deep breath. "I met her...I don't know when. Maybe two years ago?"

"That sounds about right."

Conrad nodded. "Yeah. She'd come over here to work the

summer in a bar. She was really cool. Everyone liked her and she made friends real easy. I think I must've met her one night in her bar. I knew some friends of hers and we got introduced. You know, the usual thing."

John nodded slowly.

"She told me she was really enjoying being away from home and being independent. Away from her friends and family. I got the impression she was somebody who liked travelling, being on the road, not tied down." Conrad paused and inspected the end of his spliff, blowing away a piece of part-burned cigarette paper. "I wondered if she was running away from something, or someone."

"Oh yes? Why do you think that?"

Conrad looked up at John. "Everyone who comes to this place is running away from something," he said seriously.

"What do you mean?"

"Look, think about it for a minute. Why would you come here? Really?"

"Because it's a nice place to stay?"

"Bullshit. There are a thousand nice places to stay between here and, I dunno, London, or New York. Thousands. All of them nice, and none of them have the crap that's going on down here. Why," he asked, pointing his finger at the table, "would you choose here? Specifically."

John shrugged his shoulders. "I don't know."

"Well, I'll tell you, Harrison. Because you want an adventure," he said emphatically. "You want to get away, to escape. You want to find something, or someone, that's a bit different from the norm, a bit out there. Or maybe you want to find yourself."

"So why are you here," John asked.

"Me?" Conrad laughed. "Me? Oh, man, that's a whole other story." He caught John's eye. "And you, big guy? Why are you here? What are you running away from?" John swallowed a thousand knives that cut his soul. "It doesn't matter," he muttered, looking away. Conrad took another drag on his spliff and smiled as he watched John struggling to contain himself. "So what happened to Erin," John asked, his voice cracking.

Conrad said carried on watching the man standing incongruously in the middle of his floor. "Like I said, we all come here for a reason, and not always for the most obvious one."

"And..." John said impatiently.

"Hey man, I'm getting to it," Conrad said. He put down his spliff and looked around the room. He leaned over and pulled a college sweatshirt off the floor. Yawning, he pulled it over his head and smoothed it out over his body before folding his hands in his lap and gazing once more at John.

John sighed and looked out of the window.

"Like I said," Conrad continued, "I met her in the bar where she was working, and she seemed like just another one of those bright, easy-going English girls having fun away from home. Then we started going to the same parties and bumping into each other here and there from time to time. And one night, she asked me if it was true that I sold drugs." Conrad scratched his head and rearranged himself on the bed. "Normally, I wouldn't talk about that sort of thing in a public situation, but I knew she was cool. I told her that, yes, people had said that and that it's possible I could help her, if she knew what she was looking for."

John stared at Conrad and frowned. "Oh yes? And did you help her?"

Conrad wagged a finger at John. "Hey now, don't give me that look."

"What look?"

"That look I've seen a thousand times before. The you-corrupted-my-sweet-innocent-girl look, the look where you're thinking: She would never have ended up the way she did if she hadn't met you."

John raised his eyebrows. "Well?"

Conrad shook his head. "You know what, you couldn't be further from the truth. The truth, if that interests you at all, is that she knew exactly what she wanted. The truth is that she'd been something of a coke head when she was growing up in jolly old England, and she was rather keen on repeating the experience, don't you know." John winced. "Not only that but she was pretty keen to try out whatever else I could get my hands on. She was a proper little hedonist, was our Erin, and now she was away from her family and accountable to no one, she wanted to find out just how far that hedonistic streak could take her." John folded his arms and nodded slowly. "You see, it's not as simple a story as you thought, eh, Mr Moral High Ground," Conrad said, a trace of smugness in his voice. John narrowed his eyes and stared at him.

"Anyway, she bought some coke, which can be pretty damn good down here, if I do say so myself, and she told me she wanted to try a little crack." John's eyes widened. "Don't ask me why, but she did. It turns out she really enjoyed it." John arched an eyebrow. "Well, they do say it's very moreish," Conrad said, cackling.

"Do they indeed? And what happened next?"

"She told me she didn't want to try crystal meth, which is quite popular here, 'cos she reckoned the skag-whore look wasn't really something she wanted to get into. But she did fancy trying a little brown."

"Brown?"

"Yes, daddio. Brown sugar, China white, dope, smack...you want to hear any other names for it?"

"Okay, okay, I get it. You mean heroin."

"Yes, Mr Square, I do mean heroin. She wanted to try some of that good old letter H. It turns out that all her heroes had done it at some point and she wanted to know what all the fuss was about, and maybe find out if it really would take her to some of the places she imagined." Conrad took a cigarette from a packet lying on the sofa and lit it. "She loved it, of course. They all do. And soon she wanted more, more, more, even though she knew it was taking her over." He took a long drag and blew out the smoke, while John stared at him, unsure what to say. "But, you know what? It turns out that bar jobs don't pay that well, especially if you start becoming unreliable and don't turn up to your shifts. Eventually, she got fired and then ran out of money, like they all do in the end, if they haven't gone running back to daddy."

"So what happened next?"

"At first, she hung around here," Conrad said, sweeping his cigarette in front of him, "asking for anything left over that I wasn't going to sell or use myself. But I told her she had to pay, just like everyone else. I mean, I'm running a business here, not a charity."

John looked around the dirty room. "Yeah, I can see what you mean," he said.

"Hey, do you want to know the end of the story or not?" John stared at Conrad and waited for the American to continue. "As I was saying," he said, "obviously she couldn't pay her way. So...I put her in touch with some local businessmen I know."

John sighed. "I see," he said sadly.

"Hey, she only went on dinner dates," Conrad protested. "At first, anyway. You know the thing: accompany a lonely traveller to dinner and maybe go for a drink afterwards. Wear something nice, engage in polite conversation and make him feel special, not like the lonely fuck with too much money he really is."

"And I suppose it didn't stay that way for long?"

"You know how these things work out," Conrad said, shrugging his shoulders. "A pretty, fresh girl, all shiny and cosmopolitan? Those older guys love all that. Of course, she thought it would stay just being dinner dates and occasional trips to parties. It was easy like that, and she certainly liked the money."

"Oh yes?"

"Definitely, man. She was right back here with that first bundle of cash in her hand, buying another bag of H and a hit of crack to go on the side. Just to make it fun, you know?" John sighed. "Well," Conrad said, "we both know it was never going to end like that. One night, she slept with one of those oh-so-nice businessmen. He was young, handsome, smart, funny and damn charming, and she liked him. She thought he was different from all the rest. And indeed he was different, because he wasn't a real customer but some young cousin of the boss who was back from college for the weekend, or some bullshit like that."

John knew, with a shard of anguish, what the American would say next, and looked away.

"Of course, now she'd fucked one of those guys once, she couldn't really say no the next time, especially if she wanted to keep up her steady supply of drugs. She was young and pretty, and life hadn't worn her down, yet. So they soon made her fuck all of them, and more. Any which way they wanted, and as many as they wanted. And of course they filmed some of it and put it online, just so she'd know who was boss and that there was no way out. She was so distraught about it she ended up spending all her money on drugs just to get her through the day. At one point, she realised she was so far down she didn't know how she'd ever get back out." Conrad rearranged himself. "She was mostly down at that fancy five-star hotel, the one looking out over the sea. Do you know it? It's the one with the yacht."

John nodded sadly. "Yes. I know the one you mean. I'm staying there."

"Okay, so you know what's going on there."

"Well, I wouldn't say that exactly."

"Whatever. So, she was down there practically every night, looking after whichever guy, or guys, the gang wanted her to take care of that evening. And then, one night, things got a little out of hand."

"What happened?"

Conrad lit a cigarette and took a long drag. "I don't know exactly, but some guy got a bit rough and she must've snapped."

"What do you mean?"

"Like I said, I wasn't there, but apparently she decided she'd had enough. She grabbed a letter knife and stabbed him in the throat. More than once. Then she stole his money and credit cards and ran. I don't think she can have done a good job of stabbing him though, because he didn't die and he was able to finger her when the boys from the gang turned up to sort out the mess. And she most definitely didn't do a good job of getting away because they managed to pick her up at the airport while she was waiting for her flight."

John turned away and looked out of the window. "So they killed her," he asked quietly.

"Well, it's not as straightforward as all that, although she did die in the end."

"God damn you, man. Did they kill her or not?" John shouted.

"Look," Conrad said, "do you want to hear what happened to Erin? Because if not, I can kick you out of here and right back to where you came from." John sighed. "What do you want, anyway," Conrad demanded. "Why do you care about Erin? What's it got to do with you?"

"Let's just say I'm helping someone try to find the truth and bring her killers to justice."

Conrad looked John up and down. "You?"

"Yes," John said indignantly. "What?"

"You? You are going to bring those guys to justice?"

"Yes. That's the idea."

"Who with?"

"Someone who was close to her."

Conrad sighed. "Okay, well, good luck with that. I presume you have no idea what you're up against, otherwise you'd have never come up with such a crazy idea. Jesus Christ. Amateurs."

Conrad tidied up some ash that had fallen on the sofa. John watched him, unsure what to say next. "How do you think you're going to help her now, anyway," Conrad asked without looking up. "She's dead." He stared at John. "And for what? Because she was junky whore who couldn't pull herself together? She's not worth anyone's effort."

John leapt forwards and grabbed Conrad by his sweater, pulling him close to his face. "Listen, you selfish fuck, you may not give a damn about her or girls like her, but I do, and all I'm trying to do is help a family find justice for their child and make sure the poor girl's terrible death wasn't in vain. Nobody deserves what happened to her, whether they're a junky whore or not, or whatever you want to call her."

Conrad stared back at John. "Like I said, just like Harrison Ford in *Frantic*."

John gritted his teeth, fighting his desire to punch him in the face and trying to force himself to remember that he needed this man's help. After a few seconds, he let go of Conrad's sweater, pushing the man back on the sofa and turning away to stare out of the window. Conrad smoothed himself down and examined his packet of cigarettes, which had been crushed in the tussle.

"I hadn't finished telling you the story," Conrad said calmly.

"Oh no," John asked noncommittally.

"No. There's more to it. Before she went to the airport, she visited an old friend of hers, who she had known since she was working in the bars, back before she started on drugs and ended up being a hooker. Someone who had been there for her, after a fashion, listening to her when she needed to talk."

John spun around. "What do you mean," he asked urgently. "What are you talking about?"

Conrad cleared his throat. "It turns out that, before she stabbed her friend in the neck a second time, she made him confess to what was going on. He feared for his life, with the blood pumping out his neck and all over the carpet, so he named names, explained how things operated, who and what went in and out, and spilled the beans on how the authorities turned a blind eye for a cut of the action. And, being a resourceful and clever young lady, she taped it all on her phone. So when she went to see her enterprising friend, he made sure he kept a copy, nice and safe, even after her phone mysteriously disappeared from the police station during the investigation."

Conrad pulled a shoebox full of papers towards himself with his foot and rummaged around until he produced a small USB drive. John stared at him in amazement. "Why...why didn't you take that to the police?"

Conrad laughed. "The same reason why you're not working with the police now."

"What? You know who I am?"

"Yes, I do, Dr John." John recoiled at the mention of Jasna's nickname for him. "Don't be so surprised. Jasna was a good friend of mine too. One of the best." John's stomach tightened at the mention of her name. "And she told me everything about you. She really liked you, Dr John, more than anyone she'd ever met. I was very upset when I heard about what happened to her." John nodded, fighting back the tears. "So you make sure you use this well. I want you to get it into the right hands, and you take down those bastards, whatever happens. Okay?"

"Yes, I will." John stepped forwards to take the drive, but Conrad pulled it away.

"Just one more thing."

"What is it?"

"Make sure you keep my name out of it. I don't want to wind up being tortured and dumped behind some trash cans in a dark alley like Erin."

John nodded. Conrad slapped the USB drive into John's hand. John frowned as he turned it over and inspected it. "Why didn't you say any of this earlier?"

"I wanted to know if you were for real. I'm not going to hand that over to anyone. Jasna said you were cool, and when she said someone was cool that was enough for me, but I needed to check you out for myself first. I needed to know you were determined enough to go through with this."

John sighed and pocketed the USB drive. "Thanks," he said and reached out a hand.

Conrad smiled at the formality but took his hand anyway, holding it tight. "As they say in the movies: Take care of yourself, buddy. You're in great danger."

"Thanks, but I know how to take care of myself."

"Don't be so sure, Dr John."

CHAPTER FIVE

JOHN WALKED OUT OF THE FLAT AND CLOSED THE DOOR carefully behind him. There was no one in the corridor and he walked quickly and quietly to the lifts. He watched the numbers on the panel go up slowly as the lift approached, then, remembering the state of it, decided to take the stairs, spinning on his heel and pushing through the swing doors.

As he disappeared from view, the lift door opened and a man in a dark suit stepped out. He walked slowly down the corridor, checking in front and behind him. As he approached Conrad's door, he pulled a pistol from his jacket and armed it. The man knocked softly and listened intently for Conrad's approaching steps.

"Hey man, did you forget your bull whip or something," Conrad said as he opened the door, his voice trailing away when he saw the man. "Oh shit." Conrad tried to slam the door shut but the man jammed his foot in the gap and forced it open. Panicking, Conrad ran into the flat and to the bathroom. He slammed the door behind him and slid down to the floor, holding the door handle and breathing heavily. "Oh fuck, oh fuck, oh fuck," he said over and over again.

The man calmly closed the door of the flat and searched for Conrad. When he realised he must be in the bathroom, he tried the handle but Conrad held tight on the other side. The man stepped back and shot at the door. Conrad screamed and the door opened a little. The man forced the door all the way open and Conrad scrambled backwards and cowered by the toilet bowl. The man pointed the gun at his head. Blood was running thickly down Conrad's arm from where he had been shot through the hand and he was shaking. "Please don't kill me. I'm begging you."

The gunman said nothing.

"What do you want? Whatever you want, you can have it, just please don't kill me."

The gunman waited, unflinching.

"Look, I don't have it anymore. I gave it to that doctor. Jasna's boyfriend."

The gunman flexed his fingers around the pistol grip.

"Please. Don't kill me," Conrad begged. "I'll halve my cut of the drug money...anything. Just please don't kill me."

The gunman raised the pistol to Conrad's face.

"It doesn't have to be like this," he said, starting to sob. "We can work something out. Once you've got rid of that stupid doctor, no one need know anything, anything at all, and then we can go back to how it was before."

The gunman titled his head, apparently thinking about what Conrad had said, and then fired two shots into his face.

CHAPTER SIX

JOHN STOPPED PART-WAY DOWN THE STAIRS AND LOOKED out of the window. The glass was dirty and air leaked in through the old metal frame. There were dead flies scattered across the sill and everything was coated with dust. He gazed out over the estate and beyond, towards the luxury hotels and private beaches in the distance. He thought of Jasna, and wondered where she had lived in the jumble of flats and decaying villas that led down towards the sea. She would hate to think that he had got himself involved in all this, but what choice did he have? I just need just to link your and Erin's deaths to Charles's evidence, and we can give it all to his friend. Then we're done, and they'll go to jail. He turned the USB drive over in his pocket and smiled. Conrad. What a character. He was so sure of himself.

He turned to continue down the stairs but there was a heavy crack across the back of his head and he fell forwards, rolling down the steps to the landing below. He didn't have a chance to stop himself from falling before a leather shoe arrived in his face and his body spasmed as the pain smashed across his cheek. The tendons at the back of his neck strained and blood filled his throat and mouth. He flailed his arms and kicked his legs but connected with nothing and fell and rolled further down the stairs. A loud crack and a burning explosion in his abdomen, as if he'd been disembowelled by a white hot sword. On and on he tumbled down the stairs.

Once he had stopped falling, he opened his eyes. He was lying face down sprawled across two steps, pouring with sweat. The pain across his skull was unbearable, and his face was swollen. He watched his blood drip onto the cold concrete steps. He tried to pull himself up but, with a nauseating tear, he realised he'd been shot somewhere just above his right pelvis, although he couldn't tell how badly. As he wondered whether he could drag himself down the stairs and outside onto the grass, he heard slow, steady steps coming down towards him. He turned towards the sound, coughing and wincing with pain. He squinted, trying to see the face of the man silhouetted against the light from the window on the landing above.

"What do you want?" John croaked, staring in fear into the pistol barrel pointed at his face. The man watched him, an empty expression on his face. "I don't have any money on me. Nothing. Just cards. Look..." John reached for his jacket pocket but the man batted away his hand with the barrel of the gun. John coughed and swallowed down a slick of coagulating blood. "Just tell me what you want."

The man readjusted his grip on the gun and cricked his neck. At that moment, a large piece of wood hit him square across the back of his head. He stumbled heavily and, ignoring the pain in his abdomen, John leapt up, grabbing hold of the gun and launching them both down the stair well, turning so he would land on top of the man. The man groaned as they hit the bottom of the steps, and John looked up to see Charles, carrying an old plank, hurrying down after them with a worried expression on his face. "Enrico told me you might be in trouble," he said.

John saw the gun appear from underneath him and point at Charles. He grabbed the man's arm and pulled them both down the next flight of stairs. They fell awkwardly, the gunman on top, and John struggled to turn underneath him. He could hear Charles rushing down the stairs, a sharp crack, a fall, then nothing. When he finally managed to pull himself, wincing in agony, onto his back, the gunman was standing over him, breathing heavily and pointing his pistol at John's face.

So this is it.

The gunman breathed deeply and tightened his grip on the gun.

It's finally over.

John looked into the man's eyes and accepted his fate. Then the stairwell filled with police sirens and the sound of cars braking heavily on the grass outside. The gunman looked at the window, back at John and then again at the window. He quickly put the pistol back in his jacket, jumped over John and ran down the stairs.

Holding his bleeding abdomen, John scrambled back up the stairs, finding Charles on the next landing, gasping for breath and covered with blood. When he saw John's face, he tried to smile, but coughed heavily. "Come on, let's get you to hospital," John said. "The police are here. We need to get you to theatre immediately. He quickly checked Charles's body, finding a large gunshot wound in his chest that was bleeding heavily. His heart sank. Downstairs, the police burst through the main doors and gave chase to the gunman.

"I'm not going to make it, John," Charles whispered back.

"Don't say that. Don't give up on me," John pleaded.

"I'm cold, John. I think this is the end."

"Please," John said, tears filling his eyes. He looked away, realising that, given Charles's age and condition, it may already be too late to save him, even if they started operating straight away. "I'm sorry, Charles. I'm so sorry." John found Charles's hand and squeezed it tight.

"Promise me something."

"Yes, anything," John said.

"Don't give up on this, John, not now."

"Of course not," John said. He looked into the older man's eyes, now weak and distant. "I'm so sorry," John whispered.

"It's okay," Charles whispered. "My life isn't worth anything without Erin."

"Charles," John said urgently. "That's it. It's Erin."

"What do you mean?"

"She's given us everything we need to get them. The gang, everything."

"I don't understand," Charles said, his voice shaking. "How?"

"She got them, Charles, on tape. We have the evidence. Before she died, she recorded one of them telling her how the gangs operate, who they are and what they do, and how they evade the authorities. She did it, Charles. She is the missing link to all the evidence you have. She's cracked the case."

"My angel," Charles whispered. His face crumpled and tears ran down his cheeks. He squeezed John's hand. "Thank you," he whispered.

Charles exhaled heavily and his grip on John's hand loosened, and John knew it was the end. John sighed heavily and closed the older man's eyes. Then the strength drained away from him and he collapsed back onto the wall. Staring at Charles's lifeless body, he listened to the hurried steps of policemen mounting the stairs.

PART EIGHT

CHAPTER ONE

JOHN WINCED AS HE ARCHED HIS BACK TO INSPECT HIS wound in the mirror over the mantelpiece. It was hard to see at this distance, but it seemed the hospital had done a reasonable job of patching him up. He ran a finger over his skin and the rough, wiry stitches, wondering how many more times he could be shot in the abdomen at near point-blank range and the bullet pass straight through without causing any major organ damage. Probably none, he decided. The doctors at the hospital had told him he was extremely lucky to be alive, and he knew that it to be true. Lucky in a physical sense, at any rate.

He limped out onto the balcony. The stone was cold on his bare feet and he thought about going back in to fetch his shirt. Instead, he looked out over the hotel gardens, now silent and shrouded in darkness, and out to sea. All was still and the water shone metallic in the moonlight. There were no clouds, and the trees seemed to be painted against the sky.

Why am I alive?

He looked at the palms of his hands, which were cut and swollen. The doctors had joked that his face had looked more like the Elephant Man when he arrived at the hospital. His cheekbone had been fractured when the gunman kicked him in the face, but there had been no movement of the bone and they decided it would heal naturally. At the time, he hadn't even noticed it was broken. It must have been the adrenaline. He ran his fingers delicately over his face and wondered if he would ever look the same again. He hadn't yet been able to bring himself to look at his face in the mirror, although he was told the swelling had come down considerably.

Why am I alive? Why is Jasna dead, and Erin and Charles too, and not me?

He looked down to the bushes and concrete path below. If it wasn't for me, Jasna and Charles would still be alive. A wave of sickening guilt swept through him and he cried, tears wrung from his screwed-shut eyes then sobs heaved from his chest. But the pain in his abdomen became too much and he slid to the floor, glad of the cold stone against his burning skin.

The faces of the dead rushed through his mind, one after another after another after another; an endless procession of despair that cut him through, piece by piece, until he could take no more. He opened his eyes and stared into the infinite night. It seemed as if the stars were pushing down on him. He saw himself from above, pathetic, nothing, alone on the balcony. He was caught in a tangled web of murder and betrayal, with threads as sharp as glass, slicing through anyone they touched, leaving them bleeding and dead inside; a hollow body to be used and cast aside. I am a fly, waiting to be liquified and emptied. I will desiccate in tomorrow's sun and be blown away with the winds.

There's no way out.

He imagined reaching up to the parapet and slowly, deliberately, hauling himself upright. Then clambering onto the edge and standing, half-naked, arms outstretched, and fixing his eyes on the horizon, the rough stone and moss pushing into his feet. Then gently, imperceptibly, tipping himself forwards and, with a contraction of his ankles, launching himself off. He imagined the rush of air and the slam of concrete into his face. A flash of pain, and it would all be over. Instead, he lay and revelled in his imaginary death, a release from the web, from the tormenting loss that invaded every second of his life. He gazed up and it seemed as though the stars were falling and the night would envelop him whole.

But what is the point of all those deaths if I die too?

His mind flashed to England, to his silent home and the bustle of the hospital. How he wished he could take a plane and go back right now. How he wished he could undo it all. But his flight wasn't until tomorrow afternoon. Today was meant to have been the last full day of his holiday. He imagined a different self, rested and refreshed, coming back from a final swim in the crystalline sea, smiling at the staff on reception as he passed, then coming up to his room and packing. He imagined leaving his suitcase with reception after he checked out the next morning and walking along the busy streets, buying sweets for the nurses when he got back and taking one last meal in a local restaurant.

A light breeze passed over him and he shivered. He could never live again as he had done before all this had happened. That world was closed to him now.

Turning and pushing against the floor, he winced several times as he slowly got himself upright. Eventually, he leaned against the balcony edge, breathing heavily as he gazed out over the hotel gardens and to the sea. He listened to the slow crashing of the waves against the cliffs below the hotel. After a while, he went back into his room, aimlessly sorting and resorting his things, trying to work out what to do next.

There was a soft tap on the door. He turned and stared, his heart pounding in his chest. He waited, and the knock came again, more insistent this time. He stepped forwards to open it but then remembered Jasna knocking on his door on their final night together and he froze, seeing her face in the soft light of the corridor.

"It is me, David."

He snapped out of his reverie and blinked. He opened the door slowly, turning away from the policeman's concerned expression.

"I'm not here to arrest you," David said as he entered the room and closed the door quietly behind him.

"Good," John said, returning to sorting through his things.

The policemen folded his arms and regarded John. "You are lucky to be alive, Dr Hunter."

"Am I?"

"Yes, you are. Don't you know that?"

"Not especially."

David watched John trying to ignore him. He walked around the room and inspected the picture of John's wife on the mantlepiece. "What, may I ask, are you doing out of hospital?"

"I fancied a change of scene," John said, snatching the photograph back.

David smiled. "I'm not sure that the doctors would have agreed with your decision."

"Perhaps. However, I am a trauma doctor, don't forget. I do know what I'm doing." John stared hard at David, who gazed calmly back at him.

"They say that doctors make the worst patients. I wonder if that applies to you, Dr Hunter."

"Have you found Charles's killer yet?"

David shifted on his feet. "No, we haven't, I'm afraid to say. I have a good idea who it is, but I'm not sure we will ever find him now. I suspect he will have been got rid of, one way or another."

"Oh yes?"

"Let me put it this way: the gang he was working for is not very supportive of people who do not meet their objectives." David inspected his fingernails. "I am sorry about the loss of your friend. He was clearly a very brave man." John swallowed and looked at the floor. "He sacrificed his life for you."

John glanced up at the policeman. "Not for me, Inspector."

"Oh? For who, then?"

"For justice."

David raised his eyebrows. "Did you know that we found another dead body in that block of flats?" John frowned. "He was a young American man who we have come across a few times in recent years. I believe he was known as Conrad."

John's stomach turned and the colour drained from his face. Trying to sound casual, he asked: "How did he die?"

"Why do you want to know, Dr Hunter? Did you know him?"

"Well, I..." John stammered.

"Let me be frank with you. It was clear when we spoke this morning that you were not going to follow my advice and leave Jasna's death to us. So I asked one of my men to follow you. You were seen entering the apartment block some time before your sad encounter with Charles and the gunman, and a resident confirmed that she had seen you knocking on the American's door. So, I would like to ask you again, Dr Hunter: did you know the man we found dead in his apartment?" John's shoulders fell and he hung his head. "I can assure you, Dr Hunter, that no one else knows I am here, and what you tell me now will stay entirely between us."

John looked into David's eyes and realised that, whether he believed he could trust this man or not, he had no choice but to tell him everything he knew.

So John explained everything: all the details that he knew about Charles and about Erin; what he and Charles had been planning together; all that he had learned from Conrad; and finally he told David what had really happened between him and Jasna. At first, David stood still and listened intently, but as the story wound along to a more well-trodden and familiar path, he sat down on the edge of the bed and nodded along in recognition, lapsing into thought and drifting away from time to time. When John had finished, David let the silence unfold and grow, and the two men looked at each other, John unsure what to say next and wondering at what could be running through the other man's head.

Eventually, the policemen straightened himself up and cleared his throat. "I wish I could tell you that I can take care of all of this, Dr Hunter, with a simple click of my fingers, but I am afraid that it is not as simple as that." John nodded. "However, what I can tell you is that, for now, you are safe here in the hotel. My men are here and no one will try anything under their noses, especially after all that has happened in the last few days."

David paused. "The problem that you and I have is that the threads of power and corruption are woven so tightly into the fabric of society here that it does not matter who you are, or even who I am. Beyond a certain point, all civilisation is lost, and that pack of dogs will tear us apart without a moment of hesitation if they get the chance."

John frowned. "What I am trying to tell you, Dr Hunter, is that if I take what you have told me, even with the evidence that I have today, to anyone of authority or, worse, it gets into the wrong hands, the case will be closed and you, maybe both of us, will be dead before I can do anything about it. A judge won't even look at it because he is not going to risk his career, his family or maybe even his life when he is not perfectly sure he can get a result, and quickly."

John butted in. "We, I mean Charles and I...we were going to use a connection of his to get the evidence out there. A friendly judge, he told me. A young man who he said would take it on once we had given him all the evidence and he could make a clear-cut case. Apparently he has political ambitions and wants a big conviction to establish his reputation. But I don't know who it is," he added.

David reflected for a moment. "I think I know who you mean. There is one person I can think of in the region who was recently appointed and is certainly keen to make a name for himself. I also understand that he doesn't have any connections to the gangs, and, as far as I know, he's not married, which helps."

"Well, can we try him, then?"

"Perhaps. But, as I told you, it will have to be what the French call a *fait accompli*, with all the evidence there in front of him and undeniable. Today, now, he won't touch it, no matter how keen he is to have a successful case against the local mafia. If you get me all the evidence you talked about that Charles was putting together, with the CCTV recordings, the people coming in and out, then maybe he will look at it. Can you do that for me?"

"Yes, I think so," John said, wondering if he would be able to find everything in Charles's office. He stopped. "Oh no," he exclaimed and grabbed his jacket. Panicking, he rummaged though the pockets while David watched him in surprise. "Fuck, fuck, fuck," John said under his breath as he moved from pocket to pocket. At the final try, he sighed with relief. Glancing at David, he pulled out the USB drive that Conrad had given him. "This," he said triumphantly, "is what we need. This will take those bastards down, and the truth will finally come out about how Erin died."

"Why? What is it," David asked, standing up.

John smiled. "You'll see. Let's just say that with this and

the hotel records there's no way your judge will turn down the case."

"Should I take that now," David asked, holding out his hand.

John looked at his palm then at the USB drive. "No, I think I'd prefer to give you everything together, when I'm sure it can all go to the judge at the same time." David inspected his face. "It's nothing personal."

"Okay. I understand. I'm going back to the police station now, but I will leave a guard of two officers with instructions that you are to come and go as you please and that no one but you is allowed into Charles's office."

"Thank you." John checked his watch. "I'll start putting everything together now. I'll make sure that you have it all by the morning."

David opened the door to leave, then stopped in the doorway. "We shall avenge the death of your friend, Dr Hunter, and make sure the killers are brought to justice."

John stared in silence. David smiled and then left. John watched the door close and listened to the policeman's footsteps down the corridor.

"I do hope so," he said and put the USB drive back in his pocket.

CHAPTER TWO

JOHN STRAIGHTENED UP AND THEN SLUMPED BACK INTO THE chair. What time was it? He checked the clock on the computer screen. Almost two am.

He looked around and tried to imagine Charles working here, sitting in the same chair, slowly gathering the evidence and grieving for his granddaughter. John glanced back at the screen and the mass of data and files that crowded every available space. He knew he didn't have much more to do to gather everything together, but he needed a break. Besides, he still wasn't sure where to send it all. He decided early on he was going to pass everything straight to the judge and not David, just to make sure it stayed in the right hands. But who was it? Charles hadn't told him the judge's name before he died, just that everything he needed to know would be in his office.

John frowned. Maybe his details are here but I've missed them. Charles had thought of everything. Why not this too? Go back to the beginning. Where would be the logical place to hide them? He looked around the room again, this time inspecting the furniture and trying to imagine where Charles might have put something for him, and only him, to find. He got up and walked over to a cabinet against the wall that was full of pull-out drawers. He began at the top, methodically working his way down. He flicked through file after file, not sure what he was looking for. After checking through two drawers in their entirety, he realised it could take all night at this rate and, whatever it was he was looking for, it wasn't there.

He looked around the room again. "What am I not seeing," he said. He went back over what he had done since he had entered the office. He had checked the desk and all the drawers; he had looked in the small cupboard under the window; he hadn't checked the shelves on the opposite wall, but there were there were no suitable hiding places there.

He sat down in Charles's chair again and started from the beginning. He pulled open the top draw and, instead of pushing everything to one side and looking between the files, this time he carefully lifted everything onto the desk to go through it properly. Once he had taken it all out, he knocked the draw shut with his hip and started to sift through the files and reams of paper.

He stopped and frowned. That's strange.

He opened the drawer again and looked at it. It was completely empty. He pushed it shut again, watching the empty space disappear until the drawer banged shut on the frame of the desk. There it was again, that sound. John thought for a second. He reopened the drawer and pushed it shut again. Yes, he could definitely hear it. The sound of a file sliding backwards and forwards as he pushed the drawer shut.

"But there's nothing in there," he said, opening the drawer again. He bent down and squinted. He tapped the bottom of the drawer. It sounded thin and hollow but, then again, so do most drawers. He ran his finger all the way around the edge of the drawer bottom, the dust piling up against his finger.

That's it. There.

He pushed back his chair and knelt on the floor, wincing at the sharp stab of pain from his stitches as he bent over. Right at the back he could see a notch. John eased the drawer off its rollers and placed it carefully on the desk. He inspected the notch and then pushed his fingernail into it. With a satisfying click, the bottom of the drawer sprung open and there, waiting for him, was an A4 file with the words For John written in Charles's untidy scrawl.

He laughed and looked up at the ceiling. "You old devil," he exclaimed. "I almost missed it, you know." John looked down at the file and smiled with satisfaction. There it was, all laid out for him: every detail, typed up and organised. Everything he needed to know to find the information and how to compile it. Moreover, it specified where he should send it, as well as the precautions he should take. And there, among the papers, a handwritten note for John. The emotions welling up inside him as he unfolded it. It said that, if he was reading this, it meant they wouldn't be able to finish their journey together...

But John couldn't carry on reading. He got hold of himself and folded it back up and placed it in his jacket pocket. He stared for a moment at the file and sighed before he got on with finishing the job, now made quicker and easier with Charles's instructions. As he was tidying everything up, he remembered the USB drive from Conrad and pulled it out of his pocket. He transferred the audio file to the computer and checked that he had the right file, although he couldn't bring himself to listen to more than a few seconds of Erin's desperate voice.

There was a quiet knock on the door. John froze. He stared at the door handle, unsure what to do. Slowly it turned and the door opened a crack, and Enrico's worried face appeared. "I'm sorry to disturb you, doctor. Can I come in?"

John beckoned him in, and the Italian quickly shut the door and sat down, leaning forward and biting his fingernails. "What are you doing here," John asked. "I was told the police would make sure I wasn't disturbed."

"I think you need to finish and leave as soon as you can," Enrico said urgently.

"Why? What do you mean? Have you heard something?"

"The policeman, David. He telephoned me just now to ask whether you were finished yet. He thinks the gang will be on their way here, if they're not here already. He said the longer you stay here, the more you are at risk."

"Why didn't he phone me himself?"

"I suppose he didn't want the phone to ring in here and draw attention to the room. A phone ringing on reception is normal."

"Hmm. Did he said anything else?"

"No, not really," Enrico said. He reflected for a moment. "Oh, yes, he did say one thing."

"What?"

"He has a message for you. I don't understand it."

"Okay. What is it?"

"He said: they are waiting for you on the other side." Enrico paused. "What does it mean?"

John glanced at the computer screen and at the USB drive sticking out of the desktop, then back at Enrico. "I think it's better if I don't tell you. If anyone asks you any questions, it's safer if you don't know." Enrico looked puzzled. "Safer for you and safer for me," John said, adding: "Let's just say I think it could be good news."

"Good." Enrico watched John for a moment. "I don't think I told you, but Charles was everything to me," he said. John watched the clouds gathering on Enrico's face. "I loved him, and I don't know how I will be able to live without him." Enrico stared straight at John, trying to hold back the tears.

"I would have followed him anywhere, anywhere. But now he is somewhere I cannot go."

"I'm sorry, Enrico."

"He was the kindest man I ever met, Doctor, and he cared for me more than anyone I have ever known. He made me feel special." Enrico buried his head in his hands, adding in a whisper: "I don't think he knew how much he meant to me."

"I understand, Enrico. I'm sorry there's nothing I can do to bring him back or to make that hurt go away. But I promise you I will do everything I can to make sure he didn't die in vain and his important work is finished. I promise."

Without looking up, Enrico nodded. "Thank you, doctor. I'm sorry. I don't have anyone else to speak to about it."

"Please, don't apologise," John said.

Enrico stood up. "I shall leave you to finish," he said. John watched the door click shut and frowned. A thousand questions crowded his mind, but he shook his head and returned to the computer screen.

HALF AN HOUR LATER, he checked that there were no traces of his work on the computer before shutting it down. He put the file back in its hiding place, and buried the USB drive in a small plant pot on the desk. He pushed his chair back and sighed as a wave of tiredness crashed over him. He rub his eyes and swallowed, realising he was very thirsty. *Where can I get a drink? I can't go back to my room, and the hotel isn't safe. I'll just have to get something later.*

He walked around the desk and listened at the door. Nothing. He opened it a millimetre and peered out. The reception was empty. He pushed the door fully open and stepped out. As he closed the door behind him, he jumped as someone brushed against him. He turned quickly, his heart in his mouth, to see Enrico standing beside him, a concerned look on his face.

"I'm so sorry, Doctor. I didn't see you there."

"No, no, that's absolutely fine," John mumbled.

"I understand you are leaving us tomorrow."

He glanced around. "Um, yes, that's right."

"I am not working then, so I may not get a chance to say goodbye." John looked down to see Enrico's hand thrust towards him, ready to shake. The Italian was smiling awkwardly.

"Right, yes, of course." John took his hand and shook it slowly. "Thank you, Enrico, for everything."

"And to you too, Doctor. Have a safe trip home."

"Thank you." John tried to extract his hand but Enrico pulled him in closer. He looked into his eyes.

"I shan't forget you," Enrico said seriously. John wasn't unsure what to say, but Enrico let go of his hand and walked away without another word.

John frowned and turned to leave by the side entrance but, before he could take another step, there was a sharp bang to the back of his head and he fell unconscious to the floor.

CHAPTER THREE

JOHN WOKE UP WITH A START AND STARTED COUGHING. HIS throat was painful and he could barely swallow. His head lolled forwards, too painful to lift. Where am I? He knew he was in a chair with his hands tied behind his back. What was that smell? Coffee? He groaned and tried to open his eyes, but they were so tired and heavy. Maybe he could just fall asleep again...

Someone said something in a language he didn't understand and his head was yanked back by his hair. He grimaced in pain and blinked at a light shining in his face. His mouth was dry and thick with dust.

"Wake up," a voice shouted by his ear. Cold water was splashed across his face and he spluttered and gasped, screwing his eyes shut. His head was let go and it fell forwards, the water pouring off his face and onto his dirty trousers. After a few seconds, he gathered his strength and looked up.

A short, balding man with a flat, aggressive face and the tight body of a fighting dog was standing with his hands on his hips and scowling at him. "So, you're awake, you fuck," the man said and turned away. His accent was a jumble of Balkan, Cockney and American, and he spat his words as he spoke. "Make sure he stays awake."

From nowhere, a fist appeared and punched John in the stomach. He fell forwards and groaned, the pain exploding from his lesion and tearing through his body. His mouth watered uncontrollably and the spit dripped onto his trembling thighs. He poured with sweat and he thought he might have pissed himself. He couldn't hold himself up and he lolled in his restraints like a rag doll.

When he was able to lift himself, he saw the man was perched nonchalantly on a desk with a window behind. It was daylight. John seemed to recognise the view. "Where am I?"

The man caught someone's glance and smiled. "Haven't you worked it out yet?" John stared back at him, trying to assess how badly he was injured and whether it was serious. "You are back where it all started for you, you stupid fuck. We are in the gentleman's club you seemed to enjoy so much." John frowned. "Does that surprise you?"

John shook his head slowly, a wave of dread and fear crawling up his body. "Who are you?"

The man smiled. "Who am I," he asked, incredulously. He looked over John's head, and a couple of men laughed sycophantically. "Who am I? If you haven't guessed already, it doesn't really matter. It won't make any difference to you now," he said with a sardonic smile.

"What do you want from me," John demanded.

The man regarded John for a moment. "You are an intelligent man and I am very busy so let's not waste each other's time, eh? Just give me the evidence you gathered about my operations and I won't kill you. It's as simple as that."

"I don't know what you're talking about."

The man rolled his eyes and pushed himself off his desk. "Dr Hunter, I am not stupid and neither are you. The time for heroics is over. Everyone from your little group is dead and I know you and the hotel manager were cooking up a case against me. Now it's time to hand it all over and we can all get on with our lives."

"Like I said, I don't know what you're—"

Before John could finish there was a sharp crack across his cheek and the sickening crunch of breaking bone as his cheekbone collapsed. The shock made him delirious and the pain was worse than anything he had ever experienced. His mouth was a jumble of bone, and John watched in horror as two of his teeth fell out, taking a cascade of blood and spit with them. Tears welled in his eyes and his shoulders shook. "Cry, you fucking baby," the man shouted in his face. "Cry, because this is the last thing you'll ever cry about, you pathetic piece of shit." The man grabbed John's hair and pulled his head back. The pain across his cheek, now pulled tight, was unbearable. "Look at your pretty face, ruined." The man stared into John's eyes. "And this is just the beginning. When I'm finished, even your dental records won't identify you."

John shook with fear but he decided that, if there was going to be no way out, dying in fear was not how he wanted to go. He stared back at the man and composed himself, controlling his breathing. A steady calm came over him, and he swallowed the blood and spit that filled his throat. His eyes hardened and the anger rose within him. "Why," he whispered, struggling to form the word.

The man look confused and then laughed. "Why?" he cried back, letting go of John's head and walking away. John fell forwards but was pulled back upright by two hands and pinned to the back of the chair. "Why?" the man shouted. "Why? Think about it. Just for a minute." He stared hard at John. "Did you really think you could walk in here," he bellowed, gesticulating around him, "and smash everything up? Did you think that you could take one of my girls and ruin her, and I wouldn't say anything? That you could you take away something of mine and, when you lost your pathetic little girlfriend, you could destroy everything I'd built up over my whole life? Did you really think that?" He strode over to John's chair and stood with his hands on his knees, staring into his eyes. "That's why, you fuck." He spat in John's face.

Trying to sound calm, John said: "Did you really think you could get away with kidnapping, extortion, rape, murder?"

The man stared back at him and licked his lips. He looked over John's shoulder at the people standing behind him and started laughing. They laughed in response, and John realised that there were three other men present.

"You are very funny man, Dr Fuck," the man said. "I don't know what shit you've been watching on television, but you've got some strange ideas in your fucked-up head about how things work out here in the real world." The man straightened up and started pacing around the room. "Do you think," he said, glancing at John, "that there is such a thing as right and wrong, and justice and the law? Do you?" John didn't respond. "Let me tell you, the only law here, or anywhere for that matter, comes from money and power, and I have both. Those policemen, judges, politicians, reporters, whatever...I don't give a fuck about any of them. I buy whatever I want, and whoever I want. And if they don't want to be bought and prefer to be all moral or whatever, I make them do what I want, whether they like it or not. And if they still don't want to do what I say, I kill them..."

The man continued with his speech, but John stopped listening. The throbbing pain that consumed him was sickening, and he started to worry that he would slip out of consciousness. He tried to focus his mind on the window and the view beyond. He was sure he recognised it. Ah yes, that's it. There was the path he had climbed on that first long walk, when he had his picnic overlooking the hidden bay. He recalled the boat and the beautiful dark-haired woman who dived off the cliff, and he luxuriated in recreating her, imagining himself jumping in with her. He wished with every fibre of his being that he had never come on holiday. But it was too late for that now. There was no way out. He knew that.

Fear crept back inside of him. No, he said to himself. Don't given in to that. Not now. You don't want to give that rabid dog the satisfaction. No, you just have to face the situation as best as you can...

"Hey, hey," the man said. He strode over and smacked John across his broken cheek. John cried out in agony. "You listen to me when I'm talking to you, you fuck. You remind me of that pathetic bitch Jasna. You two were made for each other, you know. Two pathetic dreamers, two helpless fucks who had no idea what they were involved in. You were destined to be together."

The man perched on his desk. "Do you know what Jasna was to me?" John stared back, afraid of what he would hear next. "Nothing. She was nothing." The man looked at his fingernails. "She was just a thing, an object, a piece of junk to be bought and sold. Yes, she was beautiful girl and she had a great body, but that was it. Nothing more." He looked at John and frowned. "You know she was just some scum bitch from Romania? She wasn't a person. She was just a piece of meat. A toy." The anger rose within John and he struggled against his restraints. "You like it when I call her like that, don't you," the man said, smiling.

John tried to steady his mind and the man laughed at him. "Look at you. Why do you give a fuck about that stupid bitch? She was just another hooker, another dirty worthless whore piece of trash working in a strip club." The man peered into John's face. "Oh, you didn't know she was a

hooker, did you? She told you...what? That she was just a
waitress and she never got involved in all that? Dream on, you
fucking idiot. That's what they all say. Make no mistake, she
was just another whore, like all the rest of the bitches I got
working here for me. They all like to think they're not like
that, deep down inside. But they are."

The man paused, relishing John's reaction. "No one cares
about them. They work until they're worn out and then
they're thrown away and forgotten. Simple as that. Like
fucking dogs. A bitch dog, thrown out on the street when
they're all used up." He narrowed his eyes. "Why did you care
about this one? Why did you risk everything for her?"

John tried to speak, but could only cough, the blood thick
in his throat. The man said something John couldn't understand and a glass of water appeared from nowhere. His head
was pulled back and the water forced down his throat. He
coughed and spluttered and then swallowed hard, trying to
stop the blood and spit from going into his lungs. Once he
had recovered, he whispered: "Because she was special."

"Special?" the man roared. "Special?" He laughed so hard
he nearly fell off the desk and had to steady himself. "Special? Oh my god, you are fucking hilarious. You know what?
I'm even beginning to like you, Dr Fuck," he said, pointing
at John. "Special. What a joke." Then the laugh fell from the
man's face and he stared hard at John. "Do you know why
she was special?" John stared back at him. "She was special
because, once her boyfriend had taken her virginity and
showed her some tricks, he sold her to a pimp in Bucharest
and she was put to work, fucking any seedy old cunt who
came in and wanted a fresh piece of ass. After being beaten
about and raped one too many times, she ran away. But she
got picked up again and sent to London, where she found
herself in a much worse position, with no money, no passport and a debt to pay off. They got her hooked on drugs

and put her to work. And she worked, my friend. She worked hard."

John frowned, trying to stop the tears welling up inside him.

"That's not the story your pretty darling told you, is it?" John swallowed and looked away. "Well, she's hardly likely to tell you the truth, is she? You wouldn't have wanted anything to do with her if she had." The man came so close that John could taste his breath. "But it turns out that your little girl-friend had a guardian angel. Some guy found her when he was in London on business. She hadn't lost her looks yet and he could see there was a lot more potential in her than fucking hairy builders and dirty old men all day long in a tiny flat in west London. So he bought her out of her contract and took her here. Then we sorted her out, fattened her up, got her back to her best, gave her a flat, clothes and a normal life, and a steady supply of drugs and a job in the club. Jasna was our VIP girl. She was the one we'd give to the richest clients when they wanted someone special, someone who was far too pretty and clever to think that she could really be a whore. The really classy one. You know?"

The man paused. "But she was a whore, John." John looked up, surprised to hear his name. "Yes, John. Jasna, she was just another dirty whore. She worked as a barmaid most of the time, but when we had someone important in we offered her last, as the treat that no one else could afford. And she was good. Very good. There were some difficult times, when people got out of hand and roughed her about a bit, but we always sorted it out and made sure she was okay. Everything was fine, and everyone knew where they stood. Until you came along."

The man stood up and turned away. "When you walked in and started giving her all that charming doctor act, she decided she didn't want to do work any more. She missed a couple of shifts and told us she was ill. Her roommate had no idea what was happening, but that's girl's just a fucked-up crack addict. What does she know? So we followed Jasna, and she led us straight to you."

The man turned and faced John. "I wanted you dead, at first. But then I wanted to see what would happen." He laughed. "Then she made that stupid mistake of going to your hotel without our permission. Worse, she didn't have anything to give us when she left." The man reflected. "Was it a mistake, John? Or did she do it on purpose? Who knows. Who cares. In any case, we were waiting for her when she left your room and we had a little chat with her." He stroked his chin. "She'd changed, John. I don't know what the fuck you did to her, but she didn't want to talk to us. She didn't want to come back to the club and do her job. She didn't want to anything we told her anymore. So, Zoran here," the man gestured over John's shoulder, "got to work on her. He sliced her up a bit. But she still didn't want to talk. So he burned her." He smiled. "Oh, she didn't like that at all. She fought back, your little Jasna, and she fought back hard. She even managed to take Zoran's eye out."

John swallowed. The man stared at him and made sure that he was listening. "So I stabbed her, John. Me. I took out my knife and I stabbed her. Over and over again, until she was leaking blood like a fucking hose. Then we left her for dead, like an animal." The man smiled. John lurched forwards, trying to reach him. An unseen hand punched John in the stomach and he fell back into his chair, gasping for air.

"It was funny, seeing the police arrest you for it. But then I decided you might be useful to me, so I got you released." John looked up, shocked. The man smiled. "Yes, John, that was me. And I was right, you were useful. You led me straight to Charles and his little plot to bring me down, and you gave me an excuse to get rid of that prick Conrad. They're all dead now but there's still a way out of this for you. It's simple. Just give me the information and I'll let you go. You can go home and go back to being a doctor, or whatever the fuck you want to do. Who knows, maybe you can find another whore to turn."

John stared back at the man.. "Do you expect me to believe that? That you'd let me go, just like that? After all you've done?" He swallowed down another slick of blood. "You killed Erin, Jasna, Charles, Conrad, and now what? You're just going to open the door and let me walk away? It doesn't matter anyway," he muttered. "I'm already dead."

The man frowned. "What did you say?"

"I died when my wife was killed. I've been living on borrowed time ever since. All I live for now is to see you rot in jail."

The man raised his eyebrows and snorted. "Well, I'm sorry to disappoint you, but that's not going to happen."

"How can you be so sure? Why are you bothering to torture me if you aren't afraid of what I can do to you?"

The man glanced over John's shoulder and then around the room. His face became furious with anger. "Who the fuck do you think you arc?" He stepped forwards and smashed John across his broken cheek. John screamed in pain and fell forwards. The man pulled John's head back. "You little fuck, you're going to tell me where the information is, and then I'm going to kill you anyway. But at least this way I'm going to make sure you live every second of agony before you die."

The man pulled John's hands apart. "This is a little taster of what you're going to get." He yanked John's little finger back and dislocated it. John cried out. "Soon, you'll like be a zombie. The pain will be so bad you won't be able to do anything at all, you'll be trapped in it, unable to think or move, and then you'll wish to god you'd told me everything while you still had the chance."

The man held out his hand and a large serrated switch-blade was slapped into it. John's stomach sank and he knew this was the end. He thought of his wife, and of Jasna, and he slowed down his breathing. The man was still threatening him, but he blocked it out. He wanted to create a space where he could hide while the man did whatever he wanted to what remained of his body. "I am ready," he told himself over and over, and moved towards the infinite space within him.

As John was sinking away, the door of the room burst open and somewhere in the distance he heard gunfire. Someone fell heavily to the floor and the man who had been torturing him stepped back, raised his hands and pleaded for mercy. Then the man fell away and John saw David pointing a gun at him.

And then there was nothing.

PART NINE

CHAPTER ONE

In hospital, time loses its meaning. It becomes stretched out, flattened, and the days melt into endless repeating cycles that follow their own internal logic, unconnected to normal daily rhythms. Not only that, but your clothes, your telephone, your wallet, your habits, your family, your friends, your colleagues, even your decisions are taken away from you, not bit by bit but in one fell swoop.

It is a sudden and violent change in status, precipitated by a calamitous and physically destructive event. An event that, in any case, would shake us to the core and threaten our sense of self, but is given greater agency by our being stripped of all sense of identity the moment we cross the hospital threshold. In short, we become reduced, trivialised, a damaged unit in need of repair, renamed a patient and given a number. More an object of curiosity than an independent human being.

John had been kept under strict twenty-four-hour guard since he was rushed to hospital. Not that it made any difference to him as he drifted through the hours and days, ferried to and from the operating theatre for multiple operations. The doctors had mostly attended to his smashed-in cheek and the lesion in his abdomen, which had torn badly. They estimated he'd not had long to live and was lucky the police arrived in time. But John didn't want to know and he slipped gratefully into an anaesthetised half-world, where everything external became background noise. It helped him endure the constant indignities of being pushed around, injected, fed with drugs, monitored and woken up at all hours. He had been wheeled around the hospital half-naked more times than he cared to remember, and he dreaded waking up heavy and disorientated from the anaesthetic, staring at the other zombies in the stark neon recovery room.

The constant pain and discomfort was almost unbearable, and he had finally understood how pain enslaves people, reducing them to a shell of their former selves as they slide between mindless lassitude and frantic paranoia, in which the only beacon of hope is the promise of the next medication.

Once the opiates had fully taken hold, he watched himself transported into a netherworld beyond the limits of daily existence, a liminal space in which the pain continued largely unabated but he no longer cared about it or himself. He was alone, drifting on his opiate ocean, sealed into a separate, comforting space, far from everything. Nothing mattered now. They could do what they wanted to him. He simply watched, curious at how, in any other context, his medical care would constitute a form of torture.

CHAPTER TWO

HE WASN'T SURE HOW LONG HE'D BEEN IN HOSPITAL. IN THE beginning, David had visited him every few hours, first to check up on him and, once John was able to respond, to give him updates on the case.

On the night John was captured, the judge had called David at four am, as soon as he had received the files. By the time David had rushed over to the hotel, the two policemen on guard were dead and John was missing. It hadn't taken long to work out where he was being kept, but the club was guarded like a fortress. They slowly worked their way up to the office without raising the alarm before storming it, hoping they wouldn't be too late.

John was initially relieved the gang leader, who he learned was called Petrov, was alive and awaiting trial in jail. Later, he wondered whether justice would really be done or he would simply spend a few years in prison, directing his operations from inside before taking back the reins once he got out. "Maybe it would've been better if he'd been killed," John said one morning while recovering from yet another operation on his cheek and upper jaw.

David reminded John that, once John he back to his normal self, he would prefer the gang leader to face justice than be summarily killed like his victims. Besides, the judge was determined to make an example of him and ensure he never got back to power. "Unless they kill the judge first," David quipped. But what was it all worth, in the end? Whatever happened, they'd always be someone to replace Petrov, and everything would go back to square one. "If it really hadn't been worth it, you and Charles wouldn't gone to all that trouble and Jasna and Erin would have died for nothing."

Jasna. The mention of her name brought back the horror of everything that Petrov had said about her. He tried to rationalise it, to put it away, to tell himself that man was just saying those things to hurt him, that he was lying. He wanted to talk it through with David, but he didn't want to sully her memory by saying the words out loud. And he was afraid David would say Petrov's description was probably right. After all, John knew it was, deep down. Instead, he forced himself to remember their tender moments together, the touch of her hand in his, her smile when they walked back to town together before the rainstorm. That was the real her, not some tawdry facts about how she'd been exploited by violent men all her life. She was so much more than that, and always had been.

After David left, he stared at the ceiling for what seemed like hours before he drifted imperceptibly into a deep sleep.

As every night since he had been admitted to hospital, he suffered terrible nightmares filled with unspeakable violence. He woke from them horrified and confused and alone in the darkness. Every time, he tried to stop himself from slipping back into them but they lay waiting for him, ready to torture him once again until he could take no more.

CHAPTER THREE

A FEW DAYS OR WEEKS LATER, JOHN FOUND HIMSELF ALONE in his hospital room, watching dust fall through the golden rays of late-afternoon sun. Birds sang in the trees. In the corridor, a trolley rattled as it was pushed past his room. He smiled, although he didn't know why. And he was thirsty. He glanced at the clock by his bed. The orderly should be along soon to bring some coffee.

He reflected on the hospital. The staff were talented and dedicated, and always at pains to make him comfortable, but he wondered how well they had operated on him. It was not a wealthy institution and didn't have most of the equipment that would have been taken for granted in Western Europe. They had also seemed a little unsure when he quizzed them about the techniques they'd used to patch him up.

Whatever the result, there's nothing I can do about it now. I should be grateful to be alive. But the fear that he could be permanently disfigured crawled up him all the same. What if they hadn't lined up his bones properly, or sewn him up cleanly? He had studiously avoided looking at himself in the mirror when he went to the bathroom. He knew he must look terrible and didn't want to worry about the long-term outcome, even though he would have to confront it sooner or later.

He stared at the ceiling and traced the cracks in the plasterwork, clenching and unclenching his jaw. The sharp pain across his cheek was still there, and his new ceramic teeth didn't seem to fit in his mouth. He ran his fingers over his skin, sensing the hot swell of inflammation and the last of the stitches. He could tell where the teeth had been placed, which meant they must be visible. They'll settle eventually, he tried to tell himself.

He listened for the usual sounds of a busy hospital but all was quiet. It must be break time, or maybe there's an emergency. He thought about England, and home. Maybe I'll ask the nurse when I'll be discharged. Then he remembered his wife wouldn't be waiting for him when he got back and he would be alone. And what about Jasna? She would never see the life he wanted to show her.

The door to his room swung open and David stepped in, grabbing the door before it hit the wall, then closing it carefully behind him. "How are you today, Dr Hunter?"

John sat up a little and the pain flickered across his face. "I'm fine, better today. And please stop calling me that. It's John."

David smiled. "Apologies. I always forget. I am a formal man. It is why I wanted to be a policeman, among other reasons." David stood staring at John, who was propped up uncomfortably on the bed. "I asked on my way in when you will be discharged."

"Oh yes? I was just thinking about that. What did they say?"

"They said you are doing well, and the risk of internal bleeding is less. They want to take out your stitches and make sure you're not at risk, and then you should be free to go."

"That's good," John said. "Maybe in the next few days, then." David nodded and then stared at John. "What is it?"

David shifted on his feet and cleared his throat. "The gang leader, Petrov. He is going to court on Thursday morning for the first part of his trial."

John sat up a little further. "Oh yes? So soon?"

"They brought the case forward. The judge wants to get him into a more secure prison as soon as possible. They cannot do that until the case has been opened and he has given his plea."

"I see. Well, the sooner the better. So where is he now?"

"He's in a local prison, under permanent guard."

"Good." John inspected the policeman's face. "You seem worried."

"Petrov is a clever and devious man, John, and a rich and influential one. He has tried everything to bribe the guards, and when that hasn't worked he has threatened them and their families. One of my men was found dead, and another's family had the windows in their house smashed and their shop burned down. There have been attacks on the prison, and the other inmates have tried to get him out. They haven't succeeded, thankfully. He's also been trying to get the case stopped. The prosecuting lawyer has received death threats and selecting a jury has been, let us say, challenging."

"It doesn't surprise me. But he won't succeed, will he?"

"I do hope not, John." David looked out of the window.

John watched him, puzzled. "Are they still fine with me giving evidence via video link once I get back to the UK?"

"Yes, that's all okay. And we had some luck with the case. One of the lieutenants in the gang is willing to testify that Petrov killed Jasna in the hotel passageway."

John sat up, his heart racing. "Really," he asked incredulously.

"Yes, we offered him immunity and he leapt at it. I think

maybe he wants to take over some of Petrov's empire once the old guard are in jail."

"That's fantastic news." The image of Jasna waiting at his bedroom door, timid, her eyes lowered, came back to him and he wasn't sure whether to laugh or cry. He glanced at David, who was staring back at him. "So why do you look so concerned?"

David frowned. "Petrov has, as they say in the films, 'taken out a hit on you'."

John smiled at David's turn of phrase, but the meaning made his stomach turn. "Okay," John said. "Do you know any more?"

"No. Just that he wants it done as soon as possible, and that the person who succeeds will be rewarded, richly. It seems he is not so keen on you anymore," David said. John swallowed and looked away.

David walked over to the window. "Of course, we will do everything we can to protect you. I have doubled the guards at the hospital and there is a man on permanent watch in the corridor outside." He turned back and stared at John, but John wasn't sure what to say and the two men fell silent. The policeman started pacing around the room. "However, it is impossible to be one hundred percent vigilant at all times, even with every precaution, and I am afraid that a determined assassin will find a way through. You should know, John, that the longer you stay here, the more you are in danger. If there is any way you can bring forward your discharge and come under my prospective custody, that would make things easier."

John straightened out his bedclothes, wondering whether he would be able to convince the hospital to discharge him straight away, although he knew they would be reluctant. "I will try, David," he said. "To be honest, I would prefer not to leave until I have the all-clear from the consultant. But I obviously don't want to stay here a minute longer than necessary, especially if my life is in danger." John smiled weakly and David nodded thoughtfully.

"In any case, you're safe here for now," the policeman said. "It would be too risky for them to try anything straight away. There's too much attention on the case and Petrov is more focused on trying to escape than killing you."

SOMETIME LATER, the evening gloom invaded the room and gave space to the fears that turned over and over in John's mind.

The registrar popped his head around the door. John immediately pressed the younger doctor on when he could be released. He looked doubtful. "I don't know, Dr Hunter. We are worried about some of the lesions in your abdomen. They are healing fine but slowly, and you could be at risk of internal bleeding if you left before you were ready."

"I understand," John said, trying not to sound impatient, "but I will be careful and I would come back immediately if I had a problem. I do know what I'm doing."

"Yes," the doctor said, drawing out the word. "I know that, and I do not want to contradict you, especially as you are more senior than me." John screwed up his face, hoping he hadn't come across as patronising. "But I have to tell you that, even with your clinical experience, you may not know straight away if you develop internal bleeding." John nodded reluctantly. "Also, I think you would probably get on a plane if you left the hospital, maybe straight away," the younger man said with an impish smile. "I would be uncomfortable about you flying unaccompanied at this stage."

John knew the doctor was right, and he knew he would have said exactly the same thing to a patient in his position. Should I tell him why I want to leave, that my life is in danger? He hesitated, watching the doctor checking his notes.

"I'm desperate to go home, you know."

The young man stared at him curiously and then smiled. "Of course you are, Dr Hunter. I do understand that." He put the notes back in the slot at the end of John's bed. "I know you want to leave. Anyone would, especially after being here so long. But my first duty is to you as a patient." The doctor cleared his throat. "Let me tell you this: I will go away and phone the Professor. He can maybe think of something we can do to help you. But please understand that there are going to be no miracles tonight. You are still quite sick, Dr Hunter, even if you feel better today."

The doctor smiled, bowed his head slightly and left the room, closing the door quietly behind him. John sighed. Maybe I could just discharge myself? I could walk out of here right now. As long as I'm careful, I should be okay. Then he thought about what the doctor had said and imagined himself slumped on the floor in the airport, already too late to be saved.

"If that happens, I may as well have been killed by the hitman."

CHAPTER FOUR

OVER THE NEXT FEW HOURS, JOHN TRIED NOT TO THINK about anything, but images of his wife, of Jasna, of Charles, Erin and Conrad crowded his mind in an endless roll call of the dead. He tried to concentrate on the television, but he couldn't understand anything, and the gaudy, over-lit shows just underlined the tomb-like gloom that surrounded him. After a while, he clicked off the television and listened to the faint hum of the hospital and the occasional car that passed outside his window.

There's nothing to do but to wait.

The registrar had popped back to say that he'd had the Professor on the phone. He would be down from the operating theatre later on that evening to talk about John's condition and when they thought they could discharge him. The registrar again stressed how he understood why John wanted to leave.

But you don't, though. Not really.

He stared at the window, now a black mirror reflecting only his bleakness. He thought back to when he was lying on the stone balcony at his hotel, and the stars that pushed down on him. I wanted to kill myself. The notion seemed a little strange now, like the recollections of a different man in a different time. Who was that me? All he wanted to do now was stay alive so that something good would come out of all the suffering.

He lay back and tried to relax. The touch of Jasna's hand in his came to him from across the gloom, and then his wife's. The two morphed onto one and he drifted slowly into sleep.

CHAPTER FIVE

SOMETIME LATER, JOHN WOKE TO THE SOUND OF THE DOOR opening and a trolley with a squeaky wheel being pushed in. He tried to focus his mind, but he had been so lost in a nightmare that it took him a several seconds to remember where he was.

He watched a nurse awkwardly pushing the door open with his hip and turning the trolley. Where have I seen him before? He wasn't part of the usual clinical team that looked after John, but there was definitely something familiar about him. Where could he be from? Maybe he works part-time somewhere. Maybe he's served me drinks.

Finally wrangling the trolley into the middle of the room, the nurse glanced up and acknowledged John, nodding and smiling. He motioned to the trolley and the collection of pads, bandages, antiseptic solutions and scissors that lay scattered across it, indicating that he was there to change John's dressings. John frowned. They'd already changed him that morning and he should have been okay until at least tomorrow, if not the day after. Maybe they want to check my wounds before the Professor decides whether to discharge me. That must be it. Strange that the registrar didn't say anything. Maybe it slipped his mind.

The nurse pushed the trolley alongside the bed and started busying himself with the bandages. "Do you want to take off the old dressing first and see how it is," John asked, getting ready to unbutton his pyjama jacket.

The nurse looked up and their eyes locked. With a sickening dread, John realised why the nurse seemed familiar and where he had seen those eyes before. But before he could react, the nurse hit John across the face with a metal tray. The pain in his cheek was like an electric shock and John banged his head on the metal bed frame as he jerked back, instantly disorientating him.

The nurse dragged John off the bed and he winced as he landed awkwardly on the floor, tearing the lesion in his abdomen. The nurse took a gun from inside his uniform and pointed it straight at John's face. John, panting heavily and trying to gather himself, looked up and stared into the man's eyes. But instead of the empty resignation that had gripped him in the stairwell, he was angry. While the nurse adjusted his grip on the pistol, John swung his leg up with all his might, catching the man full in the crotch. The nurse staggered backwards, doubled up and moaning in agony. John leapt for his gun and tried to prize it from the man's hand, but his fingers were too strong and they stumbled around the room, the nurse staggering while he tried to hang onto the gun, then punching John in his side, making John cry out in pain. John flailed around with his free hand, but he barely connected with the man as he dodged behind him.

After several punches, the pain became too much and the mist began to descend. John's grip on the gun barrel was loosening, and he wondered how long he could hold on for. They turned and John tripped over the wheels of the bed, stumbling backwards. The nurse got John in a headlock and they danced around the room as he tried to force the gun towards John's face and John using whatever strength he had left to stop him.

As they passed the nursing trolley, John grabbed desperately at a pair of long scissors, almost dropping them, then taking an eternity to turn them in his hand. Once he had his fingers through the holes, he flipped the scissors over and stabbed the nurse as hard as he could below his ribcage, forcing his hand deep into the man's side, then yanking upwards and opening the scissors wide to cause as much damage as possible.

The man fell back, groaning, and dropped the gun. John kicked it away and stared at him, now prostrate on the floor and gasping for breath, the scissors still embedded in his side and dark blood already pooling on the floor.

Every one of John's instincts told him he should treat the man's wounds and save his life, but he forced himself to see him for what he was. He glanced at the scissors and then pushed the thoughts away, clearing his mind. He steeled himself and kicked the man in his side with all the force he had left in his body. The man cried out in pain and then fell unconscious.

John stared at him before falling to his knees and then the floor, the pain in his abdomen too much to bear. Panting and retching, he knew the bleeding must be bad and he would have only minutes before it would be too late. He pulled himself up onto his hands and knees and, seeing double, tried to spot the emergency cord. By the bed, you idiot. It's always by the bed. Nauseous and too dizzy and disorientated to lift his head, he crawled over to the wall, using the bed for support and searching with his free hand for the thin, woven cord.

His vision fading, he grasped at thin air and then collapsed.

CHAPTER SIX

You stand before ancient doors, chained but half-open, inviting you in. You pass through them and are in the swell of a black ocean, her hand in the breaking surf, reaching out from a long-forgotten memory.

She lies among the flowers, dead or sleeping. Her face becomes the wings of a magnificent bird, and she is an angel leading you down into an ancient tomb.

Her face appears from the water, panic in her eyes. She stands on the clifftop, a storm enveloping her. The tears run in rivers from her closed eyes, where the waves roll in from the misty shores.

She appears from the shadows of a black forest, and is eclipsed by the darkness. Three doves fly up from the gloom. They become her crossed arms and she bursts into flames.

You stare at the sea beyond the stone balcony, and she bows her head beneath a burning tree, now a candle melting over her hands. Her face, suffocating beneath a death shroud, raises up towards you from the dark earth, her mouth open in panic as she gasps for air.

JOHN'S EYES SPRUNG OPEN. The room, dark and unfamiliar,

lay heavy upon him, and he struggled to understand where he was. He tried to sit up but the pain was too great and he fell back, panting, the sweat pouring out of him.

He stared at the ceiling, barely visible in the feeble light cast from under the door, and tried to remember. Nothing came, save the horrifying image of her suffocating face emerging from the dark earth. He tried to push it away, but it overwhelmed him and he sank back into a fevered nightmare.

Soon, he breathed deeply and regularly once more, the occasional twitch flashing across his face. Only the faint hum of the hospital air conditioning broke the silence, and the quiet rustle of the guard adjusting his position on a chair by the door.

CHAPTER SEVEN

"Wake up."

A voice, disembodied, drifting across the dreamscape.

"Wake up."

There it is again. Curious. I wonder where it's coming from.

"Wake up."

A rush of light and his shoulder being shaken. A female face, half familiar, close to his, and the reality of a room. What room?

"You have to go, now."

What? Who is she? And then it came back in a flood: the hospital, the room, the operations, the fight, the cord...

"What?" He struggled to form the words. "What did you say?"

"Dr Hunter, you have to get up, now. You have to leave here."

Her face is so close. What is she sa...?

"Now, Dr Hunter. It's an emergency, someone is coming to kill you."

His eyes sprang open and he saw her for the first time. "What did you say?"

"Someone is coming to kill you, from Petrov. You have to get dressed and leave."

He looked around. A detective and two nervous-looking policemen with semi-automatic weapons were standing near the door, now wide open. He searched for David then stared at the nurse in panic.

"It's okay," she said, John noticing her heavy accent for the first time. "They're here to help you. A car is coming for you, to take you to safety, but you have to go now, otherwise it'll be too late."

She pushed back the covers and he swung his legs out of the bed on autopilot, wincing as he straightened up. "But, but how do you know that there's someone coming to kill me?"

The nurse glanced at the three men. The detective stepped forwards. "An informant tipped us off. He phoned David to say they've sent two people to kill you, tonight."

John sat on the edge of the bed, shaking his head and frowning. "I don't understand."

"Dr Hunter, Petrov has escaped prison and wants you dead. They're coming to kill you. It's as simple as that. You have to leave here. Now." The detective shouted the last word and John jumped. Glancing at the three men and their guns, he dressed as quickly as he could, wondering whether this was finally the end.

Once he was ready, the two policemen went ahead while the nurse and detective helped him to walk down the neon-lit corridors he had previously passed only on a trolley.

Outside, in the cold night air, he looked up at the black sky. There were no stars, only undulating clouds racing across the darkness. He looked around and realised the hospital was overlooking the town and the sea. He thought of the hotel and the balcony. Jasna's face appeared before him, but he pushed her away.

The nurse and the detective led him around the side of the hospital, where an old Mercedes was waiting for him, it's engine running and the back door open. He froze. How do I know if I can trust these people? What if they aren't really policemen? What if she isn't a nurse? If I get in, will I be driven away and shot, left to rot on a hillside? He glanced at the nurse, who was gently tugging at his arm, and the detective. He looked at John and frowned. "It's okay," he said. "The car is for you."

Is it? In what sense?

He looked across the hospital car park and to the town beyond. A sports car was speeding silently down the hill opposite, its tyres smoking as it rounded every bend. "That's them," the detective said urgently. "You have to go now." John hesitated again and pulled back. What if that car is the police and they're coming to save me, and it's these people who are the gang?

The driver of the Mercedes twisted in his seat and stared at John. "Oi," he shouted, "what the fuck are you waiting for? Get in, for fuck's sake, or we'll all be dead."

John snapped out of his reverie. "Yep, sorry, coming." With the nurse and the detective holding his arms, he hobbled over to the car as quickly as he could. The roaring engine of the sports car became ever-louder and, as he fell into the seat and pulled the door shut, it swung around the corner in a screeching wail.

"Oh fuck, they're here," the driver said and slammed the car into gear. They shot forwards and John stared out of the back window, watching the sports car swing around as it negotiated the car park entrance and then straighten up to follow them. The policemen opened fire but it did nothing to slow its progress.

"They said there's an exit up this way," the driver said, glancing in his mirror. "We'd better find it or we're fucked." The Mercedes shot down a ramp and onto another level of the hospital. The sports car was close now and John could see the faces of the people inside. A hand appeared from inside the car carrying a gun and a shot was fired.

"Ah, here we go, that must be it." Their car swung around a corner. John was thrown across the backseat as they dived down a ramp and landed heavily, before swinging around and heading for a narrow track leading back up to the main road. The sports car was initially left behind, but was soon back on their tail, and John stared at it through the back window, mesmerised by the steady approach of death.

The Mercedes swung violently right and left, throwing John around in desperate agony. "I'd put my seatbelt on if I was you," the driver said casually. Panting hard and sweating, John straightened up and clipped himself in. "Don't worry, I used to be a rally driver in my time off. I'll soon have us out of here."

They shot forwards and slalomed nimbly between two parked cars, before executing a perfect handbrake turn and accelerating hard up a narrow, uphill street. John glanced back at the sports car, which was struggling to keep up but hanging doggedly onto their tracks, disappearing then reappearing as they rounded each corner. A small, muscular man was now sitting on the sill of the near side door and shooting at them, his face contorted in hate.

CHAPTER EIGHT

THE MOONLIGHT SPARKLED ACROSS THE WATER AS THE BAY opened up before them. John pushed himself further into the backseat of the car and watched the coastline spread out like a painting. He shifted slightly, wincing at the pain and wishing he could lie down.

He had been grateful for the driver's breath-taking skills as they shot through the town. The sports car had stayed in close pursuit for as long as possible, but they'd finally sold them a dummy as they overtook a cement truck and their pursuers had crashed heavily, flinging the small, muscular man into the road. John was horrified but the driver didn't even react, and they sped along the main road and soon left the town behind.

So much death.

John thought back to his fight with the hitman and shuddered. A few days afterwards, David had told him that the guard outside his room had been found dead in a cupboard. By the time John had collapsed, the alarm had been raised. He was rushed to theatre and underwent several hours of surgery to close a rupture in his large intestines that the doctors said would certainly have killed him.

The hitman, however, had had only surface trauma and was taken into custody a couple of days later. When he went to the local prison to await trial, an inmate stabbed him in the throat with a sharpened toothbrush the next morning, and he was left to die on the floor of the prison canteen.

"He knew it would end that way," David said with a shrug. "He'd failed to kill you, twice. The first time was forgivable but they would never let him get away with failing again."

JOHN WATCHED THE MOONLIT, crystalline bays come and go, beating time to their journey. He ran his finger across his cheek and wondered if he would ever look the same again. He had been horrified the first time he had dared to look at himself in the mirror. Aside from any leftover swelling, his cheek and jaw were obviously not fully aligned. He imagined how his mother would react when she saw him, and how long he could realistically put off seeing her. I've been away for two months, after all. I'll ask one of the dental surgeons to see if they can fix it.

As the car swept around a bend and headed up into the mountains, John remembered the note from Charles. He pulled it out of his jacket pocket, unfolded it carefully and read it from beginning to end, tears in his eyes. How he wished he could tell him how everything had turned out, to share all that had happened. Maybe it's for the best he doesn't know. He would be so disappointed if he knew Petrov had escaped, after all they had been through.

John reflected. Would Erin's death, and Jasna's for that matter, ever be avenged? Would anyone ever face justice? It doesn't seem likely. Now now. He sighed deeply. And what of Petrov? What will he do? He's already come after me once, surely he won't just leave it at that. And what of his empire? At least that must be in tatters.

He carefully folded the letter and put it back in his pocket. Glancing up, he saw the driver looking at him in the rear-view mirror.

"Sorry, we didn't get properly introduced in all the rush. I'm John."

"Yes, I know," the driver said, smiling. "I'm Bill. Well, William, but everyone calls me Bill."

"How did you know to come for me, Bill?"

"You mean at the Consulate?"

"Yes. Who told you I was in danger?"

"Your policeman mate, David. He called us a couple of weeks ago to ask if we could get you out the country, once you'd recovered enough. We don't normally do that sort of thing but, given your circumstances and the obvious risk to your life, we decided we could make an exception." Bill smiled. "And when we got a call last night that they were coming for you, we thought we'd better get a move on."

John looked out of the window, watching the sea drop away as they climbed further and further into the hills. "What about Charles and his family?"

"As far as I know, they repatriated his body and informed his daughter he'd died. I don't think they went into detail about what happened and what he'd been up to. They didn't want to interfere with the case, if something got out. Although that seems a bit academic now. I think they said he'd died in an accident." John nodded. He wondered when he would have the strength to see her and explain what Charles had done in Erin's memory.

The two men fell silent and John stared out of the window. After a while, the driver glanced in the mirror again and cleared his throat. "You did something very special, you know."

"Did I?"

"You risked your life to bring those people to justice. Maybe they've got away with it for now, but you two broke that gang. They're finished. You should be proud of yourselves."

John caught Bill's eye and looked away. He gazed at the sea far in the distance, sparkling in the dark silver light, and the clouds that raced across the sky, but he saw nothing.

ABOUT THE AUTHOR

L. A. Davenport is an Anglo-Irish author. He sometimes lives in the countryside, far away from urban distraction, but mostly he lives in the city. He enjoys long walks, typewriters and strong black coffee.

To find out when L. A. Davenport has a new book out and get the latest updates, visit his official website at Pushing the Wave. He can also be found on Tumblr.

To keep up to date with all the latest news, sign up to L. A. Davenport's official email newsletter, and receive a free short story.

ALSO BY L. A. DAVENPORT

No Way Home

Dear Lucifer and Other Stories

Made in the USA
Monee, IL
19 May 2020

31426600R00164